"I've changed my mind about a divorce,"

Rhone said. "Nicky needs a family. If you want your freedom, you're going to have to fight me for it."

Shannen's eyes narrowed; then she shrugged. "If that's the way it has to be."

"Perhaps I'm not making myself clear. We're still married. You need me. And I'm moving in."

"The answer is no. *N-O.*"

"Lady," Rhone said, "it's not up for discussion."

❦

"ALL I NEED is filled with danger and intrigue, hurt and hope. When a marriage is broken, it takes a strong man and woman— willing to look beyond the surface and into each other's hearts—to pull it back together again. Shannen and Rhone are two such characters. The reader will root for them, as I did, to rediscover the love that never really died."

—Robin Lee Hatcher, author of
Liberty Blue

Dear Reader,

What a lineup we have for you this month. As always, we're starting out with a bang with our Heartbreakers title, Linda Turner's *The Loner*. This tale of a burned-out ex-DEA agent and the alluring journalist who is about to uncover *all* his secrets is one you won't want to miss.

Justine Davis's *The Morning Side of Dawn* is a book readers have been asking for ever since hero Dar Cordell made his first appearance. Whether or not you've met Dar before, you'll be moved beyond words by this story of the power of love to change lives. Maura Seger's *Man Without a Memory* is a terrific amnesia book, with a hero who will enter your heart and never leave. Veteran author Marcia Evanick makes her Intimate Moments debut with *By the Light of the Moon*, a novel that proves that though things are not always what they seem, you can never doubt the truth of love. *Man of Steel* is the soul-stirring finale of Kathleen Creighton's Into the Heartland trilogy. I promise, you'll be sorry to say goodbye to the Browns. Finally, welcome new author Christa Conan, whose *All I Need* will be all *you* need to finish off another month of perfect reading.

As always, enjoy!

Yours,

Leslie Wainger
Senior Editor and Editorial Coordinator

Please address questions and book requests to:
Silhouette Reader Service
U.S.: 3010 Walden Ave., P.O. Box 1325, Buffalo, NY 14269
Canadian: P.O. Box 609, Fort Erie, Ont. L2A 5X3

ALL I NEED

CHRISTA
CONAN

Published by Silhouette Books
America's Publisher of Contemporary Romance

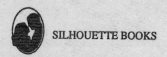

SILHOUETTE BOOKS

ISBN 0-373-07678-9

ALL I NEED

Printed in U.S.A.

CHRISTA CONAN

is the writing team of Vickie Conan and Christine Pacheco.

Vickie states that writing has always been her favorite mode of expression. The magical power of words, how they create images that excite the mind and imagination, never ceases to fascinate her. More than anything, she loves romance and happy endings.

Christine doesn't remember a time when she didn't write, and was thrilled when she finally sold a book, believing that reading is a universal link that can bring all our dreams and hopes together.

Both writers live in the Denver area with their husbands and children, along with numerous animals.

For our loving families—
whose encouragement never wavered.
For Chris—
whose hand joined mine, reaching for the same star.
And especially for Vickie—
whose belief and talent made a dream a reality.

Chapter 1

Suffocating waves of heat rose from concrete and asphalt, enfolding Rhone Mitchell in their embrace, making it difficult to breathe.

Stalled cars backed traffic for blocks while out-of-sync signal lights congested intersections. Tempers flared. Blaring horns competed with angry shouts and screeching rubber.

When Rhone's cab stalled, too, he'd given up hope of arriving at his office in air-conditioned luxury. Now, on foot, he regretted not letting the driver call him another. Still several blocks away, downtown Dallas shimmered like a mirage.

Rhone muttered under his breath, wondering what was so terrific about breathable cotton. The white shirt and khaki slacks pressed against his damp body like a second skin. The back of his neck itched, dark brown hair sticking to it, sweat turning natural wave into loose spirals.

Welome home.

Rhone sneered at the thought. Within minutes of his plane landing, he'd rebelled at his reentry to civilization. After returning from Colombia, he'd spent a month recuperating in a rented house on the Northern California coast.

And at the moment, he wanted nothing more than to prop his bare feet on the deck railing, a cold brew in hand, and watch the sun set over the Pacific. Instead, in exchange for the ever-present ocean breeze, he would have to settle for a cool shower.

But even that would have to wait. Business before pleasure, however basic.

Among the cluster of high-rise buildings, Rhone spotted the one that housed his office. He groaned as lunch-hour pedestrians surrounded him, slowing his progress.

With thoughts tuned to the upcoming meeting with his partner, Rhone felt a twinge of reluctance. He considered how Doug Masterson would take the news that Rhone intended to resign. For good, this time. Undoubtedly, Doug would be disappointed. Rhone felt only relief. Solitude had forced him to face facts.

He should have quit while he was ahead. Had tried to, but just couldn't turn his back on unfinished business. He'd botched it. The realization that he should have recognized the trap was a bitter pill to swallow.

Rhone had piled a heap of guilt onto himself because of the failure. He'd risked his life as well as that of his friend...Doug, who'd rescued him from his incarceration in hell. Besides, Rhone was tired of his life-style. Tired of the ugliness and damned tired of the nightmares.

He wanted roots, space. And freedom. Things he'd once taken for granted. Somehow, Rhone vowed, he would find a way to pick up the threads of his life, recreate something meaningful.

Nudging through the crowd to the revolving door, he sighed with relief, a blast of cool air greeting him as he entered the forty-story building. Crossing the lobby, he nodded to the armed guard. Along with a group returning from lunch, Rhone stepped into the elevator.

Too late he realized his error.

Before he could react, the doors closed. The soft whooshing sound might as well have been the clank of metal against metal. Immediately, his head swam and his chest tightened familiarly. He groaned silently. *How could you be so stupid?* It was happening again, and he was powerless to stop it. Seconds stretched into eternity.

He leaned into the corner, resting against the paneling. Sunglasses, still in place, concealed his anguish. The nightmare that so often awakened him in a cold sweat collided with reality, prompted by the confinement of the elevator. He remembered another time, another place.

As though sensing his weakness, the swirling black void descended, distorting perspective, mingling past with present. He was confined in a concrete coffin, three feet wide by five feet tall. A six-inch square at the top had been the only source of air. He remembered the heavy stench of sweat, blood and fear.

At the time, it hadn't occurred to him it was his own.

Rivulets of perspiration had dripped down the sides of his face, across the strap of leather around his neck. The heat tightened the leather like a tourniquet, choking him. With hands and ankles bound, he was helpless to save himself.

Breathe, Mitchell. Deep, slow breaths. Think about something else. Think about Shannen. Rhone struggled, reaching deep in his mind for the memory that had ended his terror so many times before.

His sense of survival forced him to fight the dark void threatening to consume him, to drive him to his knees. He envisioned viridescent eyes, more green than blue, with tiny flecks of gold. Hair the color of sunlight with streaks of mink brown framed a face that was delicate planes and angles. He remembered soft curving lips, a smile that prodded hidden dimples into view. And her skin... He could almost feel the smooth, silky texture.

When the elevator swished to a stop at his floor, it took every ounce of his strength to exit with dignity and walk to the rest room around the corner. Once there, he collapsed against the wall, legs weak and shaky. Cold ceramic seeped through his damp shirt. He closed his eyes on a wave of nausea. Then he breathed deeply, slowly, forcing his lungs to fill with oxygen, willing his stomach to settle.

As the blackness diminished and his senses cleared, he opened his eyes. He knew a trace of illness would linger for several hours. It always did.

Rhone splashed cool water on his face and neck. Close, confined or crowded areas had never bothered him before—until Colombia.

In his mind he still heard the drug-ridden taunting laughter of the man who had directed his brutal punishment.

Jack Norton had been more rabid animal than human, the substance that yielded his wealth eating away at his sanity. The real kicker was, early in his career, Rhone had worked with Jack. Then Jack's life fell apart. He had been in hock up to his ears. His wife left him for another man. Jack saw greener pastures, most likely thinking a fortune would bring his wife back. The quicker the better.

To this day, Rhone didn't think Jack had recognized him.

Rhone wanted only to forget. But as time went on, the past returned to haunt him. He may have escaped physically, but mentally, he was still a hostage. Gritting his teeth, he wadded the paper towel into a tight ball and threw it. It landed in the trash can with a dull thud.

Heading down the hall, he paused at a door marked Suite 801. Using a coded key card, he entered. Gloria, their secretary, looked up from a desk littered with files. Her ageless eyes sparkled when she saw Rhone.

"Well, well. Look who's back." She stood, coming around her desk to hug him. Hands on his arms, she leaned back to scrutinize him. "Gads, darlin', you look awful."

Rhone grinned and opted for a half-truth. "My cab broke down about a mile away and I walked."

"In this heat? Knowing you, I suppose you paid full fare anyway."

"Don't tell anyone," he whispered. "It might ruin my image."

"Rhone. I thought I heard your voice." A sandy-blond counterpart to Rhone leaned against the doorjamb. At six foot three, Doug's eyes leveled with Rhone's, then narrowed, taking in the pallor beneath his friend's tan. Silent communication born from years of working together, of protecting each other's backs, of saving each other's lives, passed between them. Giving an imperceptible nod, Doug turned back into his office.

Rhone followed Doug, then closed the door behind him.

"Your vacation didn't help," Doug said flatly.

"The coast was fantastic. It was the elevator I could've done without."

Doug laughed. "Old habits. And everyone thinks you take the stairs for exercise."

Rhone gave a rueful grin, appreciating Doug's ability to make light of a dark memory. "Yeah, well, *everyone* should see you when a spider invades your space." Bypassing burgundy-upholstered chairs, Rhone strolled to a window, gray carpeting absorbing the sound of his footsteps.

"Ah, but I had you to protect me."

"Sure." Rhone laughed. "Until you took away my machete."

With a smile, Doug sat, crossing his ankles over the corner of his desk. He linked his hands behind his head, his expression turning serious. "I tried to reach you earlier. When I got no answer, I figured you might be heading back."

"No more overseas assignments, Doug."

"Can't say I'm surprised. You tried to tell me before, but I wouldn't listen. Just couldn't believe you really wanted to give it up."

"I don't think I ever could completely. I've decided to put in for a permanent Stateside location." Rhone gave a shrug and grinned. "I guess I still need the action, but on a more domestic basis."

"I wouldn't let the home boys hear you say that." At Rhone's answering laugh, Doug went on. "Where are you planning to relocate?"

"I've been encouraged to consider returning to New York. I haven't decided yet."

"So." Doug spoke with a nonchalant tone. "Where is Shannen these days?"

Rhone's gaze sliced through the space that separated them. "I don't know. Besides, she has nothing to do with my decision."

"I was hoping she had everything to do with it. You two had a good thing going."

"On the surface I suppose it appeared that way."

"Come on, Rhone. Surely you can work out your differences. I'd hate to see you throw it all away without trying."

Doug's comments struck a nerve. Rhone had thought of little else but his estranged wife. In a word, Shannen was the reason he hadn't yet decided where he wanted to settle down. At the same time, he knew she wouldn't appreciate his proximity. Not at this late date.

"Colorado." Rhone's voice was distracted, distant.

"Excuse me?"

"I found out last week Shannen's in Colorado. She took back her maiden name of Richardson. I never anticipated she'd do that. Her phone number is unlisted. She works from her home near the mountain community of Dillon, about sixty miles west of Denver. Keeps a low profile. Apparently, she's sharing the house with a woman who has a kid. Does that sound to you like Shannen is interested in a reconciliation?"

Rhone continued, not waiting for Doug's response. "I don't think so. She made it as difficult as possible for me to find her. The message is clear."

"Aw, hell, Rhone. I've seen you work around, over and through any obstacle thrown in your path. And now, one hundred ten pounds of femininity stops you cold." Doug shook his head. "My guess is your conscience is bothering you. I can only imagine you must have been a real jerk."

Rhone winced, returning his gaze to the window. A jet crossed his line of vision but it was the anger and pain in Shannen's eyes the last time they were together that he saw.

It was true. He'd thought he could have it both ways. A wife, a home, eventually a family. On the flip side, he could carry on with his job, doing what he did best: thriving on the danger, flirting with death, expecting Shannen to sit home. And wait. Thinking only of himself, he'd given no thought to the stress, the anxiety he'd put her through.

When Shannen demanded he choose between her or his job, he'd laughed at her uncharacteristic show of assertiveness. He'd been so sure that's all it was. A show. Rhone winced again. When he'd finally returned home, Shannen was gone. There had been no note, no forwarding address.

Rhone changed after that, though for some time he'd denied Shannen had anything to do with it. He denied that when she left she'd taken a part of him with her. There was a gap in his life, an emptiness that he'd tried to fill by taking on back-to-back assignments. He took stupid risks. Made serious mistakes.

Agreed to go to Colombia.

There, caged like an animal, he'd been forced to face his feelings, confinement becoming as much self-inflicted mental torture as it was physical abuse. He'd vowed to find Shannen, to somehow find a way to make it up to her. If she would let him. He knew she had once loved him. He also knew the possibility of her rejection would be the most difficult risk he'd ever taken.

It was this same mental fencing that kept him from deciding where he wanted to go. He was at a crossroads, unsure of whether to follow his heart or his head. And yet, he always came back to the same conclusion. It *would* be a shame to walk away from Shannen without trying to make amends, never knowing what the outcome might have been.

Rhone sighed. Changing the subject, he turned back to Doug. Weariness edged Rhone's words. "Any particular reason why you tried to reach me in California?"

Doug's expression turned grim. He motioned Rhone to a chair closer to his desk. Once Rhone was seated, Doug answered. "Yeah. At six o'clock last night, Jack Norton's twin brother, Jimmy, became a free man."

A string of colorful adjectives filled the silence. "Mandatory parole?"

Doug nodded.

Irritation rankled. Norton—the clichéd bad penny. Rhone curled his lip, thinking that once again he had to put his future on hold. But on the heels of that thought came another.

Maybe Jimmy's turning up again was a blessing in disguise. Maybe it was the opportunity he needed to exorcise the past, to exorcise the nightmares once and for all.

"Jimmy will be coming after me."

"Not if he values his freedom," Doug said.

Rhone's neck rested atop padded leather. He stared at the ceiling, the tone of his voice matter-of-fact. "He blames me for his brother's death. To Jimmy, I was the man in charge of the operation that killed his brother, and that's enough." He sat up again. "Kill me and he's evened the score. It would be worth spending the rest of his life behind bars."

"There was a spray of gunfire. No one knows who killed Jack. Could've been one of his own men."

"It doesn't matter. Not to Jimmy."

"Okay, then, we'll go after him."

"No. He's my problem. Not yours."

"Are you crazy?" Changing positions, Doug leaned forward. "Jimmy will have enlisted Jack's army of throat-slitting scum to back him up."

"I disagree." Rhone picked up a pencil amid the clutter on Doug's desk. "Jimmy's different. Jack felt powerful when he could order others to do his dirty work or fight his battles for him. Jimmy's a loner. He's sly like a rattlesnake and meaner than a school of piranha that's caught the scent of blood. Not hard to figure why Jack is dead and Jimmy is still alive."

"Regardless, we started this ugly mess together. We'll finish it the same way."

They glared openly, each defying the other to argue, neither willing to back down.

The buzz of the intercom interrupted their stalemate.

"There's a man on line one demanding to speak to Rhone. Says it's a matter of life or death."

The pencil laced between Rhone's fingers snapped in two.

"Norton." Rhone and Doug spoke in unison.

Rhone stood. "We'll take it on the box."

Doug turned to his computer, punched keys in rapid succession, then nodded.

Pushing the button on the speaker phone, Rhone elicited a lazy drawl. "Mitchell."

"Don't bother with a trace," the muffled, distant voice advised. "I know exactly how much time I have."

"What's on your mind, Norton?"

Jimmy gave a low laugh, the sound reminding Rhone of Jack. Unconsciously, Rhone's hands curled into tight fists.

"I want you to suffer. The way you made me suffer. Before I put you out of your misery, Mitchell, you're gonna know what it feels like to lose someone—"

"Norton, wait!" Rhone couldn't help the note of desperation.

The line went dead.

Both men cursed. Doug raised his arms in frustration. "Just a few more seconds, I would've had him."

Instant rage, unlike any he'd ever known, shook Rhone to the core. His voice reverberated with it. "Never mind. I already know, if not where he is, where he's headed." A white line formed around his mouth. He felt the constant flicker of muscle along his jaw, and his gut twisted with the effort to harness his anger, maintain control.

He had to get to Norton first. Dear God, before it was too late.

When Rhone spoke again, his voice was raw with a strangled mixture of ice-cold fear and boiling fury. "The son of a bitch is going after Shannen."

Chapter 2

"Maa-Maa!"

The sound of her son's childish excitement stole her attention. Smiling, Shannen glanced up from the drafting table in time to see him struggling to push to his feet. Stubborn determination glittered in his eyes.

"You can do it," she coaxed softly.

Shannen held her breath as her fifteen-month-old knotted his face into a furious frown of concentration. She uncurled from her position, cramped muscles complaining from the hours she'd worked without a break.

"Maa-Maa?"

"I'm right here, honey," she promised, slipping from the chair and kneeling on the floor. "You can do it, Nicky." Shannen worried her lower lip as she studied him, not wanting him to give up as he had so many times recently. "Walk to Mommy."

With a plop, he landed on the floor.

She fought the urge to rescue him, knowing she had to allow him to take these first steps into the world by himself...as much as she wanted to shield and protect her precious gift forever.

"That's it," Shannen encouraged as he grabbed hold of the coffee table. She didn't mind that dull fingerprints marred the shiny surface.

Once steady, he reached out a foot, then instantly pulled it back again.

She chuckled. "You can do it, honey."

Nicky flashed a grin before tentatively moving one foot forward. Shannen knotted her hands by her sides, positive that this afternoon he would walk to her.

He let go of the table.

Arms, bent at the elbow and raised to shoulder level, reminded her of a baby sparrow she'd once watched as it peered over the edge of its nest in a towering ponderosa pine.

Nicky wobbled. Her stomach performed several flips. Then, slowly, carefully balancing on legs as stiff as a robot's, he took his first step...and his second. Tears of joy stung her eyes.

On the final step, Nicky squealed with childish delight, then pitched forward into the security of her embrace. Shannen laughed, hugging him close and pressing a kiss on top of his still-downy soft hair.

Truly, she thought, times like these made everything worthwhile. Unable to contain her thrill, she scooped him up and called for Maria. After all they'd been through together, Maria deserved to share in the excitement.

"*¿Sí, señora?*"

"Watch," Shannen said, standing Nicky next to the coffee table.

Gone was the frown, replaced by a huge grin. Shannen's nod of encouragement was the only cue Nicky needed. Eagerly he performed his new skill once again.

No matter how old she got, Shannen knew she would never forget these precious moments. It seemed like only yesterday he'd been a tiny, helpless infant. She swallowed the lump in her throat at the thought that, all too soon, these moments would also be yesterday's memories.

From the doorway, Maria applauded enthusiastically. "*¡Muy bien!* Very good," she repeated in English. "In a day or two, we run to keep up, *sí?*"

Shannen grinned up at the housekeeper. "Better make that an *hour* or two."

While Maria finished preparing lunch, Shannen took Nicky outside. Holding her son's hand, she met his proud grin with one of her own. Slowly they walked the length of the deck, the sun-warmed redwood feeling good against Shannen's bare feet.

Nicky paused, pointing a childish fist.

"Hummingbirds," Shannen supplied. She sat him on the railing where he could better see the miniature birds flitting around the feeder. Wrapping her arms around his middle, she held him securely in place.

She wished he would always stay small, innocent. She dreaded the day when he would question the other half of his heritage, question the whereabouts of his father.

As the image of Rhone Mitchell came to mind, Shannen quickly shoved it away, reminding herself he was part of her past and that's where he would stay. She didn't want Nicky to care. With unashamed selfishness, she wanted to be all he needed. Just as he was all she needed.

He turned inquisitive eyes to hers. "Pay?"

"Play," she corrected. "We'll play until lunch is ready." Lifting him, Shannen caught the fresh scent of baby shampoo and powder. "Mmm, you smell good."

As Nicky was recently prone to do, he took her face between his palms. Puckering up, he planted a wet kiss on her cheek.

Shannen's heart swelled.

Reaching the small patch of grass behind the house, Shannen lowered Nicky to his feet. She held his hand, aiding his balance over the uneven ground, guiding him to his stockpile of yellow metal trucks and assorted cars.

"Vroom, vroom," he said. Letting go, he sat, already absorbed in his make-believe world.

Shannen rested her shoulder against the bark of an ancient tree, new leaves providing shade from the glare of the cloudless Colorado sky. Here in the Rocky Mountains, the air was clean and clear, the sky bluer than any place she'd ever seen. She'd attended college in Colorado and loved it then. Returning had been one of the few benefits of leaving Rhone.

Damn. Why was he intruding on her thoughts today?

Maybe because the older your son gets, the more he resembles his father. The thought was as accurate as it was unwelcome. Further, it was laced with guilt.

Her husband had no idea Nicholas existed.

Stoically, Shannen told herself Rhone had made his choices and she wasn't one of them. She had needed more from him than he'd been willing to give.

Threatening to leave Rhone had been tough, painful, because in spite of everything, she had loved him. Following through had been agony.

Shannen had made it as difficult as possible for him to find her. She'd done it to prove how serious she was about not settling for less. But all the while, she knew with his connections he could find her. If he wanted to.

Now Shannen didn't want him to find her, fearing what he would do. She had kept his son a secret too long.

Despite the early-summer warmth, a cold chill crept up her spine and found root in her soul. Rhone could be a formidable man when crossed. No, better he never knew about Nicky.

"Lunch, *señora!*"

"Thanks, Maria. Be right there." Cupping her hands to her mouth, Shannen called Nicholas. "Nicky, time to eat."

"Uh-uh." Animatedly, he shook his head. Just watching the motion gave her a headache.

"Uh-huh," she affirmed, pushing away from the tree and letting blades of grass squish between her toes.

Nicholas rose on all fours, pushing his bottom upward. On wobbly legs, he stood. Squealing, he tried to run. Before his lack of coordination toppled him, Shannen swung him off the ground.

He giggled.

She laughed, grateful she'd been blessed with this child.

As she carried him up the stairs, she shuddered, remembering how, at three months premature, his life had hung in delicate balance. During those first tenuous weeks, the scales had threatened to tip the wrong way. And during those weeks that had seemed like months, Shannen had spent every available hour at the hospital, constantly hovering nearby, silently prodding her tiny son to fight. Ultimately, the pediatrician credited Nicky's survival with her vigilance and his own will to live.

The day she took him home was the happiest of her life, but there'd been no one to share it with. Then, as now, Shannen felt a conflicting mix of emotion and adamantly refused to acknowledge the part of her that missed Rhone.

"I made his favorite today," Maria said, setting a plate of hot dogs and mixed vegetables on the table.

Shannen placed Nicholas in his high chair and tied a Colorado Rockies baseball bib around him. She and Maria smiled, silently acknowledging that he wore more than he ate. He seemed so excited by his efforts, Shannen didn't have the heart to help him.

Finally Nicholas blinked and yawned.

"I'll put him down for his nap," she told Maria, wiping Nicky's face and hands.

"But your deadline..."

"I only have an hour or two of work left to do, and I can send it by overnight express."

Maria shook her head, clucking. "I don't know why you hired me."

"So I can spend more time with Nicky," Shannen tossed over her shoulder, an appreciative grin tilting the corners of her mouth.

Her foot barely touched the first step leading to Nicky's bedroom when she heard a vehicle pull into the drive. Not expecting anyone, Shannen frowned, turning toward the door.

She juggled Nicholas onto her left hip and stood on tiptoe, looking through the peephole. She didn't recognize the primer gray pickup.

A man climbed out, moving around to the passenger side. Brilliant red hair, piled high, met Shannen's curious perusal. Dressed in tight jeans, the woman who emerged stood as tall as the man. Her knitted top stretched across a well-endowed chest, leaving little to the imagination.

The man had dark hair, straight and over his collar. The sides and front were slicked back, revealing a high forehead. Where the woman's jeans were faded, his looked like they had yet to meet a washing machine and fabric softener. Under the navy corduroy jacket, Shannen couldn't help but notice creases down the front of the pale blue shirt—as though he'd just taken it out of the package and put it on.

Unimpressed, her frown deepened. She didn't have the faintest idea who they were; and whatever they were selling, she wanted none of it.

A refusal already forming on her lips, she swung the door open.

Recovering from his surprise, the man lowered his hand from the brass knocker, speaking before Shannen had a chance. "Afternoon, ma'am. Sorry to bother you. My, my, that's a handsome boy you have there. Bet you and his daddy are real proud."

Immediately, Shannen regretted opening the door. She stiffened, hugging Nicky tighter. Looking into the man's eyes made her skin crawl. They were dark, bottomless pools—cold and calculating. Shifting, they seemed to assess everything and miss nothing.

"Whatever you're selling, I'm not interested." She spoke firmly, hoping to hide her nervousness. She stepped back to close the door.

Boldly, the man stuck a scuffed boot against the jamb.

"I'm with McPherson Realty, ma'am. I'm sure you're busy. This won't take long."

Shannen glared, a surge of anger overriding her concern. In a flash, the months of self-defense training Rhone had insisted she take—would have insisted every woman take if he could—rushed back. She'd scoffed at his reasoning then, thinking she would never have cause to use it. And now, more than two years later, she wasn't sure if she remembered how. She prayed she wouldn't have to find out.

"My client here," the man continued, nodding toward the woman, "is interested in buying your house."

Taken aback, Shannen gave the redhead another thorough inspection. She didn't look like the type who made her living on the right side of the law; certainly, she didn't appear able to afford anything remotely resembling Shannen's house.

She returned her attention to the man. "My home is not for sale. Now if you'll excuse me..." Shannen's expression dared him to defy her the right to refuse.

His jaw clenched, then he smiled. A smile that never reached his eyes. "Think about it," he said. "I'll check back, in case you change your mind."

"Don't bother. I will *not* change my mind."

The man shrugged, his glance resting on Nicholas. "You say that now. Who knows what can happen...in a day or two?"

"*Señora,* who do you talk to?" Maria called from the kitchen.

Disgust and irritation rippled through Shannen's reply. "No one." She closed the door on the man's smirk, the woman's pout.

"The audacity of some people," Shannen grumbled. Turning the dead bolt, she headed for the stairs.

Nicholas yawned again. Snuggling against her neck, he slipped his thumb into his mouth.

In his room, Shannen feathered a blanket—one that Maria had quilted—over his small, sleepy body and gave him a kiss.

"Ba," he demanded.

"Bear," she said, and retrieved the small stuffed animal from the corner of his crib. "Sweet dreams, my baby boy," she said softly. For the next few minutes, she stood in the doorway, watching the easy, rhythmic rise and fall of his breaths. Breaths he'd once struggled for. Occasionally, still did. Being born too soon had weakened his lungs. A common cold or sniffles from seasonal allergies turned into bronchitis and pneumonia within hours of onset. She kept a supply of medication on hand to help prevent those complications. Although the chance he would develop asthma was high, she preferred to think of it as a phase he would eventually outgrow.

Shannen returned to her drafting table, forcing herself to concentrate on finishing the project. Over an hour later, she stretched and took a final glance at her work. Her critical eye was pleased with the job she'd done. A degree in graphic arts and fluency in six foreign languages had proven a profitable combination. Better still, she could work from home.

Piling the papers together, she prepared a package for overnight shipment. After telling Maria her plans, Shannen climbed into the driver's seat of her four-wheel drive vehicle. She inserted the key in the ignition and hesitated, glancing at the house. *Her* house, she thought, brimming with pride. Hers and Nicky's. Finding the log two-story and the rustic setting had been a dream come true. They were surrounded by forest and wildlife, a welcome contrast to the high-rise apartment she and Rhone had shared in New York. It wasn't hard to understand why she'd been approached to sell. Shannen supposed there were those who would, if the price was right.

The Realtor's dark, piercing eyes that had seemed to mock her nudged Shannen's thoughts. She shook her head, trying to dispel the mental picture.

Before she could, a shiver traced across her shoulder blades and down her spine. Her breath caught and held. A spontaneous, undeniable feeling of being watched made her spin around in the seat.

For several seconds, she peered into the woods, looking for movement.

She saw no lurking shadows, nothing out of the ordinary. A hand over her heart, she gave a shaky laugh. Apparently, the stranger had unnerved her more than she'd realized. Come to think of it, the company he worked for didn't sound familiar. To ease her mind, Shannen jotted the name and made a mental note to check it out while she was in town.

Shannen drove down the steep dirt road until she reached the outskirts of Dillon—a mountain community big enough for her to remain as anonymous as she wanted, yet have the conveniences she needed. Including a doctor.

Dr. Jonathen Peterson was more than Nicky's physician. She considered him a good friend, though not long ago he'd made it plain he was interested in far more than friendship. Shannen might have been, too, if the circumstances were different. As Jon frequently reminded her and failed to understand why, she still had legal ties to Rhone. She'd explained that initially, she'd pursued a di-

vorce but wasn't now because she was afraid Rhone would
find out about Nicky. Jon discounted her fears of what
Rhone might do, arguing that any judge would side with
her. Shannen wasn't so sure.

Furthermore, as if her life weren't complicated enough
where men were concerned, she knew it was a matter of
time before Jon demanded she make a choice. Though she
couldn't blame him, she didn't much care for being on the
receiving end of ultimatums.

After dropping her envelope at the post office, she
drove to Jonathen's clinic.

"He's been expecting you," a young receptionist
greeted. "Come on back."

In Jonathen's office, Shannen took a seat, grabbing the
magazine she'd left there last time. A few minutes later,
he entered, his blue eyes offering a welcome that a part of
her wanted to accept. The less sane part. The same part
that had fallen for the cool, handsome looks of Rhone
Mitchell.

With abstract interest, Shannen noticed Jonathen made
no motion to remove his lab coat or the stethoscope
draped around his neck.

"Sorry, Shannen," he said, a smile of regret tinting his
eyes. "I'll have to take a rain check on that cappuccino I
promised you. I had a couple emergencies this morning,
and I'm running behind schedule."

"I understand. We'll make it another day." She tried
not to show her relief. Today she just wanted to be home.
The harder she tried to forget about the real-estate agent,
the more his strange visit replayed in her mind. It was on
the tip of her tongue to tell Jon about it, but as he'd said,
he was busy.

"About our dinner date tomorrow, I'll pick you up—
say sevenish?"

"That's fine," Shannen said, rising. "Oh, before I go,
I need to get a prescription refill for Nicky."

Jonathen scribbled some indecipherable hieroglyphics on a piece of paper, scrawled an illegible signature across the top, then ripped the sheet from his pad. "Bring him by for an official visit soon."

"I will," she promised, folding the paper in half and slipping it into her purse.

At the drugstore, while she waited, Shannen asked the pharmacist for a phone book. She checked companies in the realty section.

There was no listing for McPherson.

"May I use your phone?" Shannen asked, somehow managing to keep her voice level. At the pharmacist's nod, Shannen punched in the number for Information, her finger shaking.

"I'm sorry, ma'am," the operator finally said. "I don't show a listing for McPherson Realty in the area."

Trying to slow the frantic pounding of her pulse, Shannen replaced the receiver. Immediately she grabbed it back and dialed home. One ring. Two. "Come on, Maria," she urged. Three rings. "Answer."

The recorder clicked on.

Shannen made every effort to stifle the panic that tried to claim her while she paid for the prescription.

The police. Should she call the police? Walking briskly to her car, she discounted the mental suggestion. Her tendency to be overprotective was based, she knew, on an ever-present fear of losing Nicky. She'd come so close when he was born, she'd never completely recovered. On more than one occasion, she'd played into the cruel games of her imagination.

Still, the need to know Nicholas was fine had her driving as fast as she dared.

Shannen parked in the driveway and grabbed the keys from the ignition. She slammed the car door, heading for the house.

"Maria! I'm back!"

In the answering silence, Shannen noted that no scent of dinner filled the air. Maria usually started cooking by now. "Maria?" Probably upstairs with Nicky, Shannen told herself.

At a jog, she took the stairs two at a time, only to discover the nursery empty. She pulled aside the colorful drapes and glanced out the window, hoping to see her son and Maria in the backyard. When she didn't, Shannen called the housekeeper's name again and headed downstairs.

Shannen's pulse had added a few extra beats and her breaths came in shallow bursts. *Calm down,* she warned herself.

Earlier thoughts of Rhone returned. Fear of his discovery had her momentarily gripping the banister. But if Rhone were here, surely his vehicle would be parked out front.

Dark, shifting eyes superimposed over Rhone's image in her mind.

The Realtor. Oh, Lord, had he made good his threat and returned? "What if he's hurt Nicky and Maria?" Her voice cracked on a wave of sheer terror.

She gulped a drink of oxygen, repeating to herself that she was being irrational.

But Nicky was the light of her life.

Shannen rushed into the kitchen. The echo of her footsteps sliced through the eerie stillness in the vacant room. Something was wrong. She felt it.

"They must have gone for a walk," she said aloud, as if the sound of her voice would calm her. After all, her house sat on two acres of land, most of it heavily forested. It wasn't inconceivable that Nicky and Maria would be out of sight.

An acrid smell met her nose and she looked toward the stove. Smoke was rising and the odor was getting worse.

Tentacles of fear strangled what little optimism she'd clung to.

She grabbed for a pot holder, switched off the gas and pulled the burning aluminum pan from the stove. Obviously it had only been filled with water, in preparation for the peeled and sliced potatoes on the cutting board. Shannen knew Maria wasn't irresponsible enough to leave the stove unattended.

The smoke detector let out a belated, alarming shrill.

"Maria!" Shannen's voice had risen to a hysterical octave.

The noise of something crashing to the floor vibrated through the kitchen. Startled, Shannen jumped.

Following the sound, she gave no thought to danger as she ran to the pantry, yanking open the door. Maria, eyes frightfully wide, mouth gagged, hands and feet bound with blood-restricting knots of rope, lay on the floor. Several cans of food lay scattered around her. Somehow she had managed to kick them off the shelves.

"Oh my God!" Rushing to the woman, Shannen tried her best to untie the gag. She fumbled for several long seconds before giving up and hurrying to the kitchen for a pair of shears.

By the time she'd freed the housekeeper from the strip of cloth, a thin line of blood trickled from the corner of Maria's mouth. Ripping open a package of paper towels, Shannen took one, dabbing it on the small cut. "Where's Nicky?" she demanded, adrenaline threatening to steal what remained of rational thought.

Maria babbled in her native language.

"Maria!" Shannen's tone was sharp. "You've got to calm down and tell me what happened."

Tears gushed from the woman's eyes.

Shannen repeated herself in Spanish. Maria continued to cry and shake her head. Shannen drew in a breath, dragging air deep into her lungs. Taking the woman by the shoulders, she carefully enunciated, "Where is Nicky?"

"Gone. They . . . they . . ."

"*¿Sí?*" Shannen prompted, desperate.

"They took him. He's gone, *señora*. I tried to stop them. . . ."

Shannen's entire body began to tremble uncontrollably. "Where? Who? When?"

Tears poured from Maria's eyes.

The smoke detector continued to shriek, adding fuel to Shannen's panic.

She forced herself to sever the ropes slicing into Maria's skin. Bleeding welts showed the brutality of her son's kidnappers. No matter what, Shannen knew it couldn't be Rhone. He couldn't have changed this much.

Shannen closed her eyes against chaotic, overwhelming emotion. She had to think. Think. Even if it was the last thing she wanted to do.

"We've got to save the *niño*," Maria muttered miserably.

Shannen clenched her fists, not caring that her nails cut into her palms. Scared and angry, she forced herself to her feet. With eyes glazed by hot, unshed tears, she groped for the phone and punched the three emergency digits she'd prayed she'd never have to use.

Then she sank onto the floor, knees curled to her chest and began to cry, her body convulsing with huge, aching sobs.

Rhone's fingers tightened around the steering wheel of the rented four-wheel drive vehicle. He'd made good time in the air, but the trek up this damned mountain was slowing him down considerably. The narrow winding road had more curves than a well-built woman, he fumed. Each was concealed by a veil of jutting rock formations that were barely visible in the opaque darkness, demanding more of his attention than he wanted to give.

Instead of hours, it felt like days since Jimmy's phone call. Immediately following it, Doug had made arrangements for a Learjet to fly Rhone to Colorado. Having the carry-on bag Rhone had taken to the coast with him, he hadn't wasted time going home to repack. Doug promised to catch a flight first thing in the morning.

Rhone had gladly accepted Doug's assistance. With Shannen's safety at stake, Rhone would take all the help he could get.

But what if he was already too late? What if Norton had gotten to Shannen first? *What ifs* Rhone couldn't bear to think about and yet, couldn't purge from his mind.

With bitter frustration, he leaned his head against the back of the seat. The crisp breeze that floated through the opened window surrounded him—a welcome change from Dallas. For a moment, his glance strayed toward the sky. At this altitude, the stars were unbelievable, looking close enough for him to reach up and grab.

Shannen was a stargazer, he remembered. And a dreamer. She found joy in things most people took for granted. He smiled. Once, together, she cast a wish on a shooting star. More the realist, he'd played along at her insistence, to humor her. To his way of thinking, though, no star could have compared to the one he'd held in his arms that night. They still didn't, he decided.

An obscure dirt side road brought Rhone back to the present. Reversing, he illuminated the street sign with his headlights. Pinewood Drive. He felt a stirring of anticipation as he turned. And on the heels of anticipation, icy fingers of dread teased his composure.

Without the lights of other traffic, the darkness became all consuming. The stars and the crescent moon did nothing to light his way. What appeared to be dense forest lined the road.

Desolate.

Secluded.

Whatever had possessed Shannen to live in such seclusion? He didn't like it. Not one bit.

Apprehension gained momentum the longer he drove, the closer he got to his destination.

About a mile and a half later, lights from a house beckoned through the trees. Slowing down, Rhone looked for an identifying house number on a mailbox, post, anything. There was none. He turned anyway, sensing the house that was situated in the clearing was Shannen's. His approach startled several deer. With graceful leaps, they disappeared among the trees.

In the beam of his headlights, he saw the prefabricated log two-story. Following the drive to the north side of the house, Rhone frowned, parking behind a white sedan. He noticed the chrome spotlights, the government license plate. Looking beyond the cruiser, he saw a four-wheel drive with the local police emblem and another vehicle belonging to state patrol.

He cursed savagely as panic shot through him. He'd arrived all right, but too damned late.

Chapter 3

"There ain't no one comin' after us, is there?"

Jimmy Norton glanced from the rearview mirror to the buxom redhead next to him. "If there was, don't ya think I could handle it?"

"Yes, Jimmy."

"I'll tell you what I can't handle—that Mitchell brat's wailin'. If you don't shut him up, you're gonna wish someone was comin' after us. Got it?"

"Yes, Jimmy."

"Yes, Jimmy," he mimicked. He shook his head with disgust. Blocking out the racket, Jimmy reran the events of the past twenty-four hours through his mind, relishing each.

Hearing fear in Rhone Mitchell's voice had been the highlight of the day. Jimmy snickered aloud, mentally patting himself on the back.

But his pleasure was short-lived. In the confining cab of the truck, the baby's wailing reached a screaming pitch.

* * *

At a sprint, Rhone's feet touched one of the five steps leading to Shannen's front door. Graphic pictures of restitution flashed through his mind. To hell with common courtesy, he thought. Ignoring the brass knocker, he reached for the knob.

A faint rustling of dried brush, then a muffled snap of a twig diverted his attention.

Reflexes took over. Withdrawing a knife from the narrow leather scabbard in his boot, Rhone stood perfectly still, every nerve taut, ready to spring. Keen awareness honed to delicate precision from years of training focused outward—waiting.

The deer he'd seen earlier could have returned, but his instincts told him no. Experience in the jungle had taught him well the cadence of wildlife. Human footsteps sounded completely different.

At exactly the right moment, Rhone ducked and turned. With minimum exertion, he knocked his opponent's weapon to the redwood porch. A grunt, then a moan followed as Rhone bent the man's arm at an awkward angle, holding the blade of steel against exposed flesh. It would take a second, Rhone thought. Only a second.

At that moment the door swung open.

Immediately, Rhone came to two conclusions. One, he didn't much favor looking down the barrel of a .357. Two, as light fell, Rhone identified who he held in his death grip. Muttering a string of oaths, he released the man.

Chagrined, Brian Yarrow rubbed his neck, as though needing to reassure himself it was still intact. "Trust me when I say," he told the patrolman, "Rhone Mitchell isn't someone you want to point a gun at."

"Rhone Mitchell?" the patrolman asked, holstering his weapon. "I've heard of you. DEA?"

"At one time. Among other things."

With a cursory glance at Brian, a special agent he'd trained, and no apology, Rhone sheathed the knife. "Where's Shannen? Where's my wife?"

Rhone strode past the patrolman, not waiting for an answer. Brian hustled to catch up. "Your wife? Then that would make the kid... Mitchell! Wait a minute. There's something you should know."

With single-minded purpose, he ignored Brian. Crossing the foyer, Rhone heard a female voice.

Shannen's?

Without calling attention to himself, he paused at the entrance to the living room.

A dark-haired woman, presumably Shannen's roommate, sat next to her. Facing away from Rhone, Shannen responded to the officer's questions in a tone that said she'd already answered them more than once. Irritation rippled through him. Rhone cocked his head, trying to decipher the words and failed. Her voice was thick with unshed tears, husky with many already shed.

"If you leave me now, I won't be here when you come back."

The last exchange between them replayed in his mind with relentless accuracy. Her voice had sounded exactly the same. Rhone didn't have to see her face to know there would be a haunted expression in her eyes. The question was, Why?

Across the room, the officer looked up and spotted Rhone. Shannen stopped midsentence, following the officer's gaze. Rhone was reluctant to meet her eyes, afraid of what he would see and yet, he was unable to look away.

A whisper of warmth altered her stunned expression. All too quickly, the warmth was replaced by confusion, then, accusing anger.

Tears streaming over her cheeks, Shannen jumped from the couch. Golden hair hung to her shoulders in disarray, dark circles under her eyes punctuating pale skin devoid of makeup. She looked as though she'd been through hell, but to him, she was beautiful. She would never be anything less. He stepped forward and placed his hands on her shoulders, speaking her name.

She shook off his touch, as though finding it repulsive. "Damn you, Rhone Mitchell. Isn't there any place I can be safe?"

In the face of her anger, Rhone almost laughed out loud, his relief was so great. Norton hadn't yet made good his threat—though, obviously he'd made contact with Shannen, voicing his intentions and terrifying her. For that and crimes only Rhone and Doug knew about, Norton would pay. When he made his move, they would be ready.

Brian stepped up behind Rhone. "We've put an APB out on Norton. Shannen . . . that is, Mrs. Mitchell—"

"Ms. Richardson," Shannen said through clenched teeth.

Watching her, Rhone's eyes narrowed. So, that's how it is, he challenged her silently. *We pick up where we left off.*

As if in a daze, Rhone comprehended the rest of Brian's words.

"What's this about an APB?" Rhone fired the question. Breaking eye contact with Shannen, he turned on Brian, voice dropping to sea level. "What the *hell* is going on?"

Brian's glance flickered between Shannen and Rhone before settling on his superior. "Ms. . .er, Richardson and her housekeeper gave us enough details for a composite sketch. They also identified Jimmy Norton's photo."

"Any particular reason why?"

Tension ricocheted through the room.

Rhone didn't recall Brian demonstrating as much hesitancy at the academy. Quite the contrary. *Cocky* and *obnoxious* were words that came readily to mind. As Brian's instructor, Rhone took credit for reforming the kid's overinflated ego. A trait that would have gotten him killed sooner or later. Sooner was a *definite* possibility if he didn't speak up, Rhone thought, with ill-humored impatience.

Apparently taking pity on Brian, Shannen squared her shoulders, confronting Rhone.

"There's been a kidnapping. *Your* ex-con was here earlier, posing as a real-estate agent." Shannen paused. Twisting her hands, she took a deep breath, then continued, "He came back later while I was in town. Maria, my housekeeper, didn't see him when he was here the first time. The description she gave the officer this evening matched mine."

"You're absolutely certain it was Norton?"

The look she gave him shot holes in any hope Rhone had she was mistaken. He didn't like the idea Norton had been so close to Shannen that he could have reached out and touched her—or worse. Where she was concerned, explicit knowledge of what Jimmy Norton was capable of made Rhone break out in a cold sweat.

He redirected his line of questioning. "Maria lives with you?"

"Yes."

Rhone frowned, recalling the information he'd been given after he'd ordered the trace of Shannen's whereabouts. The same information he'd passed on to Doug earlier—that Shannen supposedly shared the house with another woman who had a kid.

"Then the child is hers?" Rhone asked. It didn't make sense. Why would Norton take the kid when taking Shannen would have been a direct hit?

Looking over his shoulder toward Maria, Rhone thought she looked more the grandmotherly type, but who was he to say? Maybe the kid was her grandson.

His eyes narrowed as he studied the disheveled woman huddled in a corner of the couch. For the first time he noticed that the outer edge of her mouth and lip were swollen and discolored. She stared blankly across the room, her fingers knotted tightly in her lap. It wasn't her tense knuckles that arrested his attention. Bruises, dark blue with streaks of red, encircled both wrists. The chasm of hatred Rhone felt widened dangerously, evoked by the man who had dared to inflict such blatant abuse.

When Shannen didn't offer confirmation, Rhone looked back at her, speaking more sharply than he'd intended. "I'll need a picture of the child."

"How do you know it was a child that was taken?"

"Come on, Shannen." A ring of impatience surrounded his words. "With my resources, there's very little I don't know."

Shannen's chin tilted, though her voice quivered. "Then why ask me, when you already know it all?"

Rhone ground his teeth, impatience giving way to full-fledged irritation. "Because I'm lacking details that were apparently considered too minor to pass on." Silently, Rhone cursed the responsible investigator.

"Minor... details?" Each syllable was clearly enunciated in a monotone that held a jagged edge of tightly controlled anger.

He flinched. "I'm sure you're close to the child and understandably, you're upset." Rhone changed his tone to gentle coaxing. "I can't help if I don't know who I'm looking for."

"Who asked you to help?"

"When a known... felon threatens to harm a member of my family, that's all the invitation I need. If you have a problem with that—tough. The fact Norton screwed up and took the child instead of you doesn't make me any less involved. I will do everything I can to get the child back unharmed and put Norton behind bars where he belongs.''

Shannen stared into space somewhere over his left shoulder. Grief and despair battled for prime time, wreaking havoc with her calm facade.

''You're looking for a fifteen-month-old boy,'' she finally gave. ''His name is Nicholas. Sometimes we call him Nicky.''

Her shrug belied the fury that sparked from the depths of green-blue eyes that turned on him.

''There's a few additional *minor* details you should know. Nicholas is extremely susceptible to upper-respiratory infections—'' Shannen's voice broke. She swallowed rapidly before continuing, flinging the words at him as though holding him accountable for their meaning.

''Nicky often requires medication. If he doesn't get it, his condition can become life threatening within hours.''

Rhone sighed. He knew it wouldn't matter that Nicholas belonged to someone else; the hurting would be the same. Shannen loved kids. She always had. In fact, she couldn't stand watching movies when, on-screen, a kid's life, or that of an animal, was in jeopardy.

Shannen had wanted a baby, his baby, she'd said. But the timing had been all wrong. Unfortunately, Rhone hadn't been able to explain the reasons to Shannen. And when he could have, it was too late. She was gone. In the span of a heartbeat, he knew he would give anything to turn back time, to right the wrongs. To love her the way she deserved.

At the moment, she looked lost, alone and afraid. How like her to hide her feelings behind a mask of anger. How like human nature. A common reaction, considering fear and anger were kissing cousins. Wanting to offer comfort, Rhone ran his hand up Shannen's spine.

He sought her nape and the tense muscles he knew he would find there. Gently yet firmly, he massaged them between fingers and thumb.

A circuit of tremors shook her slender body, the circuit passing and connecting within himself.

She could deny all she wanted that nothing existed between them. Furthermore, it was of no consequence to him what name she'd chosen to use—it was as much a lie as were her efforts to convince him she was immune to him. Had the circumstances been different, he would have taken great delight in pointing out her transparency.

"The picture?" he repeated.

She moved away, again distancing herself from his touch. "Do you think we could, um . . . talk privately?"

Rhone deliberately took his time pocketing the small notebook and pen. He watched Shannen nibble on her bottom lip, remembering the nervous habit that had clued him in to stormy seas on more than one occasion. As though reading his mind, her glance darted from his. Rhone would have sworn she was hiding something, could have sworn he'd caught the foul scent of true confession. Quickly as the thought came, he discarded it. As usual, where Shannen was concerned, he was jumping to conclusions.

Her words reminded him they weren't alone and Rhone glanced around the room.

Not bothering to hide their interest, their audience appeared to hang on every word. Rhone scowled and the officers shifted, a clearing of throats breaking the tense silence. A terse command was on the tip of Rhone's tongue when Brian interceded. Ordering the men outside, Brian escaped with them.

"I'll take Maria upstairs to her room," Shannen said, her tone reflecting the countenance of exhaustion and despair she didn't try to conceal.

He sighed again, wanting to take her in his arms, to re-assure her, to take into himself her devastation and anguish if only she'd let him.

"There's coffee in the kitchen," Shannen added. "Help yourself."

A shot of Jack Daniel's held more appeal, but Rhone doubted Shannen stocked anything stronger than her favorite diet cola. Other than an occasional glass of wine, he recalled she rarely indulged. Coffee would have to do.

Her arm around the small dark-haired woman, Shannen paused next to Rhone. "Maria, this is my..." Faltering, Shannen's glance flew to Rhone's.

"Husband," he supplied smoothly. Without regard for Shannen's obvious discomfort, Rhone took Maria's hand into his own.

Maria's expression told of her pain and regret. "I am so sorry, *señor.*"

In Maria's native language, Rhone explained she had nothing to be sorry for, that she'd done nothing wrong.

"I should never have opened the door," she added, her tone resentful and unforgiving.

Rhone understood only too well the feelings of regret that tormented her. "Do not mourn yet, Maria."

A small cry escaped her bruised lips as she flung herself at Rhone, hugging him with desperate strength.

Surprised, he hugged her back, his glance seeking Shannen's over Maria's head. A flicker of compassion briefly warmed his wife's expression, but whether it was directed at him or Maria, Rhone couldn't tell.

Shannen moved forward and gently pried Maria away from him to lead her toward the stairs. Rhone watched them ascend, listening to the calm and soothing tone Shannen used to reassure the housekeeper.

In the kitchen, he poured coffee. He took a sip of the black liquid, pacing the length of the room. Something bothered him. Something he couldn't quite put his finger on. More annoying was the fact that he sensed whatever it was, was ridiculously obvious. Like a forgotten word that resided in memory barely out of reach.

Restless, he set the mug down, sloshing coffee over the rim. Unlocking the window over the sink, he opened it and breathed deeply. The night air, crisp and scented with pine, offered a measure of relief.

Rhone felt rather than heard Shannen's approach behind him. He turned, leaning his hip against the tiled counter. "This is as private as it gets. What's on your mind?"

It didn't take long to figure she was in no hurry to share with him. He watched as she filled her own cup and doctored it to taste, the spoon clanking against porcelain as she stirred far longer than necessary. He was on the verge of yanking the metal utensil from her hand, when she rinsed it and laid it in the sink. With effort, he held his silence when she grabbed the dish cloth to wipe up the coffee he'd spilled. It was crazy, but for reasons he couldn't begin to fathom, he refused to make whatever she wanted to say easier by encouraging her.

"About Nicholas..." Shannen stared into the cup she had yet to drink from, her hands wrapped around it like a vise. "He isn't Maria's child."

Rhone had to lean forward to hear her last remark, so softly did she speak. The tension, the restlessness he'd felt earlier returned tenfold. "What *exactly* are you saying, Shannen?"

"Nicholas is..." She put her coffee down, not meeting his gaze. "...Mine."

The floor falling away beneath him couldn't have shaken him more. Without thought, he took her by the arm and pulled her closer. "Yours and who else's?" he managed through clenched teeth. The thought of Shannen lying with another man sucked all rational thought from his mind, leaving a red haze of fury in its intense wake. "Adultery is grounds for divorce, but then, that's what you've wanted all along."

Shannen glared, the tone of her voice mocking him. "Desertion is also grounds."

"You should know all about desertion."

She gave a firm tug, freeing herself from his grasp. "Oh, that's rich. If you'll recall, you left first."

"I had a job to do." Dammit, why was he defending himself to her, knowing now what he knew?

"What about *me*, Rhone? *I* needed you."

Wearily, he closed his eyes for several seconds. "I don't expect you to understand."

"How could I? You never gave me a chance. While my life was an open book, yours was always one huge secret. God, how I resented that."

"Security," Rhone said.

"Oh, yes, it's all coming back to me. Wouldn't want to tell the little wife any security secrets. Can't trust her to keep her mouth shut. Never mind that I had security clearance of my own."

"That's enough." His tone brooked no argument. "Above all else, your safety was my number-one concern."

Paying no heed, Shannen raised a brow, speaking with a caliber of spunk he hadn't heard before. "Sure it was. Let's ignore the fact you were gone seventy-five percent of the time. Of course, to ease your conscience, you did shove those self-defense lessons down my throat. As you can see, they did a lot to save my son from the raving lunatic who took him."

"Maybe if you'd been here, they would've helped." The moment the words left Rhone's mouth, he wanted to call them back.

What little color had been in Shannen's face fled. As he moved toward her, she held out her hand to stop him.

Rhone halted. A razor-sharp edge of pain lanced through him with the knowledge she didn't want him near her. Not now. Undoubtedly, not ever. He saw the self-made promise of a future with her, which had kept him alive in the past, waver on the brink of destruction. Shoving it over the edge was the vision in his mind of Shannen with another man.

He took a deep breath and then another, letting each out slowly, willing his anger to ebb and numbness to take over.

"We'll find your son, Shannen." After that, you can have your divorce, he promised her silently. He would have spoken the words aloud, but even under the circumstances the finality of their meaning was more than he was prepared to deal with.

"Desperately, I want to believe you." Shannen's eyes implored his, then became distant. "Don't make promises you might not be able to keep. Besides, I'd rather hold on to my hope than your promises."

Being on the receiving end of a firing squad would have been easier to face than Shannen's command of the English language. He regretted that he'd given her the power to hurt him so deeply. Worse, he knew she was right. Her words evoked memories. Rhone remembered promising that he would quit taking on so many assignments, that he would spend more time at home. Promises he'd meant to keep.

He gave himself a mental shake. Wallowing in the past was getting them nowhere.

"Tell me what happened this afternoon." He spoke with a quiet, even tone, making sure Shannen couldn't interpret censure in his voice.

She massaged her temples, squinting with discomfort.

Unerringly, Rhone opened the door of the cabinet to the left of the sink and reached for the bottle of aspirin.

Shaking two into his palm, he handed them to her with a glass of water.

"Thanks." At his direction, Shannen sat down at the table.

Sitting across from her, he reached for her hand. "Tell me," he said again.

She fidgeted, trying to withdraw her hand from his grasp, but he didn't let her.

Shannen spoke in a hollow tone, relating the events of the afternoon. "Then, while I was in town, Maria says a woman came to the door. Her car had broken down, and she needed to use the phone. When Maria turned to lead the woman to the phone, a man followed the woman inside. He grabbed Maria. She fought him and claims she scratched the side of his face."

"Norton?"

Shannen nodded. "Maria says he made no effort to conceal himself at any time."

Maria was lucky to be alive to tell about what had happened, and Rhone knew it. He doubted Shannen's fate would have been as good had she been home. Her knowledge of self-defense was limited at best and would probably have only served to incite Norton rather than deter him.

"Nicholas is only a baby." Shannen said. Dry-eyed, she stared down at their interlocked fingers. Rhone knew it was the image of her child that she saw. *Her* son. Damn. Nicholas should have been hers and . . .

Rhone breathed in shallow gulps.

Silently calculating, he realized it was entirely possible Nicholas was his son, too.

Yarrow's hesitant muttering when he tried to waylay Rhone from bursting into the living room came to mind. At the time, his fear for Shannen had absorbed his concentration. He'd heard Yarrow, but the words hadn't registered.

Rhone wanted to ask, needed to know, but the words froze in his throat. Denial that Shannen, after all they'd shared, could be so devious as to keep his son a secret, battled with the cold facts of logic.

If Nicky wasn't his son, then Shannen had wasted no time in lining up a replacement, but that didn't jibe. *Easy* wasn't a word he would have used to describe getting to know Shannen intimately, especially since she had proven to him she was the living and breathing definition of old-fashioned values. That was two years ago, though, Rhone reminded himself. People change.

Shannen squeezed his hand in silent communication. He knew she wanted him to tell her everything would be all right, but as she herself had said, she would rather cling to her hope than his promises.

Likewise, he would rather cling to denial that Nicky was his than accept the idea she could so heartlessly, purposefully deceive him.

Rhone swore succinctly. He *had* to know. Taking a deep breath, he released Shannen and sat back in the chair. "I want to see a picture of Nicholas." His piercing gaze defied her to deny him.

He would see the proof before he would give Shannen the opportunity to lie by asking her.

For pulse-stopping seconds, Shannen stared at him. She seemed about to say something, then changed her mind. Rising, she moved as though in slow motion to a bookshelf in the adjoining dining room. She retrieved a framed photo and with reluctance evident in each step, returned to his side. Hesitating, she held the photo close to the midsection of her body. Her eyes met his as he firmly eased the picture from her grasp. In the virescent depths, he saw the truth before he ever glanced at the five-by-seven he held.

With a sick feeling, he lifted it to the light. His hand shook as he stared at the miniature replica of himself.

Without a doubt, Jimmy had seen the same similarities. Had capitalized on them.

"I want you to suffer."

Jimmy's words ran rampant in Rhone's mind. He felt an acute sense of rage at the cruel injustice of involving an innocent child in a cold-blooded scheme for revenge. Thinking that Nicholas was Shannen's child had been horrifying enough. That it was also Rhone's child was indescribable.

This time, Norton, you've gone too far. You've made a grave error. One that eternal hell—and I—will see you pay for.

Rhone raised a finger to the glass and with a slow, gentle touch, outlined the face of his son. His voice was rough with inner torment, barely above an incredulous whisper. "It's possible you could have left me not knowing you were carrying our child. For that, I could have forgiven you."

He battled an urge to make Shannen suffer—and lost. He glanced up, not trying to conceal raw anger and bitter resentment. Rhone saw her draw back as though he'd slapped her. He didn't care. "You've gone way beyond omission, Shannen. You've robbed me of the first fifteen months of *my* son's life.

"For that, I swear, I will *never* forgive you."

Chapter 4

"Shut that kid up," Jimmy demanded.

"I'm trying." Naomi sent him a pleading look.

"Maa-Maa!"

"Shuddup!" Jimmy snapped. He extended his hand toward the small neck. It would be so easy....

"No!" Naomi yelled, her words barely audible over the screaming. "If you kill Mitchell's brat now, it'll screw up everything."

Jimmy sneered, then pounded his fist on the steering wheel. "Then shut him up before I do."

"I think he's hungry."

Jimmy rolled his eyes.

"You'd better see about findin' someplace where we can get a bottle or something. Diapers, too."

He swore.

Driving to a small convenience store, he made Naomi go inside, taking the kid with her. He ground his back teeth together when she came back out, asking for money. Having to use *his* money to buy the stuff infuriated him.

But Mitchell would repay. In more ways than one. Oh, yeah, Jimmy would see to that. It'd been his promise to Jack before he died.

Jimmy shook out a cigarette and held the lighter to the end long after the flame started to burn the tobacco. He released the flint wheel.

Before taking a deep drag, he laughed in the quiet of the cab.

"Got it," Naomi said, juggling the door, a package and the baby.

Jimmy made no move to help. Before she was situated, he dropped the transmission into Drive and floored the accelerator. Jimmy wanted to reach his destination soon, so he could put phase two of his masterfully crafted plan into action.

The sound of Rhone's voice, rubbed raw with emotion—hurt, anger and a myriad of others she couldn't identify—scraped painfully across Shannen's conscience. She'd known keeping their child a secret would hurt him if he ever found out. Never in her worst nightmares had she imagined his tone would be this ragged, this tormented.

"Why, Shannen?" he demanded, voice hoarse, yet echoing around her as if he'd screamed at her. Dropping another octave, he said, "Why didn't you tell me?"

She noticed he gripped the picture frame tightly, the long length of his fingers biting into the glass with a force she thought would shatter it.

He took a step toward her.

She retreated.

Rhone stopped. His head lowered and from the distance, she saw how his gaze arrested on the features of their son, the same features that so closely resembled Rhone's own. And then she saw his shoulders tremor.

A knot formed in her stomach. No, it wasn't possible. The man who'd always been tough and dependable, rugged and aloof couldn't possibly possess this kind of emotional depth.

Every instinct told her Rhone couldn't possibly be crying. "Rhone?" When he didn't answer, she took a hesitant step forward. She wanted anger, accusations, anything but this silent punishment. They'd had plenty of experience fighting, arguing. They'd done it as much as they'd made love. But this...

Shannen didn't know what to do, what to say. Never had she felt more helpless. She twisted her fingers together in front of her. The cuckoo clock in the room ticked off each second, escalating the tension, the unspoken hurt. She spoke his name again, forcing the single syllable around the ball-size lump in her throat.

Rhone looked up then. Shannen recoiled.

She saw moisture in his eyes, but no tracks from tears. He cried, but not on the surface where it showed. She could see the bottled-up pain that demanded release, but knew he wouldn't give in. God forbid Rhone would lose control and be human. Then, sadly, she remembered discussing this very subject with him once.

Rhone had told her he'd been taught showing emotion made men weak and vulnerable. As a youngster, he had cried at the loss of a pet. And had been beaten for it. Rhone had sworn to her if he ever had a son of his own, he would teach the boy that it took more guts for a man to cry than not to. As for Rhone himself, he'd said it was too late, that some things just couldn't be changed.

If she had thought the sound of his tortured voice would destroy her, Shannen knew the sight of his anguished eyes would haunt her forever. The knowledge that she could have saved him this pain seared her heart.

The glass protecting her son's likeness shattered, startling her.

"Damn you, Shannen," he said, seeming to see all the way to her soul.

She shook her head. Anguish and despair nearly doubled her over.

"Why didn't you just cut out my heart and feed it to me with a spoon? The result would have been the same." He balled his hands into fists at his side. "No," he corrected. "That would have been merciful."

The thread of hope had been tenuous, but deep down she'd never given up. Never stopped praying for the miracle that would bring them together again. Until now. The realization that she'd clung to a dream that couldn't be left her empty. Like the nursery upstairs, like the space beside her in bed every night.

"Look at me, Shannen." When she didn't, he repeated, "Look." Drawing in a deep breath, he finished, "Take a good look. I want you to see what your selfishness cost me. Cost us."

Slowly, knowing he wouldn't be satisfied until she did as he demanded, she forced herself to stare up at him. She winced.

Anger, resentment and guilt churned. With a flick of her wrist, she wiped her tears. "You seem to be forgetting one very important fact, Rhone Mitchell. It's because of *you* Nicholas isn't here tonight. You. Not me."

"Had I known Nicholas existed," Rhone bit out, "none of this would be happening. I would have made certain of that."

"How? By 'imprisoning' us in protective custody? Or maybe you had the relocation program in mind." Shannen gave a bitter laugh. "Thanks, but no thanks. Being stalked by your enemies, needing to be prepared to run and hide, was never—still isn't, my idea of a quality life. In part, that's why I left you. That and your overzealous dedication to your crusade for world peace. The danger you thrive on terrifies me. It destroyed our marriage, destroyed our opportunity to be a family."

He opened his mouth to speak, then flashed her an ominous glare instead. Just as she remembered, Shannen knew Rhone also recalled a similar conversation they'd had two years ago. Only, then, she'd been flinging "what-ifs" at him. Now, reality had turned that argument into a living nightmare.

Her insides twisted when he knelt. Helplessly, she watched as he tenderly fingered the picture, shaking it free of the shards of glass. Still on one knee, he met her own pain-filled eyes. "I will find Nicholas, so help me God. When I do, don't think for one minute that I won't share my son's life. It's time he knows who his father is."

Shannen spoke, her voice barely above a whisper. "You can't have him, Rhone. I won't let you take my baby away from me. He's all I've got."

"And more than you deserve." Full-bodied rage seemed to surge through him. With a speed that denied his six-foot-three frame, he shot to his feet and demolished the distance separating them.

She backed up until she collided with the log partition behind her. Unable to support her own weight any longer, Shannen leaned against the wall.

Shannen knew one thing without a doubt—whatever Rhone had seen, had experienced during the two years since their last meeting, changed him. The changes went deeper than the physical, but right now she didn't have the energy to contemplate beyond the surface.

As he towered above her, hardened resolve reflected on features that seemed to have aged a decade. The dark brown hair brushed back from his face was laced with strands of silver, a color that hadn't been there before he left for the mission that killed their marriage.

Deep lines accentuated lazulite-blue eyes. And he'd lost weight. His cheeks had a slightly hollow look—not that any of these things made him less attractive, she thought distantly. If anything, the aura of tightly leashed power made him more appealing. And threatening.

"I wanted to tell you," she confessed on a strangled whisper, "that I was pregnant."

"Why didn't you?"

"I tried, in a roundabout way. I told you I wanted to have a baby. Your baby. But you made it clear a family wasn't in your plans."

"Those plans weren't intended to be a permanent arrangement," he said through clenched teeth. He placed his palms against the wall above her shoulders, pinning her. "But, then, you didn't exactly give me the chance to alter them, did you? You just naturally assumed I wouldn't want the baby."

She flinched at his savage curse.

"Who do you think you are? Who gave you the right to make that decision?"

"You didn't have time to be a father," she defended, refusing to cower at his verbal attack.

"I would have made time."

She gave a bitter laugh. "You'd have managed to make time for your child, but couldn't for me?"

Shannen watched as his eyes narrowed with something close to loathing. He cursed again and straightened, though he didn't move away.

How stupid of her to think honesty might have bridged a portion of the gap between them. Yet, being honest with herself, she admitted she'd always known he would have tried to make it work.

His sense of responsibility had been the first thing she'd fallen in love with. But it had also been the one thing that had plucked the bloom of romance from their relationship, petal by petal, until not even a withered stem remained.

His fingers bit into the tender flesh of her upper arm. Pain, more emotional that physical, shot through her. She knew he held her with less strength than he possessed, less power than he probably wanted to exert.

Shannen cocked her chin back, reminding herself he was the one who had walked out on her.

She met his gaze, ice to ice, unspoken pain to unspoken pain.

"Tell me about Nicky." Rhone's voice was ragged, raw, tinged with exhaustion.

"You're hurting me," she said softly.

He blinked, only marginally loosening his grip. "Tell me," he repeated.

Immediately, pictures of Nicky came to mind, one tumbling over another. All the firsts: the first time he rolled over and sat up, his first smile, first tooth. The first word he said, "Maa-Maa." And only today, his first steps.

Precious moments she'd known would one day be cast in memories. Were they all she had left?

Shannen tried to give voice to the words Rhone so desperately wanted—needed—to hear and couldn't. The pain was too great, fear for Nicky's fate, all consuming. Tears blurred her vision as she sent a pleading glance to Rhone.

Apparently misinterpreting, abruptly, he released her. On a swift pivot, he strode from the room, each step punctuating his anger as the heels of his boots met the tile.

The sound of drawers opening, doors slamming, had Shannen bolting from the kitchen.

At the door to the living room, shock and disbelief held her in place. A side of Rhone she hadn't seen before alarmed her.

With a frantic fury, he dumped contents of desk drawers and built-in storage cabinets into a pile on the floor. With the toe of his boot, he paused only long enough to sift through the debris. Apparently dissatisfied, he turned to the bookshelves, volumes falling helter-skelter in his wild search.

Tears streamed, her heart breaking into a million pieces as she was forced to come to terms with the extent of the damage she'd done to her husband.

A crashing vase spurred Shannen forward.

So intent was she on rescuing Rhone, saving him from himself, that it didn't occur to her that probably not even Doug would have approached.

"Stop it. Stop it!" She took their wedding album from his hands before he could give it a toss, laying it aside. Wrapping her arms around him, she hung on tight in an attempt to restrain him, knowing full well her strength was no match for his. He tried to push her away and almost succeeded.

His gaze riveting on hers, murderous rage poured like liquid fire.

"I'm sorry. I'm so very, very sorry." Her voice broke.

Shannen felt him sag onto her, the beat of his heart pounding against her own. She tried to support him as they sank onto their knees amid the rubble.

His breathing ragged, he took in a gulp of air, then another. Dark brows drew together, and a muscle flickered along his jaw as he struggled to mask naked emotions.

He finally won, but not before Shannen identified each. They were gut-wrenching, soul-breaking feelings she recognized only too well.

When he spoke, hollow acceptance laced the same anguish that filled her. "Do you hate me so much?"

"No. Oh, God, no, Rhone."

Gaze leveled with hers, he released a long sigh. "At this moment I can't offer you the same reassurance."

She closed her eyes. She couldn't blame him. "I know," she whispered.

Their differences were vast, seemingly irreconcilable. They each came from opposite ends of the same pain. An innocent child was in the middle. Through no fault of his own, his parents stood divided, neither knowing how to right the wrongs of the past.

But she had to try, Shannen thought. More for Nicky than herself, she had to try.

She stood, extending her hand to Rhone. "Come with me. There's something I want to show you."

Seeming to debate, he watched her in wary silence. Then reaching a conclusion, he rose unaided in a lithe motion. She hadn't really expected him to take her hand.

At the stairs, when he did, she was surprised and grateful. She needed his touch, a connection with his strength. Obviously, he needed the same in return.

The grip of his fingers tightened, but no more so than hers as they stood on the threshold to Nicky's room.

Shannen glanced upward, saw Rhone's eyes rove with a hunger she understood and yet, with one she couldn't begin to imagine. She followed his glance as it came to rest on the mobile of cartoon characters above the crib.

A painfully empty crib.

"Come on," she coaxed, her voice thick. Stepping forward, Shannen drew Rhone with her. She released him and crossed the room to the bureau. Opening the top drawer, she withdrew a brightly colored baby book. In it, she'd recorded every highlight of their son's growth and development.

Shannen turned, offering it to Rhone.

His eyes met hers, and for a moment she saw a flame of warmth, a flicker of eagerness that gave her an inkling of what it could've been like. Should have been like.

When he'd settled in the rocker, Shannen turned on the lamp, offering more illumination than the night-light. She headed for the door, thinking he would want to be alone.

"Don't go." His tone was hoarse, barely above a whisper—as though speaking louder would banish their fragile truce.

Over the next hour, Rhone pored over the pages, asking a multitude of expected questions. Sitting cross-legged on the floor nearby, she answered, often having to shove the words past a throat grown tight.

"He's sweet, Rhone, so sweet. He can't go to sleep at night until I cover him with a blanket and give him a kiss." Her lower lip trembled. "Nicky's such a happy baby, smiles more than not."

Shannen gave a short, self-conscious laugh. "I probably sound like a boasting parent who thinks she has the perfect little angel."

"Not at all" came his husky reply. "You sound like the proud and caring mother that I'm sure you are. That I've always known you would be."

With a brief nod, she realized she'd needed his assurance that he thought her a good mother, not one whose neglect had somehow caused the tragedy they now faced.

"You can't blame yourself, Shannen."

How like him to tune in to the direction of her thoughts. He'd always had the uncanny ability.

"As you say," he continued, "if anyone is to blame, it's me." Self-recrimination clouded his eyes.

"We've said a lot of things tonight in anger." She gave a tired sigh. "We need to bury the hatchet, concentrate on getting Nicky back safe and sound. Right now, that's really all that matters."

"You want a divorce."

Rhone's abrupt change of subject caught her off guard. The words seemed almost tangible as they and the depth of their meaning hung between them. Distracted, feeling numb to everything but her missing child, Shannen was uncertain at the moment of what she wanted, or how to respond.

"Don't you?" She turned the tables.

She met his watchful gaze, couldn't begin to interpret his thoughts. Then he looked away.

"Again, as you say, getting Nicholas back is all that matters." He returned his attention to the book in his lap.

Twice, Rhone laughed at his baby's comical expressions, forever captured on film. The deep rich sound prompted memories of the good times she and Rhone had shared. They seemed so long ago, she thought, with a niggling of wistfulness.

For the most part, he stared silently, completely absorbed in reconstructing the first fifteen months of his son's life. Began creating a bond, if that was possible.

Apparently feeling somewhat requited, Rhone closed the book. "Nicholas hasn't been baptized." He made the statement in a tone that didn't criticize. If anything, he sounded relieved.

Nevertheless, when she looked up, she didn't bother to hide her startled expression. In a way, it surprised her that Rhone had mentioned the ceremony, that it would matter, considering what he did for a living. Then it occurred to her it was because of what he did that made it so important. At least, partly.

"I thought about it. Wanted to, but I . . . It didn't seem right."

"Good," Rhone said. "A father should attend his son's christening. I would've hated to miss out. I'll look forward to it."

Shannen accepted his hand, letting him pull her up. "Rhone, what if—"

He shook his head. "No. Don't even think it. We will have Nicholas back. Soon."

The emphasis he placed on the word *we* helped shore her up. Someone else had as much at stake as she.

Returning to the kitchen, Shannen reached for the carafe, refilling their cups with coffee. Her back to Rhone, she said, "At the risk of irritating you, I've got some questions of my own."

He moved closer, taking the cup she offered. "I'm sure you do." He hesitated, then added, "I'll answer what I can."

"This is all because of Jack, isn't it?" she asked, referring to Jimmy's dead brother and Rhone's ex-colleague.

Indecision warred on grave features. "What do you know about Jack?"

"Having been an interpreter for the United Nations, I, too, have friends in high places who have kept me somewhat informed. That shouldn't come as a big surprise."

"It doesn't. I suppose what does is the fact you bothered to keep tabs on anything that remotely involved my activities."

"Don't flatter yourself," she retorted, ignoring his fleeting smirk. "And quit trying to change the subject. This is about revenge, isn't it? Somehow Nicky and I got caught in the middle."

His voice was riddled with regret. "Believe me, I'd give anything not to have to put you through this."

Shannen felt a stab of guilt. "I know. I do believe you." But try as she might, she couldn't stop holding him accountable.

Rhone shifted, looking anywhere but at her.

"We may have had our differences, Rhone, but through them all, I know you were always concerned for my safety, even if I wasn't as sure of your love."

"Shannen—"

"Don't." She groaned, pressing her fingers to her temples, trying to erase the stubborn throb there. "The past is over. And right now, I need to focus on the future and Nicky's well-being."

Rhone looked as though he intended to say something else, then stopped.

She didn't give him a chance to regroup his thoughts. Didn't give herself a chance to ponder anything but preservation. "How did Jimmy Norton know where to find me?"

"Jimmy just got out of prison. We know for certain he has used the same contacts Jack did."

Shannen, who'd started to pace, stopped midstride. "These contacts . . . they're still running around, free?"

"Notice, I said, 'has used.' We thought we had . . . removed them all. A couple were his roommates in prison. Trust me. When we find this one, he'll meet the same fate as his comrades."

She didn't ask what that would be, didn't want to know.

"And as for you, Rhone, how did *you* know where to find me?" she asked softly. "Amazing, when you think about it. It didn't take the bad guys any time at all while it took you two years. But then, of course, that would be assuming you'd tried before now, and we both know better."

His muscles tensed visibly. "I didn't expect you to change your last name."

"I wouldn't have if you'd been a real husband," she tossed back, refusing his offer of guilt.

"So much for burying the hatchet, huh, Shannen?"

She was exhausted and knew it. She needed to sleep, wanted to wake up in the morning knowing the ugliness, the terror had been nothing more than a horrible dream.

Picking an argument with Rhone was an excuse to avoid the agony of facing the fact she wouldn't be tucking her baby in his crib tonight. Wouldn't be kissing his soft, warm cheek, or feeling his wet attempt at a kiss in return.

"For months I waited for you." Her breath caught on a sob. "I wanted you to find us, and now it's too late."

With a sound akin to a growl, Rhone reached for her. She twisted away, resisting, but his strength was overpowering. Her body shook with silent sobs.

She might have imagined the feather-light touch of his hand on her hair. Beneath her ear, she heard the strong, fast beat of his heart. Oddly reassuring in a world that was anything but. And his scent, the one that had haunted her those first nights alone when she couldn't sleep, teased her again.

He was the last person she wanted comfort from and, at the same time, the only one who could provide the comfort she needed. She sniffled, thinking that odd paradox had always described their relationship. It still did.

"What happens next?" she mumbled against his chest.

"We wait for Norton's next move."

"That's it? Wait?"

"By dawn, two dozen law-enforcement officials will be scouring the area. I'll be setting up a command post here. I'd like to get you away—"

"No."

Shannen heard the depth of his sigh, the resignation in his voice when he said, "I thought that would be your reaction, but I can't promise you'll be safe here."

"I'm not asking for promises, and I'm not leaving. Besides, what if Jimmy tries to make contact? For ransom or something?"

"The only thing Norton wants in exchange for Nicholas is me."

Unable to hide her alarm, Shannen leaned her head back to look up at Rhone, tried to read his masked expression. "What are we going to do?" she whispered.

Expecting to hear an outline of his plans, she was again taken aback. "When this is over, I'll give you the divorce you want," he said instead. There was no emotion in the quietly spoken words, the delivery of each distancing them more than ever.

Is it what she wanted? Shannen felt as though a fist had landed on her stomach. If it wasn't for the support of his arms, she might have reeled.

"I know you tried to serve the papers—"

It was true, she had, but she'd done it more to get his attention. A childish ploy, but the only option she'd been able to come up with. "Doug said you were on your way home from Colombia."

"Home?" He gave a short laugh. "Needless to say, I didn't stay long when I discovered you'd left and had filed for a divorce. If my not signing the papers caused you an inconvenience, I really could've cared less.

"Not long after that, I was asked to make a final trip to Colombia. I got back last month. So, take it for whatever it's worth—when I had the chance to track you down, I was too damned angry. And when the anger subsided, I was too... far away."

He released a long sigh, one that Shannen believed echoed her earlier sentiment and her unspoken fear that, in reality, it was too late to make amends.

What happened in Colombia, Rhone? she asked silently. Where have you been since you got back? What happened that changed you, destroyed our marriage and stole my husband—my son's father, from us? Shannen ached to verbalize the words but knew if she did, he would tell her nothing. Theirs was a relationship based on secrets. And secrets were no better than lies. Spawned by distrust, one built on another in an endless pursuit to hide the truth.

She couldn't help wondering what it would have been like had things been different.

Rhone said nothing, as if he, too, were afraid of inflicting any more damage with words.

And in spite of everything, she realized his mention of a divorce now felt like a dreaded threat.

* * *

Less than a hundred miles away, Nicholas stuffed a fist into his mouth and curled the other into the dirty mattress. Lifting his head, he whispered the word that had always brought security and warmth into his life. "Maa-Maa?"

Chapter 5

Black faded to gray as long-awaited dawn battled over
the horizon.

Rhone had worked most of the night, calling in favors,
ordering equipment and going over topographical maps,
desperate to find any hint of where Norton might have
gone.

He despised feeling helpless, detested the fact that at the
moment, Norton had the advantages. Truth was, though,
both Norton brothers had been trained as survivalists.

But then, so had Rhone and Doug. Most things considered, they were evenly matched with their enemy, but
not in ways that counted. Norton's purpose was strictly
revenge, and ultimately it would catch up to him. Rhone
was willing to bet his life on it. Motivated for the wrong
reason, consumed by it, Norton would make a fatal mistake.

That thought brought a quick, feral grin to Rhone's
mouth—the only sense of satisfaction he'd felt since getting Norton's call.

Rhone wiped a hand across his whisker-roughened chin. He had slept little that night, but it was enough. Years of conditioning had changed his internal clock. He couldn't remember when he'd last slept through the night. Even when Shannen had slept in his arms, he'd spent hours each night awake. He'd been content to watch Shannen dream as she'd snuggled against him, her body warm, replete from their lovemaking.

His mind drifted from maps, plans, mental checklists.

God, how he had missed Shannen. Rhone had never known anyone like her before she came into his life. No one had remotely interested him since.

Knowing she slept only a few paces down the hall did nothing to help discourage the direction of his thoughts.

For them, making love had been far from dull. Whether playful or intensely serious, every time had been a new experience. He'd cherished every moment they shared, knowing deep down, as Shannen had, that each could be their last.

For the most part, to Rhone, the possibility of being killed in the line of duty had seemed unlikely—a possibility he couldn't afford to think about. But then, in the darkest hour of night, when Shannen stripped him of his defenses, he recognized his mortality as, unerrantly, she'd reached inside to touch his soul. With sweet, trusting abandonment, she'd laid hers open to him.

Rhone's body tensed with aching need. He groaned aloud, throwing back the sheet that covered him. The early-morning chill that wafted from the window he'd opened the night before breathed over his heated skin, the result equal to that of a cold shower.

Unfortunately, he thought, it had little effect on the memories that threw his imagination into overdrive. Memories best left buried. Shannen—and now, Nicky— were his own weaknesses. Weaknesses that would see him dead if he wasn't careful.

In one fluid motion, he rolled off the bed, landing lightly on his feet. Still dressed, he headed downstairs to the kitchen.

When the scent of brewing coffee filled the air, he turned toward the bathroom. After showering and putting on jeans, scarred leather cowboy boots and an old dark blue T-shirt, he paused on his way to the back door to fill a mug with the dark liquid. Brian's snores drifted to Rhone. No light sleeper there, he assessed irritably, tucking a 9 mm into his waistband.

Unable to be confined for long, and needing space, Rhone stepped out onto the redwood deck. Orange and pink highlighted the sky, the vivid colors creating a dramatic backdrop for the still-snowcapped peaks—peaks that stretched with stark majesty toward the heavens. Leaning his hip against the railing, he sipped and swallowed, enjoying the view, the space, the quiet. He breathed deeply, slowly, liking the mingling scent of sage and pine.

It could almost lull a man into a false sense of security. But not him. He had too much at stake—knew just how cunning his opponent truly was.

Rhone Mitchell wouldn't make the mistake of underestimating Jimmy Norton. Especially not when Nicky's life was at risk.

The thought of the child sent a never-before-felt sense of pride through Rhone. By damn, he had a son! A fact he was still in awe of, one that had yet to sink in. An undercurrent of feelings overrode the anger and the hurt Shannen had inspired with her omission, sweeping him along with a force he could no longer fight.

When he thought of Nicholas, joy, pure and simple, filled Rhone's heart to overflowing. Nothing could compare to the sense of pride he felt. It was deeper than pride of accomplishment. More accurately, he decided, it was a sense of being blessed. The miracle of life was a gift.

After the horrors he'd witnessed, the death and destruction, the gift of life was all the more precious. That he'd been fortunate to share in its creation amazed him, thrilled him. Left him incredibly humble.

He regretted not being here when Nicholas was born. Above all, he regretted that Shannen had felt the need to exclude him. It took two to make or break a marriage, he knew, and he could no longer ignore that he'd certainly been a large part in its demise. He'd been deluding himself by blaming Shannen.

Rhone slammed his empty cup on the railing, shattering the ceramic. He turned toward the stairs. Impotent frustration, compounded by a feeling of not being in control, bottled up inside, demanding release. Needing strenuous exercise, he set off at a brisk pace.

As he'd told Shannen, Rhone intended to be a part of Nicky's life on a regular basis. If he took a position in the Rocky Mountain field office, he would only be roughly two hours away.

The sound of rushing water coaxed Rhone along as he followed a trail through the dense cover of aspen and evergreen, conducting a perimeter search.

Rhone swung around, sensing a presence. Automatically he reached for his weapon.

"It's beautiful up here," Brian said, emerging from the cover of trees. "Makes it almost possible to forget the ugliness."

Rhone replaced his gun. The image of the man who threatened the safety and well-being of his family—Norton—who held the power to destroy all that was meaningful, blotted out everything else. Rage, barely leashed, unfurled, seeking an outlet. Soon, Rhone thought. The unspoken word was both threat and promise.

"Thought you'd want to know—Doug called. He's landed, and he's on his way up."

Rhone started back toward the house.

Yarrow quickened his pace. "I wanted to find you, too, to talk to you about . . ."

Rhone tuned the younger man out, focusing instead on an outline of a plan.

Now that he knew for certain who and what they were up against, Rhone's gut feeling was telling him loud and clear to get ready.

Norton's game was psychological warfare. Rhone knew the rules, knew Norton would attempt to lead them on a wild-goose chase, using Nicholas as the bait. Unless Rhone missed his guess, they would hear from Norton within the next forty-eight hours.

By then, he would have his own trap in place. Every agency in the state—hell, in the nation—would be in on the manhunt, at his beck and call. In times of emergency, agencies hung together like family. He'd never been more grateful for anything.

He knew it would seem like forever. Rhone gnashed his teeth together, detesting the hard truth that for now, Norton had him in the palm of his hand.

Brian's solo dialogue caught and held Rhone's consideration.

". . . you understand, you're too close, too involved to be objective. Of course, your input would be greatly appreciated—don't get me wrong. So here's what I was thinking."

Rhone gave a snort. Stopping, he faced Brian. "Don't." His voice was low, carefully controlled.

Brian frowned. "Don't what?"

"*Think.* Just do as I instruct and we'll get along fine. If you have a problem with that, get the hell out."

Brian kicked at the dirt with the toe of his boot, reminding Rhone of a chastised little boy.

Then Brian looked up, a hint of a grin pulling at the corners of his mouth. "Now that I have your undivided attention, mind telling me what your plans are?"

With a slow shake of his head, Rhone decided he had to hand it to the kid. Few dared push their luck with Rhone. The fact that Yarrow did—always had, come to think of it—indicated to Rhone maybe, just maybe, there was hope for the kid after all.

"Target practice," Rhone answered.

"I just recertified—"

"Not you. Shannen. I want you by the phone in case Norton calls."

Brian raised a brow. "Shannen knows how to shoot?"

"She will by nightfall, although I'm sure she'll be as stubborn about learning as she was before."

"You're not letting her come with us, are you?"

"No. She's staying here." Rhone's eyes narrowed, considering his options. "With you," he decided.

Rhone was confident he and Doug could accomplish their goal relatively quickly without Brian's help. Yarrow would have been an asset, but Rhone felt better knowing Shannen wouldn't be alone. While he expected an argument from her, under no circumstance was Shannen accompanying them. The danger of getting hurt was too great a risk, one that Rhone wasn't willing to take. Besides, without someone here to watch her, Rhone knew she would try to follow.

Brian seemed about to object, then shrugged. "If that's the way you want it." There was a grain of disappointment in his voice.

"That's the way it's going to be. Need I say that if any harm comes to my wife..."

His glance level with Rhone's, Brian's voice hardened. "You taught me well. I know the routine."

Rhone gave a curt nod.

Beyond Yarrow's shoulder, Rhone watched Shannen. He'd seen her come out on the deck and look around. For him? Spotting them, she moved to the steps and descended. Apparently, something caught her attention as she abruptly changed directions. Rhone saw her bend.

For no longer than a split second, he felt a tingling sensation, an eerie awareness. He took it for what it was: a warning.

Even so, nothing could have prepared him for the agonizing scream that shattered the silence.

Instantly, Rhone knew the bitter taste of fear.

With several hundred feet separating them, Shannen was exposed, vulnerable. Rhone crouched, his eyes scanning the perimeters of the property, his hand instinctively covering the weapon nestled in the waistband near his spine.

Aspen leaves hung motionless in the still air. Shielding his eyes from the sun, Rhone saw only the movement of scurrying chipmunks. At last satisfied, he stood.

"No! Dear God, no!" The mountains deflected the mournful chanting of Shannen's voice, sending it back round again with haunting clarity.

Rhone broke into a run, Brian sprinted after him.

On her knees, Shannen picked up a small stuffed bear from where it lay facedown in the dirt. That the bear was a favorite of Nicky's was evidenced by the matted appearance of the brown fuzzy material. Afflicting torment, both hers and his own, squeezed Rhone's heart. He watched as she turned the bear over, meticulously dusting it off.

"When Nicholas was three months old, I bought this for him. The size seemed so right for his tiny hands. He refers to him as Bear. Original, huh?" She continued, not waiting for his answer. "Sleep is out of the question until Nicky has Bear snuggled in the crook of his arm. I can't tell you how many times he's sent me to find Bear at naptime or bedtime." Her words caught on a half laugh, half sob. "Too many to count. Not nearly enough to last a lifetime."

Shannen brought Bear to her chest, hugging the toy tightly. Tears streamed unheeded. With soul-wrenching repetition, she cried out Nicky's name as she rocked back and forth.

Maybe it was because he knew Shannen so well, or maybe because he loved her so intensely. Whatever the reason, Rhone felt what she was going through. Felt the ache of empty arms that longed to hold their son.

Gently, firmly, Rhone reached down and drew Shannen to her feet. "Oh, God, babe, don't." His own voice was thick, grating.

For a flash of a second, anger and regret dissipated. With fierce need, his arms encircled her, pulling her snug against his chest. Bear caught between them, Rhone felt her lean into him, needing his warmth, his strength, as much as he needed hers. Seeming to sense it, she reached around him, hugging him back.

Rhone had no idea how long they stood that way, not that it mattered. Thankful for Brian's quiet retreat, Rhone gave himself up to the moment. He didn't want to think. He wanted only to savor the feel of the woman he held.

Her golden-brown hair lay against his cheek, soft and silky. A delicate scent of rose filled his senses. With her arms stretched upward, the short-waisted sweater bared a crescent of skin. With his thumb, he grazed her smooth warmth.

Rhone felt a faint shiver, felt the tiny bumps that raised in response to his touch. With the length of her body against his, she had to be aware of his own response, but she didn't pull away. God, he wanted her. It was more than a physical need. So much more. He drew in a ragged breath.

Shannen had to want him on the same level, unconditionally for the same reasons. And it had to be forever, or not at all.

He leaned back. When Shannen raised her head, Rhone framed her face between his palms. He saw her reluctance to let go and felt a glimmer of hope. And he saw so much more.

Gone was the child-woman he'd married. Gone—the innocence from life not yet experienced. In her place, he saw a woman who knew the meaning of hardship and success, heartache and joy. And love. In the natural course of life, the changes he saw were inevitable. Rhone didn't want to think about having had a hand in speeding up the process. He didn't want to think at all.

His gaze fell to her mouth. He remembered shared kisses. Hot and fiery. Slow and sensual. Nipping and teasing. He swallowed a groan. Meeting her eyes, Rhone caught the answering flicker of desire. He could have imagined it, it was gone so quickly.

He bent, brushing her forehead with his lips. He thought he heard her sigh as she slid her hands down his back. They came to rest on his lower spine and Rhone felt her stiffen. He released her, allowing her to take a step away.

"Still armed and dangerous, I see."

The momentary tenderness vanished, as if it had never happened.

Though he heard no censure in her tone, her words brought to mind repeated arguments from the past. Shannen hated guns, hated what they stood for. Though she'd married him knowing what he did for a living, she had eventually quit trying to hide her resentment of his having a gun in their home.

And only just now did he realize why.

Rhone reached out, tucking a strand of hair behind her ear. "Life is fragile, fleeting. The gun was a constant reminder, wasn't it?"

Shannen tipped her head, eyes widened with surprise. "You'll never know the hell I went through. Self-induced, maybe, but nonetheless, terrifying." She started to say more but stopped herself.

Rhone didn't push the issue. It was a beginning. He felt encouragement that the door she had closed and locked between them was opening, slow inch by slow inch. If he'd learned nothing else in Colombia, he had learned the value of patience and faith.

Shannen glanced down at the bear she still held, then back up at him. "I'm glad you're in charge of the search."

"We'll get through this. We *will* have our son back."

Shannen nodded. "I need to help. I can't stand being idle—it's driving me crazy."

Rhone debated how much to tell her. He wanted her cooperation, but he didn't want to scare her unnecessarily. "I'm not certain if you figure into Norton's plans or not, but I think you need to be able to defend yourself. Norton's M.O. includes a mini-arsenal. Fancy footwork and well-aimed punches can't stop a bullet, Shannen."

The color drained from her face. "Nicky—"

"—will be all right." Rhone placed his hands on her shoulders, hoping he wasn't lying. "It's me he really wants. He's using Nicky as a bargaining tool, and I have no reason to doubt he would use you in the same fashion."

"You want me to learn how to shoot." It was more a statement than a question.

"Yes. I know how you feel about guns, but..."

Rhone paused, watching a gleam of anger kindle in Shannen's eyes. He felt a measure of relief. In fear, there was weakness. Preying on weakness was Norton's strong suit. But in anger there was strength.

"I'll do anything to get my son back. Teach me," she said. Her tone was positive, the words spoken without hesitation.

* * *

Shannen noted the look on Rhone's face with a brief flash of satisfaction. His jaw had dropped, nearly imperceptibly, and if she hadn't known him as well as she did, she might have missed the subtle change in his expression.

The fact she still read his features so easily twisted another knot into her already-tight stomach.

"You're sure?"

She nodded tightly. "Yes." She said the word sincerely.

"But..."

Shannen held up a hand. "I'm tired of the bad guys having all the advantages. And I promise you this, Rhone. If I ever get a chance to hurt the bastard who took my son, I will. Teach me, Rhone," she reiterated, each word ripping a new shred in her heart. "Teach me to shoot."

The surprise inched from his face. Resolutely, he nodded. "Yeah," he agreed. "I'll teach you."

She stiffened her spine. Never again would she be a victim. Never would she run from life and hide...even if it meant confronting her husband head-on.

"Ready to start?"

A frisson of something...anxiety maybe, traced through her. It'd been too much, too fast. "I need to shower first."

He gave her a curt nod. "Half an hour?"

"Okay." She turned away.

"Shannen?"

Her husband's voice was raw. Ragged. Slowly she pivoted, until she looked at him again. "Yes?"

"I'm..." He raised a hand as if to touch her, reach for her, then dropped it helplessly at his side. "I'm sorry."

Unable to force a response, she merely lifted a single shoulder. This time, he let her go.

In the shower, she closed her eyes as if the motion could—for only a second—shut out the horrible things that had happened. Even warmth couldn't chase away the chill that had held her in its grip since she'd returned home yesterday.

With determination, she squirted shampoo into her palm, the foaming lather spreading over her fingers. Events and sensations replayed themselves, and the harder she fought to suppress them, the more forcibly they hijacked her mind.

Maria.

The ghoulish grip of anxiety.

The pure panic of fear.

The despair of loss.

Her baby.

Rhone.

Their baby.

Against her will, she remembered the day that had started it all. She'd glanced up to see a stranger intently perusing her, a devilish gleam of something that might have been seduction teasing his eyes. The corners of his lips curved up slightly, easily, as if accustomed to the motion. Windswept hair had drooped lazily across his forehead, barely avoiding a flirtation with his eyebrows.

He'd leaned against her desk, close. Closer than she felt comfortable with, yet strangely, it wasn't close enough. When he'd spoken, she'd been lost. His tone held a sexy undercurrent of gravel that made his voice both rich and seductive ... reminding her of warmed brandy on a cold winter's night.

But it was the words he'd uttered that indelibly seared her memory so that they were as fresh and compelling as they'd been years ago.

"I hear you're good. At what you do."

"Excuse me?" she asked, after clearing her throat.

"I was hoping to take advantage of your, er, skills." His brows had knitted together. "Languages."

Before she recovered, he pushed to a standing position and extended his hand. "Rhone Mitchell. Gloria Jacobs referred me. Says you have security clearance and that you're more fluent in languages than anyone else around here."

Without conscious thought, she'd allowed him to take her hand. She'd felt the hard ridges of calluses on his palm, the strength in his grip and the corresponding heat that chased up her arm.

He held her hand longer than needed. Longer than he should have. And if it hadn't been for the inopportune ringing of the phone, she wouldn't have noticed.

She extricated her hand, reached for the phone and tried to concentrate on what the caller was saying. It took a lot of effort. The Middle Eastern caller spoke in a blend of English and Arabic, a combination she usually followed effortlessly. Yet, when Rhone Mitchell made himself comfortable in the worn-leather chair across from her desk, concentration was the last thing on her mind.

The call took forever. But Rhone, intently studying her with a single-mindedness she envied right then, didn't seem to care that the seconds were melding into minutes. She wrapped the phone's cord around her finger, then swiveled in her chair.

Finally, turning back to place the phone in the cradle, she read the expression of humor on his face that said he knew exactly why she'd turned away. Instead of experiencing embarrassment, though, Shannen felt as if they'd shared a secret. Rhone had a way of doing that—making her feel special.

Rhone leaned forward, again teasing her with a subtle scent of spice. An adventurous gleam in his eye, an attitude that bordered on cocky, set him apart from anyone else she'd ever known—attracting her in a way no one else ever had. He'd smiled boyishly, then slipped a document across the table.

"Can you translate this?"

She did. Then felt ill. For the first time, the job she'd done wasn't pleasant, the words were sick and twisted, a horrible combination that made her fingers feel dirty. She finished reading aloud, dropped the paper, wiped her hands on her pants, then looked at the man across from her.

His expression was intensely sober. While he revealed nothing more, she sensed a deadly combination of power and anger that he held in check.

"Thank you," he said, the tone clipped. With deft motions, he folded the paper along the creases, then dragged his thumbnail across the same creases again, as if he didn't want the paper to unfurl. He shoved it inside his suit coat, then stood in the same, single motion.

Shannen knew she wanted to see that expression erased from his features. She didn't know why, didn't know why she should care, but she did. "Mr. Mitchell," she said, halting him at the door.

He pivoted, one hand still on the knob. "Yes?"

"I..." She lifted her shoulders helplessly. She didn't act this way. And didn't know what to say next. "Never mind. It's not important."

Rhone gave a curt nod, then closed the door behind him with a decisive click.

It wasn't until then that Shannen noticed how empty her office was. How empty her life was.

When the phone rang not three minutes later, she'd grabbed it, knowing it would be him. Had known she would agree to see him.

Now she regretted ever meeting him. Regretted him being the one to father her child.

She released a shaky breath. Turning off the taps, she jerked back the shower curtain. Tiny streams of water trailed over her face. Not until she tasted salt did she realize she'd been crying. With a groping hand, she pulled a towel from the rack.

Burying her face in the soft cotton, she prayed for strength, struggled for control. Knew she wouldn't be worth a darn without either.

Quickly she blow-dried her hair and dressed, striving for the same resolve that seemed to come so easily to her husband.

On her way out the door, she paused.

A picture of her holding Nicholas on her lap caught her attention. Nicky tilted his head back, glancing up at her, mirroring her laughter as they swung on the tire attached to a tree in the backyard. Shannen swallowed the clot of pain in her throat.

Her eyes closed as she waited for the stabbing sorrow to subside. Stoically, knowing she would be no good to either Nicholas or Rhone if she allowed emotion to wash over her again, she stiffened her spine, willing a sense of purpose to take over.

Chapter 6

Shannen walked down the stairs, her hand lightly gripping the banister. She heard the rich sound of Rhone's voice, heard the agitated tone.

She heard another voice and immediately recognized the calm, controlled pitch. Doug Masterson. Rhone's partner was like family, but joy at seeing him again was instantly quelled as their conversation registered.

"But, damn it, Doug—this is *my* family we're talking about."

Her insides twisted in response to his extreme emphasis on the word *my*.

She rushed down the remaining stairs.

"And you're too personally involved, partner."

"Hell, yes, I'm involved," Rhone snapped back with a bolt of vehemence. "What do you want me to do, sit back and play tiddledywinks while we wait for something else to go down?" For emphasis, he slammed his fist into an open palm.

At the doorway, she cleared her throat, then entered the room. It amazed her that Rhone held the ability to instantly school his expression into one of supreme confidence.

"Shannen," Rhone said, the word flat and hollow.

Their gazes met.

More than time and distance separated them. An emotional gulf yawned between them, as if they'd never at all been close.

Doug took the brave step of trying to breach an uncomfortable situation. "You're looking good."

She didn't reply.

"That's what people always say when they can't think of anything else," Doug admitted, moving forward.

Shannen returned the small smile he gave, accepting his hug. Spotting his duffel bag by the door, she said, "Maria, my housekeeper, is leaving today to visit her family in Denver. I know she wouldn't mind if you took her room."

Doug nodded, accepting.

She swung her attention back to Rhone. "Is there any news about Nicky?"

The men exchanged a tense glance before Rhone reluctantly shook his head.

"I'm sorry about your son, Shannen," Doug said.

She stiffened.

"You know we won't rest until he's safe in your arms again."

Breath whooshed out of her. How much more could she possibly be expected to endure?

"Then tell me what you do know." She sent Rhone a pleading look. "And tell me why we're sitting here instead of getting out, looking for him."

The tension that radiated through the room was thick enough to slice. Apparently deciding to leave explanations to Rhone, Doug excused himself.

"Sit down."

Shannen bristled at the command. "I want to stand."

"Suit yourself," Rhone said. He watched her, as though gauging her reaction while he spoke. "Norton's a survivalist. Playing cat-and-mouse games with law enforcement is his favorite pastime. With one exception, he always wins."

When he paused, she prompted him to continue.

"We've got topographical maps of a six-state region. A second set is being analyzed by the FBI for the most likely place he's hiding. But the cold, hard fact is, we don't even know if he's in Colorado. A massive search is underway, for information, as much as for Norton. You and I could spend a dozen months searching the Colorado mountain forests and never turn up a clue."

Her throat felt raw.

"You want to hear more?"

She didn't. She did. Not in her worst nightmares had anything so startlingly awful been possible. After taking a deep breath and momentarily squeezing her eyes shut, she nodded.

"I anticipate Norton will call here. I've got to be here when he does. Equipment to trace calls is on its way, and if we can keep him on the line long enough, we'll be able to pinpoint a location. At least find out if he's still in the state. We're doing everything we can."

"So we wait." The statement was a croak, spoken with what little stamina she still possessed.

"We plan," he corrected. "We set a trap of our own. And we teach you how to shoot." With that, he strode to the table near the phone.

She gave a tight nod, grateful for an outlet, an activity to get rid of the aching, burning sensation deep inside.

Rhone spun a series of numbers, then snapped open a black box. "Come here," he told her. "Lesson's about to begin."

She followed Rhone's order, nevertheless, moving across the carpet with heavy feet. She wanted to do something, anything . . . but learn to handle a gun.

Cold fear rooted through her when she stared down at the lethal-looking metal nestled in virginal-white foam.

Then she pictured her baby, Nicky's first steps, his smile. The resolve she'd been struggling for, the strength she'd prayed for, tackled the remnants of her fear and trepidation. She could do this. She could do anything she had to if it would help Rhone get their son back.

"It's a .22," he explained. "Semiautomatic, which means every time you squeeze the trigger, a round fires." With calm efficiency, he took an empty clip from the case and opened a box of bullets.

"Watch," he said, demonstrating the technique of loading the clip. "Technically, this clip holds thirteen rounds, but you can load as few as one bullet, or if you pack them in, it'll take up to fifteen.

"Remember to count how many you put in." He patted the weapon surrounded by leather at his side. "I always load twelve bullets. That way I'm not surprised or sweating it when I'm in the field."

Rhone's calm efficiency, calculated movements were frightening to watch. At the same time, she couldn't help being impressed . . . and feeling completely safe.

"Your turn."

Suddenly apprehensive, she fumbled with the bullet, dropping it lengthwise into the open box.

"Relax, Shannen. Guns are perfectly safe, if you know how to handle them."

"Which I don't." She tried not to sound snappish, but knew it came out that way.

"Try again."

He moved behind her. Focusing on the fact she might be an asset in rescuing her son, she did as he encouraged.

"That's it."

She let out a little sigh of relief.

"Eleven more rounds to go."

With a frown, she worried her lip while painstakingly placing each rim on the slide. "Ouch!" She resisted the urge to swear when her fingers were pinched between bullet and metal.

"With experience, it becomes second nature," Rhone explained, loading a third clip in seconds, barely glancing at what he was doing.

"Easy for you to say."

"Okay, let's go outside. I found a bag of empty diet soda cans in the garage," he said, grabbing the gun case and a duffel bag.

"I take them in for recycling," she said, slipping past him where he held open the door. It took acrobatics to avoid brushing him.

"I remembered."

Neither said a single word as they crossed the grass to where he'd found a stump. Rhone set the gun case on the rotting timber, then opened the lid.

"I chose the .22 for you because it's smaller, easier to handle than a 9 mm or .357. Plus, it doesn't recoil like a bigger gun, so it'll deliver more accuracy for you."

"But is it enough...?" She couldn't finish, the thought of shooting someone making her feel sick. To combat the feeling, she pictured the man who'd taken Nicky.

Rhone nodded, an expression of understanding that needed no explanation painted on his features. ".22s kill more people every year than any other gun. The round fans out rather than just going straight. Believe me, Shannen, it'll do plenty of damage."

"I believe you," she said as bright sunlight glittered off the chrome when he took the pistol from its nest.

"Take it."

She hesitated.

"The loaded clip isn't in it. You can't do any damage yet."

He offered the butt and she gritted her back teeth. As repulsive as the task was, she had to have a working knowledge of the weapon.

"You'll be more accurate if you cradle the butt of the pistol and the base of your hand in your left palm. No, like this." He demonstrated.

Shannen followed suit.

"Legs about shoulder-width apart."

She adopted the stance Rhone showed her, then tried not to notice the intimacy as he nudged her right thigh with his hand.

"Better," he approved, "but don't slouch. Now, while I set up some aluminum cans, I want you to practice targeting a branch on that tree. Line up the barrel of the gun with the widest part of the branch, then lower the gun and try again."

Shannen did as he instructed, amazed at how badly her hand trembled even though there wasn't a single round in the gun.

"You're going to have to hold steadier than that," he said, not even glancing around.

She scowled in his direction.

"And if your concentration is going to be broken so easily with live ammo, you won't hit a damn thing. Concentrate on what you're doing, Shannen."

He was right, and had known it the same way he loaded a gun so effortlessly, with absolute certain knowledge of what he was doing.

To prove to herself—and him—she could do it, Shannen tuned out everything around her: the overhead noise of a jet, the chirping of birds.

"Now, for the real test," he said, returning and palming a clip. "Insert the magazine, like so. And make sure the safety's on." He indicated the piece of metal that would prevent the gun from firing. "But before you start, you'll need these." Unzipping the duffel bag, he took out two packages of earplugs.

They both inserted the squishy plugs, then he offered the gun to her again. She took it, remembering the smirk on Norton's face. The man had her son and God only knew if her child was being taken care of. She gave herself reassurances—whether false or not, it didn't really matter. The belief that Nicky was safe was the only thing keeping her sane.

"You practiced lining up the gun with the branch, but remember, when a bullet flies, it curves up at first, then starts to drop back down. You have to learn to compensate for distances outside point-blank range. We'll practice different ranges so you get a feel for it. Second thoughts?"

She rose to the challenge in his voice with a steeling of shoulders and grim determination. "No." The weight of the weapon felt like lead in her hand. His lecture once again reinforced the path he'd chosen. Effortlessly, he rattled off instructions, to the point that she wondered if she'd be able to absorb it all.

Rhone grinned, a lopsided number that made her heart twist. "When you've made up your mind to do something, heaven help anyone who gets in your way. Wait…" He held up a hand. "I meant that as a compliment. It's one of the things I've always respected about you."

"Don't," she said softly.

"It was a statement, Shannen, not a come-on."

The words were blunt, edged with an iciness that betrayed the warmth of the Colorado sun. She flinched. After what she'd done to him in keeping their child a secret, how could she even think he'd come on to her?

She started to frame an apology, but was prevented when he continued, "Now, take off the safety and aim at the first can."

She did. Aimed. Fired. Missed. "Damn." She glared at the gun, then at Rhone. "I thought you said this thing didn't recoil."

"It doesn't."

"Felt like it to me."

When she missed a second time, he moved behind her. His added stability gave her the confidence and accuracy to knock the next can from the post with a metallic ping. "We did it!" she said. The "we" felt natural…scary. And on the heels of that thought came another—Rhone still splashed on the same cologne after a shower.

She pushed aside all thoughts and forced herself to follow his precise instructions about reloading. With each squeeze on the trigger, her aim grew more accurate and her concentration more intense. Gone were images of everything, except for what was most important: Nicky. If it hadn't been for him, she knew she would have never even picked up the gun, let alone held it so forcefully in her grip.

When the third clip ran dry, he asked, "Ready for a break, or do you want to keep going?"

She shook her head, concentration broken. Once again, she heard the sounds of nature, became aware of Rhone's proximity.

Then the sound of an approaching vehicle saved her from answering. Immediately, frigid sweat knifed down her spine. The kidnappers? Terror held her paralyzed.

"You expecting someone?"

"No."

"It's probably Brian," Rhone said. The tight compression of his lips belied the easy tone. "Regardless, I'm sure Doug heard the car coming."

She clung to the calmness, his reassurance, like a drowning man to a lifeline.

"We'll go in the back door. Just in case." He reloaded a clip while she stared in the direction of the driveway. For the first time, she truly regretted the seclusion of the house and the fact that hundred-year-old pines blocked the view of the driveway. After ejecting the empty magazine, he slid a full one into place. "Here."

She didn't think of arguing.

"Don't be afraid to use it if you have to."

Shannen gulped. Rhone slid a much-larger gun from its holster around his waist. Absently, she wondered if it was the same one he used to lock in a safe every night when he came home—on those nights he'd actually made it home.

"Stay behind me."

Shannen fought the instinctive urge to rush past him and hurry inside to see if Nicky was back. Adrenaline, huge waves of it, rushed through her, making her palms sweaty and her knees weak.

Rhone turned the knob slowly so it didn't make a single sound. Before slipping inside, he unclicked the safety, the sharp sound making the whole situation more frightening, more real.

The drone of voices, none raised in anger, met her ears. Still, Rhone held up a hand for silence. What was going on? Suspense squeezed around her, cutting her breaths into shallow slices.

With his foot, Rhone inched open the door to the living room, gun gripped in his hands.

"At ease, Mitchell," Doug said. "I don't want to get my head blown off."

Responding to the cue in Doug's voice, obviously something both men had experienced before, Rhone set the safety, holstering his gun in a swift motion. Then he took Shannen's gun from her. Anxiety swooshed from her body even though her pulse continued at a doubled rate.

"Someone you know?" Rhone asked, extending his arm to hold the door open. "I thought you said you weren't expecting anyone."

She bit back an instinctive urge to groan. "Jonathen." On wooden-feeling legs, she walked past Rhone, into the suddenly tense room.

"Shannen, I just heard the news about Nicky—are you okay?"

Shannen was aware of the heat of Rhone's glare, Doug's open amusement as he plopped on the couch and laced his fingers behind his neck and Jonathen's concern. She felt utterly torn, utterly on display.

Jon hurried across to her, wrapping her in his arms. "You look like you haven't slept," he said, with more-than-doctorly kindness.

"Maybe a total of two hours last night," she admitted. Rhone drummed his fingers on the telephone stand, making no attempt to disguise his hostility.

"I can prescribe a sedative for you."

"She doesn't need to be doped up," Rhone interrupted.

"Please," she implored, worming her way from Jon's suddenly protective embrace.

"You must be Rhone Mitchell," Jon said, his tone resigned as he extended his hand.

Rhone pointedly, rudely, ignored it. "I am."

"I've heard a lot about you."

Rhone propped his hip on the stand and folded his arms across his chest. "Then you have the advantage. Who the hell are you?"

"Jonathen Peterson, Nicky—and Shannen's—doctor...and good friend. Not that it's any of your business. I don't recall you being around when Shannen needed you."

Shannen felt ill.

Doug vaulted from the couch, uttering a soft curse. Jon glared. Rhone stiffened. And Shannen buried her face in her hands. How was it possible for things to keep going from bad to worse?

"I'm sure the good doctor didn't mean anything by it," Doug said, centering himself strategically in the room.

"The hell I didn't."

Was it possible for the floor to open up and swallow her? Taking her to a place where she no longer felt pain, humiliation and despair?

"Look," Doug intervened. "I know you both mean well, but neither of you are helping Shannen."

Jon's shoulders drooped. "I'm sorry, Shannen. It's just that I know what you've gone through with this absentee husband of yours."

"I'm not absent anymore," Rhone snapped.

"Too bad for Shannen."

"Punch a wall," Doug warned Rhone.

"Out of my way, *partner.*"

"Stop!" Her voice, risen on a near-hysterical octave caused all three men to stare at her. "Don't you dare act like this, Rhone Mitchell. Jon's been a good friend when I desperately needed one. You have no right to treat him like this."

"Damn it, Shannen, you're my wife."

"Not for much longer."

The intake of his breath was sharp, nearly painful to listen to. She'd hurt him. Badly. Instead of stopping though, she couldn't. "You tried to dictate to me before, well, I'm through letting you run my life. When you walked out that morning, you made your decision. I wasn't a part of it."

Rhone arched a dark eyebrow. "You left, knowing full well you carried my child, *my* child, inside you."

Shannen had never before had a confrontation like this. She didn't show her feelings in public, didn't argue in front of friends. But damn it, she'd had enough. Her

missing son was the straw that broke her back. "And you
went to Colombia on some sort of avenging angel kick,
not giving a damn about me or the future we might share.
You left me, Rhone, and didn't give a second thought
about my suffering."

"You're being melodramatic."

"Melodramatic?" She almost slapped him. "Melodramatic? My son was kidnapped by a lunatic. Because of
you. I don't know if he's alive."

She choked. "Or if he's dead. My son could be dead,
Rhone. And all because of you." She glared at him.
"Don't you dare accuse *me* of melodrama."

She'd watched the changes on his face. Guilt. Re-
morse. Anger. Then he blanketed them all behind a steely
mask, though his eyes sparked with flares of warning.

"I'll have an apology for my friend," she insisted, tilting her chin stubbornly.

Silence reigned.

Refusing to say the words, Rhone held out his hand.
Jon seemed no more anxious to return the gesture, but
swallowed his pride, as well.

"And now..." Rhone said, turning back to Shannen.
With a firm grasp that didn't invite discussion, he took her
arm. "...I'll have a word with *you* in private."

She heard the terse temper in his tone, a barely veiled
threat that promised retaliation. Shannen remembered the
words he'd spoken the night before and truly comprehended how much he'd come to despise her. She remembered the old saying about a fine line between love and
hate.

She'd obviously crossed it.

Yet, still, passion existed, no matter the name. It had
always been that way—which was why she should have
severed the relationship before it destroyed her emotion-
ally. "Rhone, don't. Not like this," she whispered.

From the corner of her eye, she saw Jon try and defend her, only to be stopped by Doug's intervention.

Rhone exerted enough pressure on her wrist to make her wince. When he spoke, she recognized his tone meant business. "Let's go."

Chapter 7

Rhone wanted to strangle her.

Bitter resentment about Nicky merged with images of
another man touching Shannen, kissing her. And just how
much had she told her so-called friend about Rhone,
about their marriage? Judging from his familiarity, Peterson had implanted himself quite nicely into Shannen's
and Nicky's lives.

Rhone pictured the happy trio. And saw red. Unaware, his grasp on Shannen's wrist tightened.

"Cut the caveman act, Rhone, and let me go," Shannen said, attempting to skid them both to a stop.

He eased the pressure a fraction of an inch. Let her go
so she could run back to Peterson? "Like hell I will."

Rhone chose the path he'd taken earlier that morning.
Rounding a curve that put the house out of sight, he noticed Shannen quit struggling to free herself, walking
docilely behind him.

In a small meadow, he led Shannen toward a grove of
aspen trees near the edge of the creek. Midstride, her foot

tangled with his. The next instant, he felt the jerk of her heel against his shin above his ankle.

"What the..." His words hung suspended as Rhone fought for balance. And lost. Without letting go, he hauled Shannen down with him, sure that the surprise he saw on her face equalled his own.

The bed of grass and wildflowers did nothing to cushion his impact. Rhone winced and cursed, a sharp pain radiating from his right shoulder down his arm.

Lying on top of him, Shannen squirmed. Rhone's other arm held her firmly in place, his body, if not his mind, recognizing she was finally where she belonged.

"This isn't going to accomplish anything," she said, twisting around to look at him. "Rhone, you're hurt. You crazy idiot, why didn't you say something?"

"I did," he said through clenched teeth. "It's not worth repeating."

"Let me get up so I can help."

His anger receded as pain began to subside to an aching throb. He opened his eyes. "There's nothing you can do."

"You don't know that. I've become quite a master at giving first aid."

Nicky's name hung between them, unspoken.

"There's a pin in my shoulder," he explained, breaking the tension. "I jarred it, that's all. It'll be fine." Grunting, he added, "In a minute."

Proving it, he rolled over, pinioning her beneath him. He rested the majority of his weight on his left elbow.

"So I see." Her voice was husky, her eyes dilated. In sync, he felt the rapid rise and fall of their breaths against his chest.

"You told me well-aimed punches and fancy footwork couldn't stop a bullet. Apparently, fancy footwork doesn't stop you, either," she chided.

"Oh, I don't know. It has its advantages." He brushed golden strands away from her eyes, eyes that revealed a measure of apprehension bordering on distrust. Or was the mixture he saw a reflection of his own?

As though unable to help herself, she took the bait. "Name one," she dared.

His gaze moved over her face, following his forefinger that traced soft, delicate contours. "It helps me forget why I wanted to throttle you."

Slowly he lowered his head, placing his hands near her temples and jaw. He watched as his intentions registered, observing there was no need to apply encouragement to hold her still.

Her glance slid down to his mouth. Time and place ceased to matter. While not forgotten, never forgotten, the ugliness and terror that brought them together momentarily loosened its grip.

"Makes me forget that you insinuated Peterson into a place in my son's life that was rightfully mine."

"Rhone . . ."

Shannen's whisper was all that separated their lips.

Rhone raised his head. Her glance darted away, but not before he glimpsed what she attempted to hide. She wanted intimacy as much as he did, and not unlike him, she was afraid.

Fear had never been something he ran from. He wasn't about to start now; neither would he give her the opportunity.

With a sound similar to a growl, his lips descended to Shannen's. Coherent thought scattered.

Dreamed of . . . hungered for . . . velvety warmth.

He struggled for dominance over consuming emotion. He wanted to hurt her as much as he ached. Wanted to communicate the pain and suffering. And anxiety.

He fought for mastery of them all.

Sought to find the tenderness she always inspired.

Failed.

But found passion still soared with a strong life of its own.

Needing to punish, he claimed her lips. Demanded her capitulation.

She didn't struggle.

Instead, he felt the moment her resolve weakened, and she offered the trust of total surrender.

Punishment turned and roared, overwhelmed him, rather than her.

Something more primitive than pain claimed him and he gentled the touch. Instead of needing to inflict hurt, he gently probed, seeking her cooperation.

With what rational thought he was capable of, Rhone recognized the circumstances were crazy, causing them both to act in uncommon ways. But the sudden desire to hold and be held, to give comfort and false promises, was undeniable.

He knew he should stop, push away. Couldn't. Didn't want to. In spite of everything, he still wanted her.

With painstaking care, his lips skimmed the surface of hers, urging her to give as much as he, not wanting to go down for the count alone. Finally, with a moan as soft as a sigh, Shannen returned his kiss, knocking him in the solar plexus.

Opening her mouth, she teased his tongue with her own, coaxing an intimate mating. Her hands reached upward. He understood, and gloried in the fierce hunger she conveyed as she explored his face—like a woman rendered sightless whose lover had just returned. Splaying her fingers through his hair, Shannen urged him closer, rising to meet him halfway.

Unbidden, the image of Shannen casting her inhibitions aside for another man, for Peterson, intruded.

Abruptly Rhone tore his mouth from hers, silently cursing the direction of his thoughts. Shannen frowned, confusion chasing away exposed needs. When she opened her mouth to speak, Rhone turned his head, focusing his attention elsewhere. Only the sounds of nature filled the ensuing quiet.

A few seconds later, he glanced back, wishing he hadn't. Clearly he read her regret. He felt it, too, but in a different way. Two years of celibacy, of needing and wanting his wife, had his body recoiling painfully. He swallowed a groan. She would laugh in his face if she knew, Rhone thought.

"Does Jon kiss you like that?" Loaded with frustration, he ground out the words, wanting to put a dent in her calm demeanor. "Do you respond to him like you do to me?"

"Only you could take something wonderful . . ."

In spite of himself, Rhone's heart sang.

". . . and turn it into something cheap and meaningless."

He scowled. "Okay, so you don't want to talk about Jon. Neither do I. Let's back up to the part about us being wonderful."

Shannen shifted, pushing against him. "Let's don't."

He ignored her efforts to put distance between them. "What we had was good. You can't deny it."

"It was the best," Shannen agreed. "But great sex isn't enough."

Rhone rolled to his side and sat up. Dusting off her fuchsia sweatshirt, Shannen rose next to him.

"We had more than that," he said.

"In the beginning."

"What the hell happened? What went wrong?"

"Oh, Rhone, we've been through this. . . ."

"At the risk of repeating yourself, enlighten me."

She delayed, picking a long blade of grass. He could equate himself with the knots she tied into the narrow stem.

"The man I married was kind, caring and thoughtful. You laughed more, you spent more time at home. With me. I'll admit, I was never thrilled with what you did for a living—fear and worry were my constant companions—but I could handle it."

Rhone heard the reluctance in her voice, already sorry he'd asked.

"You changed," Shannen continued. "You distanced yourself, never letting me get too close. When I tried, you accused me of nagging. Then you'd run off on another assignment to heaven knows where. No longer did you bother to call or get a message to me that you were all right. There was no communication at all. Not when you were gone. Not when you were home."

Rhone didn't know what to say, faced with truth he couldn't deny. Or excuse. He stared at the ground, wrists dangled over updrawn knees, his back against the trunk of an aspen tree as he forced himself to listen.

"It got to the point every time you left, I felt relief. Then, when I didn't hear from you, I was sick with worry. And guilt, because our parting had been in anger. The only way I could survive and maintain sanity was in convincing myself you were fine and you'd be home soon. I'd fill myself with hope that everything would be better, be like it was in the beginning, but every homecoming, every departure, became worse than the one before."

Had he been that cruel? That heartless? Unable to see anyone's needs but his own?

He told Shannen he could never forgive her, but there was no mistaking the fact the anguish etched on her face was real.

"When I found out I was pregnant and couldn't tell you," she said rawly, "I just couldn't wait any longer. I knew I had to leave, for my sake. As well as the child's."

Shannen extended a palm, as if begging him to understand the incomprehensible.

"It wouldn't have been a good life for a child, Rhone. Kids need moms to be mommies, not mental wrecks. *I left for Nicky's sake.*"

On an emotional roller coaster since Norton's phone call, Rhone's insides twisted into a painful spasm. He couldn't call her a liar, not with the truth of her convictions in her eyes.

But he still couldn't forgive the huge gap in his life where a child belonged.

"We'd better be getting back," Shannen said softly. "I'll scrounge up something to eat."

Rhone stood. Carefully masking his feelings, he held a hand out to Shannen. Placing her palm against his, he pulled her up, considering, instead, how small and fragile she seemed. Yet she was strong and sure. Shyness had been replaced by confidence. She had grown, matured, forced to do so by the responsibility of becoming a parent and learning to provide for herself and their son.

Aside from the fact Shannen had kept Nicholas a secret lay the reality that she'd never asked Rhone for help, had never needed it.

Peterson would have been readily available.

Rhone's spark of understanding died and he sneered, remembering Shannen's earlier comment that she wouldn't be his wife much longer. Her reasoning was easy to figure. The good doctor was obviously well acquainted with Nicky, effectively usurping Rhone's role by providing the male influence Nicholas needed. While Rhone continued to question Peterson's status with Shannen, if what she said was true and he was a friend, it was hardly enough to build a marriage on. Even so, it was more than Rhone could lay claim to.

Shannen needed him now, but only for as long as it took to get Nicky back. Rhone glowered. If she had it in her pretty head he was going to walk away when this was over, he had a rude awakening in store for Mrs. Shannen Mitchell.

"By the way, thought you should know..."

A few paces ahead of him, Shannen turned when he spoke.

"Nicky's *our* son, and I've changed my mind about willingly giving you a divorce. Nicky needs a family. A real family. Full-time. If you want your freedom, you're going to have to fight me for it through every courtroom in the country."

Her eyes narrowed, then she shrugged. "If that's the way it has to be."

Irritable, he pressed further. "Perhaps I'm not making myself clear. We're still married. You need me. And I'm moving in."

Hands on hips, Shannen marched back to where he stood.

"The answer is no. *N-o.*"

Rhone copied her stance, leaning forward for emphasis. "I don't recall asking."

"It's my house. I have a say who lives in it and who doesn't."

Green eyes sparred with blue. Did she know she was turning him inside out? The heat of their anger had a reverse effect, an art Shannen couldn't begin to know she'd perfected.

"Lady, it's not up for discussion."

She cocked a brow, releasing a sigh that spoke of her exhaustion. And resolve. "Do what you want, Rhone. I no longer care."

"Did ya call her?"

Jimmy scowled at Naomi. Damn, but she was starting to get on his nerves, just like that Mitchell brat. How much did a man have to take? It wasn't fair, these sacrifices poor Jimmy had to make. He exhaled a long-suffering sigh, then drew a deep drag from a half-burned cigarette.

"Jimmy? Did you hear me?"

"Yeah," he snapped, the nicotine oozing down inside. "I hear you. I've been hearin' you for two days. Shuddup, will ya?"

"All I did was ask a question."

His fingers shook as he slammed the cigarette against the ashtray, shaking off the ashes.

Ashes.

Ever since Jack's death, Jimmy's life had been a smoldering pile of ashes. And it wouldn't be fixed until Rhone Mitchell, his wife and his obnoxious son lay dead.

Shannen knew the instant Rhone entered the living room. He'd walked silently, like he always did. But, just like in the days when they'd been together, she tuned in to him, knew without turning around that his left shoulder rested on the doorjamb. Maybe it was a subtle shift in the atmosphere, an increased awareness. Whatever, she knew, with every vibration in her body, that Rhone stood there, staring at her. Intently.

Still smarting from their earlier conversation, Shannen knew she couldn't turn around and face him. Not yet. His kiss had rattled her. Her response rattled her even more so. But it was his cool and easy pronouncement that he intended to move back in with her, be a father to Nicky, that completely unnerved her. She didn't normally consider herself a coward, but she couldn't, just couldn't, find the strength to look at him.

She knew, beyond doubt, that she didn't have the will to deny him. Not in this emotional state.

Brian cleared his throat, as if completely aware of, and uncomfortable with, the tension that swelled in the room. "Anyway, Ms.—"

"Shannen," she corrected, not wanting a repeat of the last time he'd innocently stumbled over her name. From the corner of the room, she distinctly heard Rhone drum his fingers on the doorframe.

Brian nodded. Studiously, he avoided Rhone's gaze before continuing to address Shannen. "Right. Like I was saying, your housekeeper was warmly welcomed by her family. But she was still protesting she didn't want to leave you, especially since you need her so badly." He spared a quick glance at Rhone, then turned back to Shannen and said, "Maria wanted me to be sure to tell you to call her as soon as Nicholas gets back."

Uncomfortable silence fell over the room. Rhone's fingers tightened on the frame and his knuckles whitened. Shannen slowly faced Rhone, a lump sticking in her throat.

Brian turned red.

"Thank you," she finally managed to force out.

"That is, I, er—"

"Don't worry, Brian," Shannen said, reaching out and touching the man's hand reassuringly. "We all know we'll get Nicky back safely." Her lungs felt as if someone had reached inside and squeezed. Hard. She wished she could believe her own words, believe the man posing as a Realtor truly wasn't as cold and callous as he'd seemed. But Shannen was generally a good judge of character. She'd seen his sleaziness the second she'd opened the front door.

"There's a report on that table that just came over the fax, boss," Brian said.

In a few steps, Rhone closed the distance separating them. Then he stood before her, filling her vision, consuming her senses. She crooked her head to look him in the eye. As if no one mattered, as if the world stopped, Rhone reached for her as he might have, once upon a time. His fingertips bit into the soft flesh of her shoulders, penetratingly, yet not uncomfortably.

He didn't say a thing.

With a muttered excuse, Brian disappeared.

And then Rhone and Shannen were alone.

Her mind spiraled back to earlier that day, remembering the way Rhone touched her. Kissed her. She remembered the flood of sweet yearning when his lips met hers. It reminded her of the first time he'd kissed her, walking her up to the front door of the apartment she'd shared with another woman. Always on alert, he'd opened the door, swept a cursory, yet complete glance around the vacant front room. Then he'd pinned her against the wall, letting strands of hair flow through his fingers. Just when she'd thought he intended to leave her breathless and shaking, he'd kissed her.

And left her breathless and shaking in ways she would never forget.

It'd been a repeat this afternoon. He'd had her helplessly trapped again. Shannen had known, like Rhone had known—reading her with a sixth sense—that she really didn't want to be released. Not right then.

No matter what else had gone wrong between them, physical intimacy hadn't been a problem. From the subtle shading of darkness in his eyes, Rhone obviously knew it, too.

Nevertheless, Shannen had learned that physical intimacy was a poor substitute for what she truly craved—emotional intimacy. Neither had been good at that. And since neither knew what to say, where to start, they still apparently weren't any better at emotions. Not good ones, anyway.

Slowly, as though realizing what he was doing, Rhone uncurled his fingers from around her. "Sorry."

She rubbed her upper arms. "Don't worry, it didn't hurt." Liar, her mind chided. Every time he touched her, then let go without giving her what she secretly yearned for, hurt.

Rhone raked his fingers through his hair as he paced the floor. Slowly she sank onto the sofa, letting her shoulders sag against the softness.

"Hell," he muttered, coming to an abrupt stop, his back to her. "Why does this always happen?"

She searched for the right words—heck, any words.

She found none.

"Maybe because this—" He lifted his hands expressively "—whatever it is, isn't finished between us." Rhone dropped his hands, then turned to face her. "I've never gotten over you, Shannen."

Starkness sketched between his brows. Her insides contorted into a tight knot.

"I can't be around you without wanting to touch you, hold you. Put my hand on your chest and feel your heart pound against my palm."

"Rhone, don't."

He didn't come an inch closer, not even a hint of a breath closer, yet her pulse reacted as if he'd swallowed the distance and pulled her into his arms.

Shannen gulped, emotions thrown into a tumbling turmoil. She missed her son, desperately waiting for news, each second that dragged by compounding into an eternity. And Rhone's demanding assertion that he wouldn't give her a divorce turned up the burner beneath the already-bubbling cauldron. She didn't need it.

As much as she wanted it.

Rhone stepped closer. "Don't say 'don't,' Shannen. It won't work. I won't stop." His jaw clenched into a hard line. "I want to share Nicky's life, and verbally, you can deny it, but deep down, I know you believe we belong together. You, Nicky and I."

When it appeared he intended to punctuate his statement, to prove what he said was true in a physical way, she jumped from the couch and headed for the door.

"Funny, Shannen, I hadn't figured you for a coward, not after all this."

As the door slammed behind her, the sound of his voice echoing in her ears, she realized she hadn't figured herself for a coward, either.

Chapter 8

The coffee flowed through the filter, dripping with splattering hisses into the pot. Shannen stared at it, feeling the cold that crept in and cloaked her.

Blinking and forcing herself to look away, she drained the bottom of her cup, swallowing the remains of lukewarm coffee with a grimace.

Steam escaped from the pot, the third batch she'd brewed in the last hour. If it wasn't for the fact that Brian had picked up cold cuts and bread in town, and Rhone had made the sandwiches, insisting she eat, Shannen knew she would be surviving solely on strong jolts of caffeine.

She'd spent the rest of the day—and well into the evening—holed up with the men, analyzing the scraps of information they'd received. One report said Norton had been spotted near Salt Lake City. Another put him in Durango, in southwestern Colorado. A third said he'd caught a plane out of Denver International and headed farther west. Rhone's instincts told him Norton never left the state.

As much as she hated the constant waiting, horrible uncertainty, she realized Rhone was right. They couldn't run out and blindly chase every single clue.

Nevertheless, Rhone inexorably moved toward the inevitable confrontation. He'd ordered ready-to-eat meals, had canteens and water-purifying tablets delivered. Backpacks with tents and sleeping bags had also arrived, along with weapons she'd only seen in movies, and night-vision equipment and heat-detecting apparatus she'd never dreamed existed. The latter, Rhone had explained, could help determine someone's presence merely with their body heat.

She'd asked how they could possibly carry everything if they had to hike after Norton. Rhone told her they would take only the necessities, leaving the rest. But because he didn't know for sure what Norton planned, Rhone had wanted to be prepared for anything.

Shannen glanced through the kitchen window. A charcoal-gray cargo van was parked between two motor homes. She'd seen the van come and go with regularity but no set schedule, as far as she could tell. The men who'd set up temporary living quarters on her property kept to themselves, for the most part. Their presence, both on her property and the few times they traipsed through her house to converse in muted tones with Rhone and Doug, was a constant reminder her life was anything but normal. Not that she needed a reminder. When she'd asked who the men were, Rhone had told her simply that they were the elite of the elite.

He'd gone on to assure her that if a solid clue emerged, they would be ready to act on it in seconds. She didn't doubt him.

But waiting was the most difficult thing she'd ever done.

With a sigh, she allowed the counter to support her weight—only for a few seconds, she swore. But she was so weary... such an emotional mess.

The small black-and-white television on the kitchen's island grabbed her attention as a commercial segued back to the anchorwoman at a Denver station.

"Meanwhile, topping local news, the tragic story of a kidnapped child..."

Shannen's stomach squeezed.

"Joining us live from our remote cam with an exclusive story is reporter Suzie Lord with Summit County Sheriff, Tom Jenkins. Suzie..."

The knot in Shannen's stomach became acid. She let out a soft cry, then called for Rhone.

Before the word was completely out, Rhone vaulted over the back of the couch and hustled into the kitchen. Doug wasn't far behind. Hand shaking, she turned up the volume, just as Nicky's picture flashed on the screen.

Rhone's curse was brief and bitter.

"Oh, hell," Doug said.

Shannen buried her face in her hands.

"Yarrow!" Rhone bellowed.

"... Authorities are staying mum on the issue, but our reporter spoke with Special Agent Brian Yarrow, a man many of you will remember from his work on the recent investigation surrounding the kidnapping and subsequent murder of a Colorado Springs girl. Suzie?"

"We caught up with Special Agent Yarrow when he returned the family's housekeeper to the home of her daughter, here in Lakewood."

"Front and center, Yarrow!" Rhone yelled again.

The man hurried in from his post outside the door, gun clutched in hand. Breathlessly, he said, "Sir?"

"Maybe you should watch this," Doug said.

Yarrow groaned, turning his attention to the television.

"... No comment."

"But you don't deny this is the family housekeeper."

"No, I don't, Ms. Lord, but I have no further comment at this time."

Just then, the composite drawing of Norton, taken from Maria and Shannen's descriptions, replaced Yarrow's somber-looking features. Shannen had a hard time reconciling the official, stern-faced man on the screen with the sheepish agent standing near her husband.

"Care to explain?" Rhone glared.

"There's nothing to explain, sir. I don't know how they scooped the story and didn't know they were laying in wait for me in Denver."

"And the composite sketch?"

"Rhone," Doug warned.

"And you didn't think to inform me of the press's interest?"

"It's not like that," Brian hastily assured him.

"Then what is it like?"

Shannen wrapped her fingers around Rhone's wrist and gently squeezed. At one time, he would have responded to her wishes. Would he now?

"Maybe you should ask the sheriff, Rhone." Brian loosened the knot in the tie at his throat. "I sure as hell know better than to talk to the press about your family."

"... Both kidnappers are considered armed and extremely dangerous. Anyone with information should call the Summit County Sheriff's office at ..."

Shannen had heard enough. When the phone number was superimposed over the harsh angles of Norton's penciled face, she uncurled her fingers from Rhone's arm and fled the room, not caring that the door slammed shut behind her.

"Shannen, wait!"

Rhone's tone was concerned, but it didn't slow her step. As if the tortured damnation of hell chased her, she ran up the stairs, not even taking time to hold on to the banister.

She heard his clipped instructions to Doug and Brian, telling them to get a gag order and find the sheriff, as she reached the landing.

Shannen didn't bother to lock the bedroom door. No need. A lock wouldn't stop Rhone. Not if he wanted in.

Emotion threatening to choke her, she threw herself onto the bed and curled into a ball. Her shoulders shook, but no tears came. Threatened, but didn't come.

She resisted the temptation to drag a pillow over her head and bury herself from the world and its problems. She knew it wouldn't help.

Instead, she shoved her hurt deeper by looking over at the cradle she'd never moved from her room, even though Nicholas had outgrown it months ago. Her eyes adjusted to the semidarkness, the dim glow from a night-light in the master bath aiding her. She didn't remember placing Bear on top of the tiny pillow in the cradle earlier, but there it sat.

Alone.

Lonely.

Like her.

For long moments she stared at Bear.

Then, for a reason she couldn't fathom, she pushed off the bed and crossed the few steps to the cradle. Maybe wanting to punish herself for not being there when Nicky needed her most, Shannen placed her fingertips on the intricately carved antique wood and gently pushed, watching as the cradle that once tenderly held her infant child swung back and forth.

Empty.

Bear began to topple, and Shannen grabbed for the worn stuffy. Choking back an all-consuming sob, she sank back on the edge of the bed, clutching the animal and watching as momentum continued to rock the barren cradle.

She heard the door squeak. Without turning, she knew Rhone had joined her. She squeezed her eyes closed against the stinging sensation, against the very real possibility her son might never return to demand Bear.

"Can I come in?"

He didn't wait for an answer.

She didn't expect him to.

Despite everything, despite the anger, pain, frustration and blame, she didn't want to be alone. Suddenly she couldn't face the next few hours—not without help.

Not without Rhone's help.

The door closed behind him with a nearly inaudible click. For a few seconds she didn't know where he was, if he still stood near the door, or whether he'd crossed to her.

A subtle scent of man and spice commingled in the air. Yet this time, she wasn't threatened, wasn't scared. The scent took her back to a time when everything had been okay, a time when love bloomed and the future waited, with promises and expectations.

A feeling of guilt nearly overwhelmed her as she clung to the memory of a better time. Yet, a part of her mind— she assumed it was the part meant to block her from pain—wouldn't let it go.

A gust of fresh, pure mountain air assaulted her. She opened her eyes, then faced her husband. He stood near the window he'd just opened.

He looked tired. Weary, as if the weight of the world's problems rested solely on his shoulders.

She couldn't pinpoint the cause, but knew it was a combination of her lies of omission and the fact the investigation wasn't moving fast enough for him.

A serving of guilt sought her out and dove inside.

Rhone had been right about a lot of things. If she'd ever had the courage to tell him about his son, he might have been able to prevent the gruesome events.

As much as she admitted the truth to herself, she couldn't say the words aloud.

She rubbed her hands up and down her arms. "The air's cold."

"Would closing the window truly chase away the cold?"

With honesty, with Bear pressed tightly against her chest, where she wished her child nestled, Shannen shook her head. "Nothing, except having Nicky back, would make me warm again."

Rhone rested his shoulders on the log-hewn wall, arms folded across his chest. A deceptively relaxed stance. Shannen knew better, knew the hard steel of a gun lay against his spine, knew his knees were flexed so he could move any direction if necessary.

"Do you want me to leave?" he asked quietly, words carrying to her on the crisp air, the same air that brought his scent . . . and the vivid memory of him.

He wasn't talking about forever—he'd said he'd never give her that option again. With forced bravery she met his gaze.

"Or do you want me to stay?"

In the silence, she heard the ticking of the clock, the ragged intake and exhale of Rhone's breaths. He would leave if she asked him to.

Then she would have to face the ghoulish nightmare all by herself, no one at her side to slay the dragons.

She wished she could see more clearly, needing to know what his eyes reflected that his voice didn't. "I'm afraid, Rhone," she whispered.

Silence stretched.

Then he nodded. "I am, too."

His admission squeezed past her resistance to let him stay, his honesty shaking her to her soul. "I can't stop thinking about Nicholas, can't conquer my fear that I'll never hold him again or hear him call for me." Her voice trembled. "The night is so long." She was sure she echoed his own thoughts.

"Shannen, I know how you feel about me, how much you blame me."

"And you blame me."

He inclined his head in unspoken agreement. "But I'm willing to try and put it aside—for right now—if you are."

She knew what he offered: comfort and companionship to get through the long, horrible hours until daybreak.

Agreeing to let him stay wouldn't change facts, wouldn't return their relationship to the magic they once shared. If she accepted the offer of his company, she would have to accept the offer for what it was: simply a chance to share the burden.

She blinked back a tear and whispered, "Stay. I want you to stay with me, Rhone."

She didn't bother to hide her feelings, the dim light shrouded them in secrecy, anonymity. Not that it mattered. Her voice, when she spoke, laid them bare. "I need...you. Hold..." Her voice broke. "Hold me, Rhone. Make me warm."

In a fluid motion he shoved away from the wall. Bear fell to the floor unnoticed when Rhone swept her up and carried her to the head of the bed.

Lightly she ran her fingertips over his features. Close up, she could see longing—stark and startling in its intensity, sketched across his taut face, searing her.

After setting her down, he propped pillows, then sank down on the bed behind her, pulling her close. Her back rested against his chest, her head supported by his shoulder.

It felt good, right, if only for a fleeting stoppage of time.

Rhone wrapped constricting arms around her, just beneath her breasts, with a tension that communicated his own powerful need to experience a tendril of tenderness, of closeness.

As minutes marched by, she stayed in the comfort of his arms, like she used to. The way they sat was intimate, yet not overly so. Situated this way, they'd once shared confidences and hopes for the future.

Sadly, she remembered the time right after they were married that she'd told him she wanted his child. He'd pushed her away and turned her in order to read the unguarded expression in her eyes. She'd seen a responsive flicker of excitement in his own. In that instant, she knew the man she'd chosen as her life partner would be an excellent father.

But the marriage slowly disintegrated, until she was only a shell of a person, worried he wouldn't return, terrified of all the things that could happen. She'd known what he did for a living when she smiled and allowed him to slide the engagement ring on her finger. But through the years, the band of gold had become a band of bondage, tying her to a life-style she wasn't strong enough to deal with.

And then, when she had discovered her pregnancy, she knew life couldn't continue the way it had. Hot tears of failure chasing down her cheeks, she'd slipped off her wedding set and locked it in a jewelry box, vowing to get on with her life.

Without Rhone.

The sense of success she thought she'd acquired in the past two years had been just that, a sense. Truth was, she wasn't any better without him than she had been with him.

"Penny for your thoughts," he said against her ear, breath fanning through her hair and sending a little shiver through her.

Strangely, she wanted to talk, needed to share, garner comfort. "Nighttime's always the worst, isn't it?"

He didn't answer, merely splayed his fingers across her flat abdomen.

"Shadows play on the ceiling and walls. And in your heart."

"Yeah," he agreed. "Nighttime's the worst."

Rhone held her still, waiting for her to continue, evidently sensing her need to talk. He was right, reading her with accuracy borne from years of experience.

"I can't stand not knowing if he's still alive." For a full minute, seconds ticked off by the uncaring clock, Rhone didn't respond. She knew he wouldn't lie. And offering reassurances would be tantamount to lying. "I hate sitting here wondering if he's crying for me. Wondering if he's hungry, hurt or worse. Wondering if they know how to tell if he needs medicine." She shuddered. "Wondering if he's struggling for every breath."

Rhone's arms tightened around her. Shannen realized with a sinking sensation how thoughtless she'd been. Rhone was doing everything humanly possible to save Nicky, to bring him home. A mission he was risking his life for.

Shannen struggled away, then turned to face him. "Oh, Rhone, I'm sorry." *Sorry for everything.* She reached to touch his face.

"Shh," he said. "Tonight's not about punishment. Or guilt. Right now, we just have to figure out a way to make it until dawn." She crumpled like a rag doll carelessly tossed in the corner.

With firm, unyielding pressure, he gathered her close and offered the solid support of his own body.

Even if she'd never loved him before, she knew she would have fallen for him in that very instant. There were so many things he could say, so many accusations he could justly hurl at her. Yet he said nothing.

His silence provided solace, comfort, if not healing. Rhone shifted and she experienced a sudden stab of fear that he might leave her alone to face the darkness.

"Rhone?"

"Yeah?"

"Don't go. Don't leave me alone tonight."

"I'm right here, Shannen, for as long as you need me."

"Talk to me," she said, wanting to listen to the soothing depth of his tone. But more, wanted him to share that darkest part of himself where secrets hid. "Tell me about the things that happened while we were apart. The things that took you away from me."

His shudder passed completely through her body. Though he didn't immediately say anything, his tension wrapped around them both, cloying and frightening.

"I'm not good at talking, Shannen. Never was."

"But if you truly mean to be a part of our son's life if— *when*—we get him back..." She paused for a deep breath, reassuring herself things would be okay. "... we need to be able to communicate. For Nicky's sake we have to talk."

He seemed to take in her statement. When she tried to turn again, he held her firm. "It's easier this way," he said.

She nodded, settling back against his chest. Her hand lay next to his wrist and she felt the reassuring beat of his pulse.

"I never wanted to leave, Shannen. A huge part of me recognized you were right, that the marriage wouldn't work without one hundred percent commitment from both of us. I wanted to give it. But I couldn't stay, hold you in my arms, make love to you every night and pretend that who I am isn't who I was."

What shouldn't have made sense did.

"There was no way I could live with myself if I hadn't finished what I started. I would've hated myself, learned to hate you, too."

She flinched.

Because Rhone had never been one to open up, that alone had caused more fights than anything. Shannen had grown up in a household where no one spoke with excitement or shared the daily trials and thrills. Dinner with her parents had been deadly dull, her father barely glancing up from where he read the newspaper. She remembered no passion between her parents, nothing but cold looks and limp smiles. She'd longed for a brother or sister, cousin, anyone to break the monotony.

It wasn't until her teenage years when she joined friends and their families for meals that she saw how abnormal hers was. One night, she'd calmly announced to her parents that one of her female friends had joined the French foreign legion and that Shannen intended to join her in a few weeks. Her mother had muttered something along the lines of "That's nice, dear." Shannen's father had grunted from behind the daily news, the paper not even rustling. Shannen had sworn then that *her* family life would be different, better.

Then she'd married Rhone, a man every bit as closed and remote as her father. A therapist friend had given a fancy name to Shannen's affliction. She preferred to call it blind love. This side of Rhone was different, maybe not better, but certainly a welcome change to the clam who'd only mouthed one word when questioned—"Security."

"I would have been back sooner. I intended to come looking for you—as soon as we iced Menendez." He fell ominously silent. "It didn't work out that way."

Her pulse roared in her ears. Or was that the thundering of his?

"All your hurtled accusations, your worst fears came true. Maybe it was for the best you went on with your life, not knowing."

A new chill crept up her spine. She shivered. He reached for a comforter and pulled it across them.

"You sure you want to hear this?"

"Yes."

Without being told, she knew he was about to divulge information he probably shouldn't. That he trusted her enough was a milestone.

"We got him in the end, but I wasn't so lucky. There was another minion in hiding." Rhone shrugged. "It was a trap. We lost a couple of good men that day, men I'd known and worked with, men with families."

He dragged in a jagged breath, before going on. "I could have gotten out, but it would have meant Menendez skating."

Rhone pounded a fist on the mattress. She felt his tension, his frustration and rage.

"I'd worked too damn long and hard, spent months—hell, years—in the jungle, and I wasn't going to miss my chance."

"What happened, Rhone?" She dreaded the answer, as much as she needed to hear it.

"I was taken captive."

She froze. Blood ran like ice through her veins. Captured? In Central America? She'd seen movies, read books. Suddenly, illness welled in her stomach.

"Yeah," he said, agreeing with her unspoken assessment. "It was all that, and worse."

"Your shoulder?" Tentatively, she turned on her side and reached a hand up, only to have him expertly ensnare it.

"Will never be the same, nor will a lot of other things."

This time, when she fought for release, he gave it to her. She faced him, unable to comprehend the horrors he'd endured.

Tears scalded their way down her face.

"Don't cry for me," he commanded roughly, thumbing them away. His rough skin abraded her cheek. "I don't deserve your tears. I never have."

She reached up, capturing his hand in hers. Bringing it to her lips, she placed a kiss in his palm, then glanced up at him.

"And if it had been me in your place? Would I, too, not deserve your tears? Your empathy and compassion?"

Watching her, his eyes narrowed, creating a furrow between his brows. With his mouth closed, lips in a tight line, she might've imagined his deep-throated groan.

In a single motion, he drew her against him.

Needing the man who had the power to destroy her, she inched closer, if that was possible. Heard the sound of sucked-in breath.

"Shannen?" His voice was hoarse. "Don't play with fire."

She looked at him through the distorting sheen of tears. She didn't see a cold, heartless person, who'd turned away from his wife when she needed him most. Instead, she saw a man haunted by the agonies of trying to be everything to everyone. "I'm not playing."

His gaze seemed to stare straight into her.

Her heartbeats increased. Slowly, inexorably, she moved her hand lower, until her fingers lay against his heart.

"You're worried about Nicholas," he said roughly, grabbing her hand.

She nodded. "I'm worried about you, as well."

"That's not the right reason to make love."

"I'm cold, broken spirited and have a deep need to be held, to be intimate. I think you do, too. Is needing each other, being able to offer each other comfort, so terrible? I need you, Rhone. Right here, right now.''

His nostrils flared with the effort of containing himself.

"If these aren't the right reasons to make love, I don't know what the right ones might be," she added.

"I don't want you to do something you'll end up regretting."

She smiled wryly. "I'm willing to take the chance."

"Shann—"

"Rhone, we shared a lot. Not once did I ever regret the fact we made love."

For a second, he squeezed his eyes shut. "It's different now."

"How so?"

"A lot of things have changed."

"Do you—" she hesitated, looked at him "—want me?"

He brushed her hair back from her face. "Oh, yes," he breathed. "More than you can know."

"Show me, Rhone. Make the terror, the ugliness, go away, if only for a little while. Let me do the same for you."

Rhone asked no more questions.

Cupping her face, he leaned forward. She moved to meet him halfway. Her hands skimmed along his arms to his shoulders as his lips settled over hers.

She sighed into his mouth. It'd been too long. That Rhone felt it, too, was confirmed when, in the span of a pulse beat, what had begun as gentle and tender became a raging inferno of pure flaming need.

Tilting her head, first to one side then the other, Shannen returned Rhone's kisses with a hunger that took full possession of her mind and heart.

Rhone shifted, somehow managing to bring them both to a sitting position in the center of the bed; all the while, their tongues met and withdrew in a bold, erotic dance of promise.

Shannen was vaguely aware Rhone's fingers shook like hers as they fumbled with buttons, snaps and zippers.

She moaned when Rhone drew back. His voice, rough with the same raw intensity that consumed her, spoke words that made no sense. When he lifted the sweatshirt over her head, helped her out of her jeans and panties, tossing them aside, she understood. She returned the favor. Anxious for the feel of warm bare skin, she flung his clothes the same direction hers had gone.

Incapable of thought, only feeling remained, almost more than she could stand. Every nerve responded to his questing touch, burning a trail of need so absolute, it left her trembling.

Wanting.

Begging.

At his urging, she lay down, bringing Rhone with her. Beneath her roaming fingertips, she felt the ripple of scars on his back and shoulder. She gave a tiny gasp.

His hands, positioned on either side of her head, rocked it gently, silently asking her to look at him. She blinked, trying to disguise, to contain, her anguish at the horrors and brutality he'd encountered. And failed.

"Shh," he said. "They're healed, now."

"What about the ones on the inside?" Her agonized whisper sliced through the darkness.

He rained kisses over her face. "Will heal, too, given time."

With a soft cry, Shannen pulled him to her. She ran her hands down his spine to his hips and back up again. Slowly, seductively conveying in her touch, her kiss, that everything she had to give was his. She would ask for nothing more than what he chose to give in return.

She needn't have worried. As if a gulf of years and life-altering events had never occurred, he sought and found every sensitive point of pleasure he'd once discovered, seemingly so long ago.

He stroked her breast from underneath, eliciting a soft sigh from her. When his fingertips coaxed her nipple into a taut knot, just as her insides already were, she moaned his name. Saw the flash of a grin before he lowered his mouth to suckle the hardened bud, encircling it with his tongue.

Pain so exquisitely sweet had her thrashing, reaching, grabbing. She didn't want to be the only one lost to sensual touch and crying out for relief.

Partially on their sides, facing each other, Shannen slipped her hand beneath the covers. Bending his knee, Rhone gave her the access she sought. At the same time, he tracked his fingers along her inner thigh. In achingly slow motion he moved upward.

Shannen felt his heat, hot and throbbing, as ready for her as she was for him. Her ministrations multiplied the fever, the pace of his breathing.

Rhone's moan echoed hers, his fingers finally reaching their destination. He slipped them inside, rapidly taking her to the threshold of a special place where only muted sighs were heard, burning desire and tingling sensations felt. Urgency returned as Shannen rolled onto her back. She grabbed his shoulders, encouraging him. "I... Rhone."

She read acceptance, his own readiness in a glance that locked with hers. She moved her thighs to accommodate him as he took the position that belonged to no one else. Only Rhone.

Poised above her, her insides melted as he watched for her response while he eased himself within her. She arched, wanting to drive him deeper, aching in ways she'd never forgotten, starved for his total possession.

He was a magnificent man. And for just these precious minutes, hers once again.

When his length filled her, he paused. She reached her arms behind him, drawing him closer, holding him as she often had.

In unspoken communication, they began to move.

Completely attuned to each other, Shannen found it difficult to equate the passage of time since they'd last made love.

On a gasp, the thought fled as she felt tension coil hot and hard deep inside herself.

Between breaths that mingled, from a distance, she heard his name. As he took her higher and higher, she realized she'd been the one who'd spoken it.

"Rhone," she said again.

He drove deeper into her, hurtling her closer and closer to the edge. Determined not to topple alone, she cradled his face between her palms. She drew him down for her kiss, her tongue mating with his, demanding what she'd sworn she wouldn't, giving twice as much.

When she shattered, the intensity shook her to the core of her being.

A second or two later, with a final thrust, Rhone grimaced, a moan escaping him as his own release took him down the same path that Shannen only barely returned from.

Supporting most of his weight on his forearms that nestled beside her shoulders, he leaned his forehead against a pillow. "You're beautiful," he told her. "Sweet. So sweet." His voice was muffled, raspy as he struggled to catch his breath.

Muscles still quivering, the intensity of their union lingered. Shannen thought they'd shared intimacy before. Nothing compared. Never had emotions as equally intense as her climax overtaken her in the aftermath.

Feelings she'd tried to contain these past couple days rushed to the surface. She'd been struggling so hard to be brave, to convince herself everything would be all right.

So much so that she'd succeeded on several occasions to focus on beginning to plan Nicky's christening.

Tears streamed unheeded. Her body shook with them.

Rhone immediately turned his attention to her. How, she couldn't begin to imagine, but he seemed to understand.

Rolling to his side, he took her with him, wrapping her in his warm embrace. She collapsed her head on his shoulder.

"Stay with me," she offered in the night.

He nodded, holding her even as he drew her closer and spread the comforter over them. Grateful for the warmth from the gusty wind that spilled from the open window, she snuggled against him.

An hour or more ticked by and they dozed. Eventually, Rhone stretched, as if he'd already had too much rest. When he climbed from the bed, the chill returned.

Shannen sat up and slipped her arms into the heavy terry-cloth fabric of her robe.

He slipped into a pair of blue jeans and left the top snap open. Then he paced.

Reality began to seep back in.

Needing action of her own, she slipped from beneath the covers and went to the window.

"What are you doing?"

A trace of something she had difficulty defining laced his tone. She turned back to face him.

"Don't."

She wrapped her arms around her middle. "Don't what?"

"Close that window."

The barely concealed panic made her move back toward him. Comprehension, sick understanding, pierced her. "Rhone, just what the heck happened to you in Colombia?"

It took forever for him to answer. When he did, she closed her eyes against the horror of the single word: "Imprisonment."

She sank onto the bed and drew her legs up close to her. "What aren't you telling me?"

He stood near her, back pressed against the log wall, as if needing the support.

"The cell—" he sneered "—if that's what you want to call it, was three-quarters underground. A concrete-and-steel coffin would be a more accurate description.

"As you might imagine, I try to avoid enclosed areas. Since taking up residence out-of-doors isn't a plausible solution, I have to live with it. Make do the best way I can."

She steepled her hands, then buried her face in them.

The lack of emotion from Rhone made the horror that much more difficult to handle.

He continued, as if she wasn't even there, staring at the ceiling. At nothing. "I didn't see the sun for more than a year. I wanted to mark the days somehow, but I couldn't even do that." He made a sound that wasn't quite a laugh. "Funny how the things that once mattered cease to. At one time, a steak, medium-rare with a baked potato, sounded like heaven. After God knows how long, a slab of food without bugs crawling on it and in it sounded like heaven. Prison has a way of changing your priorities."

She tightened her arms around upturned knees. "That wasn't prison, Rhone, that was barbaric."

"You got me through it."

"Me?" While she'd been living with uncertainty and regret, he'd been living in a real man-made hell. Guilt, more powerful than anything he'd laid at her feet, promised to consume her. She should have been there. Done something. Anything.

"Thoughts of you," he continued, staring at her. "Laughing. Smiling. Teasing. I relived every minute we spent together. When I thought I'd go mad from the heat, the bugs and the muscle aches, I pretended I could smell your perfume, hear you speak.

"And I dreamed. Me, who'd never indulged in a fantasy my entire life. I dreamed of you walking to me, a sexy smile on your lips, a feminine sway to your hip, an invitation in your expression." He nodded. "Yeah, I made it because of you."

Even if he eventually forgave her her sins, she knew she never would. Couldn't.

She realized that the frightening minutes of night had blended with one another, making way for the new day.

"How did you get out?"

"Doug."

She should have known. Doug would have never abandoned his friend.

The bed sagged as Rhone sat next to her, placing an arm around her shoulder.

"Rhone?"

"Hmm?" he answered absently.

Shannen drew herself tighter into a ball, as though to ward off the answer to her next question. "Did you ever cry?"

He met her gaze, head-on. "No. I was afraid if I ever started, I'd never stop."

Chapter 9

"You look like hell."

"Good morning to you, too." After opening a window, Rhone leaned against the counter, rubbing thumb and middle finger over closed eyes that felt like gravel pits.

Without asking, Doug poured a mug of coffee and slid it across the smooth tiled surface to Rhone. "Crude oil. Just the way you like it."

Rhone heard the smile in Doug's voice before he saw it. Blinking, Rhone grabbed the oversize mug and drained a good portion, grumbling that at least one of them had slept.

The double-strength dose of caffeine raced through a system that desperately needed it. As his thoughts crystallized, Rhone realized Shannen had been right about the cold. Cream-colored ceramic felt icy under his bare feet and a brisk morning breeze stirred the hairs on his chest. "Just what the devil is on your mind?" he demanded of Doug, who'd continued to watch Rhone with a half smirk.

"You."

The meaning escaped Rhone.

"You spent the night with Shannen."

"Yeah, so?"

Doug raised a hand in mock surrender. "Just an observation. You didn't show up for watch duty last night. Brian pulled a double shift to cover for you."

"Damn." Rhone ran his fingers over the top of his head, absently raking his hair into something that vaguely resembled order. "I'm sorry."

"Tell the kid, not me. I slept like a rock until an hour ago."

Rhone barely slept a wink. Not a smart move, he thought, considering it might have been his only chance.

"You obviously had better things to do," Doug decided.

"Yeah." Going for a refill, Rhone drained the pot and headed for the small dinette, the cold metal of his gun resting between the waistband of his jeans and bare skin.

Doug dumped the used filter. Replacing it, he started spooning grounds for another pot.

Rhone stared out the window, comprehending why Shannen had come here for healing. The peace and tranquillity the Rocky Mountains offered would be hard to beat. He glanced over his shoulder. "Any news?"

Mouth set in a grim line, Doug shook his head. "You know that would have been the first word out of my mouth."

"I can't stand this much longer. Shannen sure as hell can't."

"Patience has never been your forte. As I recall, Norton has been known to demonstrate even less. He'll be in contact. My guess, sometime today."

Rhone rubbed his jaw, surprised by the scrape of stubble. How long had it been since he'd shaved? A day?

Two? "Heaven help him when I get my hands on him. He's going to suffer."

Doug opened cabinet doors until he found what he was looking for. Pans rattled as he withdrew one and set it on the stove. "Want to talk about it?"

Rhone had known his friend too long to pretend ignorance. He knew Doug was referring to the previous night with Shannen. Following Doug's lead, Rhone took bacon and a carton of eggs from the refrigerator. "Shannen asked about Colombia."

"What did you tell her?"

"Just about everything." Cracking eggs into a bowl, Rhone heard Doug opening and closing drawers. "Silverware's in the one to the right of the stove."

Taking a fork, Doug turned the bacon, spiced hickory scenting the air. "That's a change."

"Figured she had a right to know."

"About time." Doug shoved the plate of bacon at Rhone. "Eat. Shannen and Nicholas need you to be a hundred percent."

His friend was right.

Voices belonging to Shannen and Brian sounded from the living room. Rhone handed Doug the bowl of beaten eggs. "I'm taking a shower."

"And miss this gourmet delight?"

"Save me some."

On impulse, Rhone sidestepped to block his wife's path. As Brian started around them, Rhone spoke to the younger man without taking his gaze off Shannen. "Sorry about last night. I'm not in the habit of neglecting my share of duty."

Brian glanced from Rhone to Shannen, stifled a smile and kept walking toward the kitchen. "No problem. I couldn't sleep anyway."

"A lot of that going around."

Green eyes swept over him, lingering on his bare chest before settling on his face.

A flash of their intimacy danced before his eyes. But that was yesterday. And now that dawn had streaked the sky, neither could deny the reality they'd forced away the night before.

"Come and get it while it's hot," Doug called.

"I'll be there in a few," Rhone told Shannen. "I was heading for the shower when you detained me."

She cocked a brow in acknowledgment of his teasing accusation. "News?"

He shook his head.

The silence said a million things.

"Shannen? You need to eat."

"Yeah," she agreed.

Not for a second did he believe she would.

Ten minutes later, Rhone wiped condensation from the mirror, wrapped a towel around his waist and reached for shaving cream and a straight edge.

Last night had been incredible. Impossible. Too many words and actions lay between them for a true truce, but last night he'd seen a part of her reasoning, hoped she'd understood his.

Unfortunately, that didn't change a darn thing.

And he had a son to think of.

With a practiced hand, he guided the razor-sharp slice of metal over cheekbones and neck. Laser-accurate thoughts returned to each detail that had been supplied by the various agencies. And what had yet to come. He'd pulled every string possible to get a copy of pertinent information from Jack Norton's file. Not that Rhone expected to discover anything new when it came, but he wasn't willing to leave a single stone unturned.

Unfortunately, nothing of value from any of his other sources had emerged. Rhone had to give his opponent credit. Jimmy Norton had done a great job of setting up a few wild-goose chases.

And the oddest thing was, he didn't seem to be working alone. Definitely not his usual style. Maybe the snake actually had a touch of human feeling for the woman who'd participated in the ruse with him. If so, Rhone had no compunction about using her to meet his own ends.

Carefully, Rhone swiped the razor blade a final time.

In the kitchen, Shannen looked up when Rhone entered. Dampness curled the ends of hair that skimmed the neckline of his shirt. Gone was the dark shadow of whiskers that had felt prickly last night. Faded jeans hugged long legs that had wrapped around hers not so many hours ago. A black T-shirt covered broad shoulders and chest from view but not from memory. For reasons known only to him, he'd opted to wear his shoulder holster instead of securing the gun in his waistband like he so often did.

Shannen got up to get his plate. Warm from the microwave, she set it on the table. "Coffee?" she asked.

"Please."

Absent was the teasing warmth she'd seen earlier. Not unlike the rest of them, Rhone's face reflected the tension they all felt. His expression was distant, preoccupied. Once again, he was the aloof professional. She, the outsider.

While Rhone and Doug included her in many of their planning sessions, she knew they shared only enough to make her feel involved. She'd seen too many glances pass between them when she'd asked questions, had listened to their vague answers that were supposed to appease her.

When Brian volunteered to clean up, Shannen insisted on helping. She didn't want to sit across from Rhone and be ignored. If she didn't stay busy, she would go crazy.

Minutes seemed like hours as the waiting game Norton insisted they play dragged on.

Going through the motions, Shannen loaded the dishwasher, her mind a million miles away. Rhone had a job to do, she reminded herself. She would have to be a fool, a selfish fool at that, not to realize that one mistake could cost him, Doug or Brian, their life. Looking beyond her own wants and needs, she put herself in their shoes and knew instantly that total absorption, total concentration was vital. *She* certainly didn't have the guts to do what they did.

Which only compounded her fears. She couldn't help it. Last night had solidified it all over again. She loved Rhone. She always had, though she'd tried to deny it to protect herself. The thought of losing her husband hurt now as much as it ever had. It hurt whether he was with her or they were separated.

She couldn't run, couldn't hide from fear. Had he been killed in the past two years, the pain would not have been less. If anything, it would have been greater. Especially when she considered the time they'd wasted in the interim that could have been spent together.

"Shannen!"

She heard the impatience in Rhone's tone, realizing he'd been trying to get her attention. "I'm sorry. What?"

"I want to explain this to you. Can you come over here?"

Drying her hands, Shannen did as he asked, glancing at the electronic paraphernalia spread over the table.

"This device will be attached to the phone," he instructed, pointing to various wires and a box. "Do not, I repeat, do not answer the phone until we tell you. We need a person over there—" he pointed "—to start the trace. Calls can't be monitored unless we're in place. Questions?"

"What if it's a personal call?"

His eyes narrowed.

Before Rhone could answer, Doug inserted smoothly, "We're not interested in eavesdropping on Shannen's private life, are we, fellas?"

Rhone's glance cut to Doug, clearly stating otherwise.

A chair scraped across the floor. "Might as well get this thing installed."

"Why didn't you install it yesterday?" Shannen asked.

"I did," Doug said. "Last night, when someone called, we discovered a glitch in the system. It'll work now."

Shannen's heart skipped a beat. "I didn't hear the phone ring. I turned the bell off on my extension when Nicholas used to sleep in my room and never switched it back on. Was it—" Norton, she thought, unable to complete the question aloud. Apprehension threatened her air supply.

"The caller was Jonathen Peterson," Doug stated flatly. "Said he'd call back today."

Shannen grimaced. Rhone didn't look up, but she saw the nearly imperceptible tightening of his shoulders.

Nodding, alternately relieved and disappointed, she crossed to the kitchen window. Saw the abandoned pile of yellow trucks just beyond the deck.

Grief washed over her anew.

Compelled by reasons she didn't explain, she grabbed a jacket from the hook by the back door.

Outside, she picked up one of the trucks and absently turned a wheel.

She heard Brian's approach and looked up.

"Nicky's?"

"His favorite. They all look pretty much the same to me." Her smile was false. To mask the building crest of tears, she focused outward, when all she really wanted to do was crawl inside herself where she could never be hurt again. "Do I sense a tad of animosity between you and my husband, or is it my imagination?"

"Maybe a bit of both. Rhone was one of my instructors at the academy. I was younger, stupid and a cocky son of a gun. He pushed and prodded me to the outer limits of my endurance. I wanted to quit but he wouldn't let me. He said he did it because he saw better-than-average potential. I figure I owe Rhone a lot. I hate to think where I might have ended up if he'd let me quit."

"He does tend to have that ability to push one to his limit."

"Yes, ma'am, I reckon you'd know all about that." Brian grinned. "I better finish my perimeter search, then I think I'll turn in for some shut-eye."

Alone and at a loss, Shannen walked, no particular destination in mind. At one point, she noticed Rhone near the motor homes, talking to the group of men who resided in them. She continued on, keeping the house in sight.

"Shannen, you okay?"

Without turning, she recognized the hint of a drawl that defined Doug's voice. She glanced around. He was alone.

"Yes. No," she answered, then shrugged, knowing he understood.

He stepped closer. Wrapping one arm around her shoulders, he squeezed, the pressure telling her he was as affected by all that had happened as any special friend or close relative could be.

Shannen knew Doug was in possession of both sides of her and Rhone's story. She'd told Doug everything the day she left New York—left Rhone. Common sense told her Rhone would have done the same, sooner or later.

"You never took sides," Shannen said. "Or criticized me."

"Quickest way I know to lose people you care about is to betray them. Not my style."

She raised her glance to Doug's. "I'm glad, because Rhone and I desperately need you now."

"There's no place I'd rather be. Keep the faith, Shannen. Believe me when I say it's the only thing you can count on to keep you strong, to get you through."

How like Doug not to make promises, but, too, how like him to share the source of his own strength.

"You would know," she said. She offered a heartfelt smile. She gave him a brief hug, then turned, heading back into the house.

Morning eased into afternoon much too slowly to suit her. She'd tried to absorb herself in a book, a mystery she'd started several days ago. Initially, it had captured her interest. Now the plot seemed ridiculously tame compared to the reality she was living. Besides, the sound of footsteps coming and going made it impossible to concentrate.

Shannen envied the men who seemed to have something to occupy them while all she had were her tormented thoughts. She tried, repeatedly, to take Doug's advice. Continually she failed.

Finding her own company less than desirable, she wandered aimlessly through the house, urging the minutes to pass more quickly.

At the entrance to the living room, she poked her head in. A quick glance confirmed it was empty. Where was everyone?

Restless, she entered the room. She straightened a stack of magazines and fiddled with a dried-flower arrangement. She paused, her gaze resting on the coffee table. Had it only been the day before yesterday Nicky had used the glass-top table for balance while he mastered coordinating his first steps? It seemed like a lifetime ago.

A lump, large and painful, formed in Shannen's throat. Looking upward, her eyes blurred. Dear God, when will this nightmare end? "I don't think I can take—"

A loud ringing interrupted the spoken thought.

The telephone! Instantly, her mind keyed in on the one person she feared hearing from. At the same time, she prayed the caller was Norton. Frantic, Shannen glanced around. She nudged the box that sat adjacent to the phone, looking for a button—something to activate the monitor. Hearing the third ring, she panicked, not knowing what to do. Her hand shook as it touched the receiver, fingers reaching around to grip the hard plastic. As she lifted it, she heard the pounding of footsteps crossing the porch, heard a shouted command to wait, but it was too late.

"Hello?"

"You want to see your kid alive again, make sure you and me are the only ones listenin' to this conversation."

Praying for the strength to pull it off, to be convincing, Shannen waved at the men who stormed into the room. "Jon," she said, feigning a warm friendly tone. "Doug mentioned you called. I'm sorry I couldn't talk just then. I wasn't feeling well."

On the other end of the line, Shannen heard the taunting laughter and felt a cold shiver race along her spine.

Doug left to go back outside, but she noticed Rhone didn't share the same respect for her privacy. Tension emanated from him as he stood near the window, his back straight, stance rigid.

"That's it. Talk to me like I'm your boyfriend. Is Rhone there? Is he listenin'?"

Acid stung Shannen's throat. She swallowed hard. "Yes, I'm feeling better, thank you."

Again, taunting laughter. "Say somethin' sweet to me, *Mrs.* Mitchell."

She turned her back to Rhone. "I'm sorry, I couldn't quite hear you."

"You got a hearin' problem, do ya?" He gave a cruel laugh. "Maybe this will help improve your listenin' abilities."

Shannen heard a rustling as Norton adjusted his receiver.

"Maa-Maa?" Nicholas whimpered into her ear. "Maa-Maa..."

She gasped. Her heart and her mind screamed to reassure her baby she was there. She said nothing. She couldn't with Rhone only a few feet away. She squeezed her eyes closed against tears she couldn't allow to fall. Her fingers shook uncontrollably as she covered her mouth to contain the agonizing terror that threatened to spill forth.

"Follow my instructions to the letter. Got it?"

"Yes."

"First. Talk to me." He laughed. "And ya'd better make it sound convincin'."

She couldn't believe what she was hearing. That she had no choice but to listen and follow his instructions sickened her. Why wouldn't Rhone leave the room? Desperately, she didn't want him to overhear, to misinterpret what she knew would destroy the fragile bond between them.

"I'm gonna count to three, *Mrs. Mitchell.* Speak up or ya lose."

The idea of saying the words to Norton was more than she could manage. Shannen turned around, her glance resting on her husband. When she spoke, with all her heart, she directed the words to Rhone, even though she knew he wouldn't understand. "Yes, you know I love you. Always have." Rhone turned on his heel to face her, his incredulous expression giving way to pure disgust. Shannen's heart twisted as she watched his angry stride carry him toward the door.

"I've heard better. Whaddas Mitchell think?"

She heard the door slam behind Rhone. Something inside her snapped. "Gee, I don't know. Why don't you ask him?" Immediately she bit her tongue.

"Maybe I will." Norton cackled. "Instruction number two. Now listen real careful. Meet me by the river to the south of the meadow on your property at sundown. Alone. If you're not alone, if you set me up or you're not there, I promise, you'll never see your kid again."

To Shannen's relief, she heard a dial tone. Weak and shaky, she replaced the receiver. How could she get away without Brian or Doug accompanying her? Rhone wouldn't be wanting anything to do with her, and the more distance he could put between them, the better. No, he would pass the duty of watching over her to someone else.

Anger, all consuming, shook her to the core. The lives of her family and friends, her happiness, her future—all stood to be destroyed at the whim of one very psychotic individual. She'd settle for just half a chance to even the score, to take him down herself.

Fury made her nerves tingle as she ran upstairs. Unconcerned that she'd get caught, she went straight to Rhone's room. On the closet shelf, she removed the box that contained the .22 and a box of bullets. Target practice seemed a good way to pass some time until her meeting with Norton. It also seemed a good way to vent some of her anger. She had no intention of taking the gun with her, but only because she had no clue as to what Norton's plans were. If, on the off chance, Nicky were with Norton, she couldn't risk her son getting hurt. Certainly not by her hand.

Arms full, Shannen turned toward the doorway. Rhone blocked her exit.

"What do you think you're doing?" he asked.

"Target practicing."

"Really? Or were you planning to shoot me while I sleep so you can pick up where you and your lover left off before I arrived? Just friends, huh?" His tone venom-

ous, Rhone shook his head when she didn't answer.
"You're a fine piece of work, you know that?"

"It's not like what you think." She couldn't help defending herself.

Rhone walked forward, not stopping until he was inches away, his eyes daring her to retreat. "Tell me, Shannen. What is it like?"

Logic told her he was hurting, but all she heard was an echo of the tone Norton had used when he'd demanded she say something suggestive. Gritting her teeth, she juggled her load and raised her hand.

The sound of Rhone's palm slapping against her wrist reverberated through the room. His fingers gripped, applying pressure that made her wince.

"Who the hell was I thinking of when I gave credit to you for saving my life in Colombia? You don't even come close to measuring up to the heroine of my dreams. Whatever there was between us, *babe,* you've long since destroyed. You can have your divorce. I don't want you. However, I do want Nicholas. I will fight you for custody, and I will win."

"No! Rhone, listen—"

"*You* listen. The next time you make a mistake like the one you made downstairs, I swear I'll put you behind lock and key."

Shannen frowned. "What are you talking about?"

"You could have compromised our son's life had that been Norton on the phone. We can't afford a single missed opportunity to trace his whereabouts. That monitor could be Nicholas's only chance at freedom."

Toe-to-toe, Shannen glared up at him. If he only knew the truth, she thought. "Then *why* didn't you leave someone stationed near it? My God, Rhone, I had no idea where anyone was. I'm not a mind reader."

Nevertheless, she saw the accusal in his eyes and pain at what he believed was betrayal. She ached to explain, but couldn't. To do so *would* compromise their son's safety.

Rhone cursed on a sigh. "Well, as it turns out, it doesn't matter, does it? Since the call was from your *friend*." He flung her wrist aside like a piece of dirty laundry. "Now, get out. I need to sleep."

Downstairs, Shannen barely glimpsed the puzzled expressions on Doug and Brian's faces. When Doug saw what she held, he moved toward her.

"I want to be alone," she told him, her voice tight and thick. "Don't worry." She gave a bitter laugh. "I promise I won't shoot anything I'm not supposed to."

After several seconds of thoughtful deliberation, Doug let her go. Grabbing the bag of empty cans by the back door, she headed behind the house to the tree stump that Rhone had used before.

Carefully she set her target, then paced her distance. As though she'd been doing it all her life, she loaded the gun with calm efficiency. Assuming the stance she'd been taught, she raised the weapon. Sighting the first can, she released the safety and paused. Her lips twitched as she remembered the room Rhone was in faced the back of the house.

Shannen pulled the trigger. Her body flinched, the sharp crack sounding more like an explosion. Her ears rang in protest, but she didn't care as she watched her target fly into the trees.

"Wear your earplugs," Rhone hollered down.

She glowered over her shoulder. "I'll just bet you take the time to put yours in before you shoot the bad guys."

"You're not shooting bad guys."

"That's what you think," she muttered, turning back around. Her jaw tightened, eyes narrowed as pure hatred coursed through her. Aligning her aim, Shannen envisioned the devil's own son, heard the repetition of Norton's taunting and cruel words.

She pulled back the trigger and, with amazing accuracy, struck her target again. And again.

How he'd managed to sleep through Shannen's racket was beyond him. With drowsy awareness, Rhone knew it was the silence that had eventually awakened him. That and daylight fading to dusk.

He swung booted feet over the edge of the bed and sat up. Yawning, Rhone glanced at the bedside clock.

Norton ought to be calling soon.

As if on cue, the phone rang.

Rhone ran downstairs to the living room. At Doug's gesture, Brian picked up the phone.

"Hold on," he said into the mouthpiece. Brian glanced up at Rhone. "Where's Shannen?"

"How the hell should I know?" he bellowed. "You were supposed to be keeping an eye on her."

"Dr. Peterson, I'll have to have Shannen return—"

Rhone grabbed the phone from Brian's hand. "Peterson, didn't I make it clear I want you the hell out of *my* wife's life? Let me spell it out for you. I don't like you calling last night, or earlier today. Or right now. And if you don't stop calling, I'm going to come over there and wrap the cord around your— *What* did you say?"

He listened, mumbled incoherently and dropped the receiver back into its cradle. Rhone's glance sought Doug.

In seconds, Doug was at Rhone's side. "The phone call Shannen had earlier—it wasn't Peterson, was it?"

"No." Rhone buckled his holster.

After checking the rest of the house, Brian returned to the living room. He gave a negative shake of his head.

"I heard the back door open and close—" Doug paused, checking his watch "—about forty-five minutes ago. I'm as much at fault as the kid. I thought Shannen had come back in.''

"She brought the gun in. It's lying on the kitchen table," Brian said.

Thank God she hadn't taken it with her. Rhone hated to imagine what happened to so many women happening to Shannen. Easily overpowered in an armed confrontation, their weapons were often used against them. It'd been the main reason he'd thought twice about teaching her to shoot, but had decided the advantages outweighed the negatives.

"I talked to Cox," Brian added. "Neither he nor his men saw Shannen leave. They're waiting outside for your orders."

Rhone gave a terse nod. "Stay here in case there's any more calls or Shannen comes back. If she does, we're on the air," Rhone told Brian, reaching for the hand-held radio.

Chapter 10

Fear made Shannen's blood run icy.

Not for the first time, she berated herself for being every kind of fool. Why had she done this?

Because you've heard enough about Jimmy Norton to know he'd kill your son without thinking twice if you brought Rhone.

It was a risk she couldn't afford to take. Wouldn't take. No matter what danger she exposed herself to.

Shadows lengthened as she moved deeper into the woods. The acres of trees had been the first thing that attracted her to the property. Now, for as many times in as many days, she regretted them. She could barely see in front of her and every noise made her jump.

Suddenly she wished she'd said something to Rhone. When she stole away from the house, he'd been asleep. Doug and Brian had been talking in the front room. She'd had to take her chances that none of the men staying in the trailers saw her. She'd done her best to keep the house and trees between herself and their line of vision. Though, if they had at their disposal a portion of the high-tech equipment that Rhone did, she doubted she'd escaped unnoticed. Admittedly, she hoped not. Otherwise she had no idea how long it would be until she was missed.

By then she could be dead.

She dug her hands deep into her jeans pockets. Norton had said to meet him at sundown. As she made her way to the meeting place near the creek, as Norton ordered, the way became more treacherous.

For balance, she pulled her hands from her pockets. Her heart thundered with panic and anticipation. In a few minutes, maybe she would see her baby again and could reassure herself he was all right.

As she carefully walked over the twisted, rotting timber and decaying vegetation, she strained to hear. Nothing. Nothing except the usual chirps of birds and chatter of squirrels and chipmunks. From overhead, she heard the drone of an airplane.

Odd that for some, today was an ordinary day. People got out of bed, went to work and were now having dinner with their families. Shannen, on the other hand, prayed both she and her son lived another day.

An involuntary shiver shimmied the length of her spine. Even if she survived Jimmy Norton, she still had to face Rhone.

She arrived near the clearing Norton dictated. It made her ill to think the man had been on her property long enough to know it so well. Just how long had he been lurking? Watching? Obviously, when he'd abducted Nicky, he hadn't gone far. The man probably got his kicks from hiding right under everyone's noses.

She stopped, ducking behind a tree. Her watch beeped, signaling the top of the hour. She jumped, then instantly silenced the noise that seemed to ricochet everywhere. Slowly, scared of what she might see, what she might not see, she peered around into the clearing.

Empty, except for a poised and alert deer nearby.

Light faded as the sun disappeared behind the peaks.

Shannen swore.

Norton hadn't showed.

Her shoulders sagged and she fought back equal measures of anger and frustration. How stupid that she'd fallen for the trick.

A snap split the air.

The deer vanished.

Then she smelled it... the cloying, gagging scent of an unwashed person.

"Don't move."

She froze. The thunder of her pulse nearly overwhelmed her. Her knees trembled. But Shannen forced herself to hold her shoulders rigid, not betraying the terror that had captured every nerve in her body.

How he'd snuck up behind her, Shannen didn't know. She must have been totally consumed with her own thoughts. "Where's my son?" She forced the words around the tightness in her throat and past the teeth she ground together.

"Safe."

He laughed, a thoroughly diabolical sound that made goose bumps rise on her flesh.

Just as suddenly, he stopped. "For now, anyway."

That was every bit as unnerving as the gloating chuckle.

"You didn't bring Mitchell, or any of his cronies, with you, did you?"

She wanted to reply with a flip answer, but couldn't get it out.

"Did you?" he demanded again.

He leaned closer. The summer breeze wrapped his stench around her so she couldn't breathe anything but his putrid odor.

Norton wrapped a hand in her hair then yanked. Hard. She winced but refused to give him the satisfaction of crying out.

He dragged her back half a step, slamming her into his body. Her cheek and neck were exposed to his yellowed, rotting teeth. The other day, she hadn't noticed just how much bitterness made him ugly, but up close, there was no disguising it. Unable to help herself, she closed her eyes.

"Look at me. I wanna see your fear."

"Never."

He laughed again.

"Where's my son?" she demanded, each word an aching effort to get out.

"It'd be easy for me to kill you, you know?" he said in an almost conversational tone. "And I wouldn't have to use my weapon to do it." With that, he shoved the unyielding barrel of the gun against her temple.

Her knees sagged.

"That's it, Shannen, baby. Let me smell your fear."

She groaned, as much from pain as revulsion.

He chuckled.

She contemplated bringing her foot down on his instep. But such a maneuver might cause him to tighten on the trigger. Rhone had taught her enough to know the gun was cocked, but not locked. A squirm might see her dead. And as long as she lived, she had a chance to save Nicky.

"Mitchell has good taste in his women."

Sickness engulfed her entire body, making her feel dirty, even the places he hadn't touched. She wanted a shower. But most of all, she wanted to be free of him.

"As I was saying," he continued easily, "with your neck stretched back like that, all neat and purty, I don't need no gun to kill you." Still gripping a handful of hair, he moved his hand so that his palm covered the column of her throat, her hair fanning about his hand.

She tried to swallow.

Couldn't.

Panicking, she started to squirm, the survival instinct consuming her common sense. She screamed, then realized no sound emerged.

She was going to die.

And Rhone didn't even know where she was. She would die with him believing lies about her.

"Fact is, rather kill you this way, then none of your blood gets on Jimmy's clothes." He laughed again.

His voice and chilling laugh reached her from a great distance.

"Ain't gonna, though."

She sucked great gulps of air deep into her lungs, the bitter taste of unconsciousness stinging her. The cooling air burned into her lungs, but it was the best feeling she'd ever had.

"Yep, much as I wanna kill you right here and now, I ain't gonna. Gonna make that man of yours suffer first. In ways he ain't never dreamed."

"Rhone isn't going to suffer if I die," she managed, throat raw and scratchy. Her words sounded as though they'd been grated over sandpaper. She wondered if the lie made them any rougher.

"Huh?"

For the first time, she saw confusion painted on his twisted features. "Rhone isn't going to suffer," she repeated slowly, trying to make each word clear. "He doesn't love me."

"He's here, ain't he?"

"So? He's here because he wants you, not because he cares about me. Or my son."

"Rhone's son," Jimmy corrected, frowning as if Shannen were stupid.

"My son," she corrected. "Not Rhone's."

"But they look the same. Any fool can see that. And Jimmy ain't no fool."

She hated this position. Her back ached and the tension of his hand in her hair made her eyes tear. Thank God for that, though. At least the sheen of moisture blurred her vision, making it more difficult to focus on his face. Her thigh muscles protested the awkward position, as did her feet as she battled for balance on her tiptoes. "No, you're not a fool," she agreed, wishing for water— anything to ease the pain in her throat. "But Rhone doesn't have any children. Think," she urged. "If you know Rhone that well, then you know he couldn't possibly be my son's father." Consciously, she avoided using Nicky's name, hoping beyond hope that the omission would somehow make Nicky safer, not reveal her utter weakness. "Rhone was out of the country. That's why I left him."

Jimmy cursed savagely.

"I don't love Rhone. I had a baby to get even with him. Harming me or the child won't get Rhone. I swear to you that—"

"Shuddup!" He kicked her in the back of the knees so that she toppled. "Let me think!"

She would have fallen completely, if not for his hold on her hair. Shannen bit her tongue to avoid crying out.

She hoped Rhone would forgive the lies, hoped she could live with herself for telling them. "Why do you think he let me come alone?" Tears that had been stinging the inside of her eyelids began to slip toward her temples. Yet she refused any other sign of the excruciating pain. "He doesn't care about me, Jimmy. How could he?"

Viciously, Jimmy yanked again. For a few seconds she wildly wondered if she'd pushed him too far. Maybe she should have kept her mouth shut.

"We'll see." The nauseating odor of his breath washed over her face. "Yeah. That's it." He nodded, then began a slow, evil smile. "Jimmy'll see." As quickly as the smile came, it vanished. His face settled into the harsh lines of a sneer. "And if you're lyin' to me . . ."

She squeezed her eyes closed.

Jimmy shoved her so she tumbled headlong into the darkened floor of the forest. She heard scampering and scurrying. Shannen struggled to stand, then gasped when he toppled her again. The wind knocked from her lungs, she lay still for several seconds.

Before she could recover, Jimmy dropped down next to her, jamming a knee in the small of her back. She fought desperately, but to no avail, except to cause him to laugh hideously.

The bitter taste of dirt stung her mouth, and pine needles poked through her clothes.

With efficient movements that proved how callous and cold he was, he pulled her hands behind her back to bind them. He tugged so hard, she thought her shoulders would dislocate.

With horrific memory, the sight of Maria's blood-stained wrists burned into Shannen's memory. Raw, consuming panic began to build. "Don't," she said, then wished she could snatch back the show of weakness.

He pulled harder.

This time she forced back the terrorized scream.

"Sit up."

"I can't."

Jimmy grabbed the tender area where her wrists were shackled, then pulled up, forcing her to her knees.

With a few quick motions, he looped a rope between her hands, then moved away so he could secure her to a tall aspen.

Crouching near her, he turned on a flashlight, propping it against a rotting branch.

"What are you doing?"

"I git so sick of women who won't shut up."

"Well, I get sick of men who feel they can bully their way into getting people to do what they want."

From a distance, she heard the crackling of branches.

Jimmy's eyes opened wide. The solid glow of the flashlight reflected off his eyes.

Insanity.

Nothing more.

His dried lips cracked into a sinister yet gleeful smile. "Thought you said he didn't care none."

"It's probably just a deer." Her heart pounded. Was it Rhone? Could help possibly be so close? Oh, please, let it be, she silently pleaded.

"That ain't no deer."

Seizing what might be her only chance, she screamed. "Rhone!"

Instantly, Jimmy's huge palm slapped over her mouth. He tutted, the noise almost a chant. "That wasn't smart. No sirree, that wasn't smart a'tall. Thought Mitchell liked his women to have brains." He shrugged. "Guess not. Maybe you're right about him not giving a damn and all." He stared at her breasts. "Course, maybe, jus' maybe, he likes what's underneath all them baggy clothes."

Bile rocked inside her.

"Now, so's you don't do anythin' so stupid again . . ." He broke the word *stupid* into two long, distinct syllables. "I'm gonna have to gag you."

She dropped her head back against the tree. She refused to beg. Refused to show him any more weakness. If she protested, he would probably just shove a rotten rag even deeper in her mouth. Resolving to be brave, wondering how in creation Rhone had ever survived the hell he'd lived through, Shannen held still, desperately trying to think about anything but here and now.

She shook her head violently when he unknotted the bandanna at his dirty throat.

Again she tried to scream, but only bit a fleshy part of his hand. Not able to conjure the calm she'd hoped, she thrashed, catching him in the groin with her knee.

She saw the supreme battle on his face as he fought not to succumb to the pain.

Good.

He deserved to suffer—especially after abducting the most precious part of her.

He cursed and grunted, but he didn't move away. "I ought to kill you right now. Nobody, but nobody, hurts Jimmy and lives to tell about it."

Shannen had every intention of being the first.

He grunted a second time, then jammed the sweat-soaked bandanna inside her mouth. Her stomach rolled violently and she gagged.

Efficiently, he unhooked his belt and yanked the leather free of the jeans loops with a sharp snap. He raised it before her. Shannen cringed.

With methodical, unhurried motions, he tied her legs together. "So you won't be kickin' nobody for a while."

He stood, surveyed her and folded his arms over his chest. "One more thing. A Jimmy Norton special touch, if I may say so." He bent to unzip a small knapsack and pulled a tape recorder from the canvas.

The eerie sound of Jimmy's mechanical laughter spilled from the small recorder.

He set the machine down, then grabbed his flashlight. "Yep, Jimmy the Brain has left his signature." He shone the light in her face until she closed her eyes to escape the glare. "Mark my words, Shannen love." With bruising pressure, he grabbed her chin between his fingers. Again his breath washed across her face. "I ain't done with you."

After turning up the volume, he disappeared into the forest, whistling as he went.

For what seemed an eternity, the sick sound of Jimmy's incessant laughter crashed through the night. She wanted to escape, needed to escape. Needed Rhone.

Oh, Lord, she needed Rhone.

"...I love you, always have..."

The tape repeated Shannen's words over the sound of Jimmy's voice.

He had recorded their telephone conversation! He'd changed it though, inserting crude obscenities.

Never before had she wished for unconsciousness to claim her. She did now.

Weapons drawn, Rhone and Doug separated, circling the perimeters of the house, looking for any clue that would indicate which way Shannen had gone.

Cox and five other agents whom Rhone had handpicked himself, based upon their reputation and unique expertise in the field, fanned out behind him and Doug.

Unspeakable fear clutched at Rhone's heart.

Not Shannen.

Dear God, not Shannen, too.

He forced himself to endure the struggle to maintain a professional detachment. A chirping whistle that an untrained ear would interpret as a cricket drew Rhone's attention. He acknowledged it, then silently pointed to a dense area of trees, watching as Doug headed for them.

With more gut feeling than familiarity, Rhone followed the path leading toward the river. Shadows blended as dusk rapidly gave way to nightfall.

The air hung still. The deafening quiet was oppressively unsettling. As though sensing the danger to come, nature held her breath in wary anticipation.

Moving cautiously, aware of his surroundings, he recalled the words Shannen had said into the phone...words he'd believed she said to her lover.

Words he now knew had been forced by Norton.

Rhone remembered the haunted look in her eyes as she'd gazed at him, directing the words to him, rather than to the slime on the other end of the phone. Could she have meant what she said?

Rhone's insides twisted, the way they had a thousand times or more in Colombia as he'd dreamed of hearing her say the same words to him once again. Had the look in her eyes when she'd turned around been a silent plea for understanding and forgiveness for what she'd been commanded to do?

He let out a long sigh. Why was it that misunderstanding and a lack of trust always harmed their relationship?

Doug circled back.

Rhone shook his head.

Then a sound, too indistinct to identify, carried to Rhone. Unaccountably, his gut clenched. That damn beast was out there. *With Rhone's wife.*

Stock-still, he cocked his head. He pointed into the forest to their right. Doug inclined his head in mute agreement. Leaving the path, they moved from one tree to another, in a practiced pattern, alternating trees, each guarding the other's back.

Rhone stopped again to listen.

A keening wail of triumphant laughter penetrated the stillness.

The softer sounds of a woman's strained voice followed.

Hair on the back of his neck rose. If . . . when . . . he got his hands on Norton's neck . . .

The mocking laughter swelled, surrounding them. It came from everywhere and nowhere at once. The hunt was on. And Rhone intended to be victor.

They rushed faster, following the same fashion as before. At a signal from Doug, Rhone dropped to a crouch behind an evergreen, acknowledging their prey was nearby.

The sickening laughter tripped through the air, once again a painful reminder that Norton had Shannen. Rhone started a prayer, then stopped. He refused to believe the universe could be so callous as to take the two most important people from his life. Shannen was okay. She had to be.

Quietly he started counting.

On three, both men spun from behind cover, guns aimed and cocked, ready to fire.

In a single glance, eyes attuned to the darkness, Rhone assessed the situation. Then cussed.

Doug did the same.

"Go to Shannen," Doug urged. "I'll get Norton."

As difficult as the order was to follow, Rhone agreed. Doug was an excellent tracker and Shannen needed Rhone, as much as he needed to hold her, convince himself she was all right.

Her eyes—reflected by the flashlight Norton had trained on her—were wild with fright. Raw, unadulterated rage raced through Rhone, making him want to chase Norton down and bare-handedly kill him.

Trembling with suppressed anger, Rhone holstered his Beretta and advanced toward her. That he was the cause of the pain and suffering she endured nearly undid Rhone.

Recrimination washing over him, Rhone dropped to his knees next to Shannen.

Chapter 11

Her gaze, wide-eyed and terrified, met his.

Rhone forced away his own anguish and acted on automatic pilot, like he had so many times before.

Hands shaking, he silenced the recorder then reached for the gag, the motion taking him close to her. With his heart hurting, he noticed the track of a single tear down her face, disappearing into the filthy fabric binding her.

Bastard.

Clenching his teeth, Rhone gently pulled the rag from her, wanting nothing more than to torch it.

"Are you okay?" he asked gently, not surprised that his voice had thickened with his own emotion.

She shook, and he knew it had little to do with the dipping temperature customary to nightfall in the mountains.

"He touched me."

Shannen sounded detached. Far away. As if she was starting to retreat someplace where no one could reach her.

Rhone swore, softly and succinctly as he unsheathed his knife and desperately sliced at the leather belt. He knew what she was going through, recognized the mind's attempt to shut out unspeakable things.

"He's got my son, Rhone."

He froze. Looked at her. And realized she was looking through him, not at him.

His breaths squeezed through pain-filled lungs. Jimmy had terrorized her as effectively as Jack had terrorized Rhone.

But damn if he would lose anything more to the debilitating grip of a twisted Norton mind.

Galvanized by desperation to hold her, Rhone sawed through the remaining bindings, then leaned toward her, cradling her as he might a child, wanting to absorb the hurt. Erase from her memory what had happened.

She didn't resist. Didn't respond. She remained stock-still, shell-shocked.

Rhone stroked her hair. "You're safe," he said in soft tones, hoping to convince himself as much as her. "You're safe. I'll never let him get to you again."

"Hold me, Rhone."

"I am, sweetheart," he whispered.

"Tighter."

He complied, closing off all regard for the cold creeping in around him. Shut off everything but the fact his wife needed him.

"Don't let me go."

"Never," he vowed. Rhone realized after Nicky was safe, Shannen might not want anything to do with Rhone again. But for now she needed him, as much as he needed her. "I thought I'd lost you, Shannen."

"I shouldn't have...should have told..." A sob tore from her.

"Shh," he soothed. "You did what you thought was right."

"But he could have . . ."

"But he didn't," Rhone supplied quietly. He expected to feel the dampness of her tears through the fabric of his clothes. When he didn't, he winced.

Except for the evidence of a single tear, she hadn't cried. He wished she would, knew the cleansing would help. Caressing her back, he softly said, "I need to get you home."

"Not without my baby."

The words were flat. Hollow.

If someone had taken a knife and systematically cut his heart into tiny ribbons, it couldn't have hurt this bad. "We'll get Nicky."

"What if Norton tied up my baby, too?"

Rhone had been imprisoned in a hellhole the size of a coffin, been brutally beaten and learned to operate as an automaton when events dictated, but nothing in his experience left him prepared to deal with this kind of emotional devastation.

"What if Nicky is crying for me right now?"

Powerless to answer, Rhone pressed a hand against her nape, resting her head on his shoulder. She still shivered, and he heard her teeth begin to chatter.

Common sense insisted he get her warm and safe, but that meant releasing her, even if it was only for a few seconds. Right now, he wasn't strong enough to do that. So he held her, offered soothing words and vows.

Two cracks split the night. High-powered rifles.

Shannen shuddered.

Rhone said nothing, praying that Norton now lay dead at Doug's feet. Rhone hoped the death didn't come quickly. Or mercifully.

A few minutes later a snapped twig arrested his attention.

He simultaneously released his hold on Shannen, moved to shield her and reached for his 9 mm. With his left hand he grabbed the flashlight and aimed the beam into the forested darkness.

"At ease."

Rhone let out his breath between closed teeth and slid his gun back into its leather holster. Doug shook his head and Rhone's facial features froze in a frown. Doug's eyes contained a murderous gleam.

"He had a white pickup this time. Got the license number."

"Stolen?"

"Yeah. Got an APB out on it. Put a slug in the back, another in a tire."

Rhone nodded tightly.

"Shannen?" Doug's voice was hardly above a whisper.

"Needs to get home."

"Want help?"

"No. Thanks."

"I'll cover your back nevertheless."

Turning to his wife, Rhone appealed to her nurturing instinct, hoping she'd respond for the sake of others, if not herself. "When you feel up to it, we need any information you can give us," Rhone said. He grimaced at that thought. Part of him wasn't sure he wanted to hear, now or later, exactly what had transpired.

She shook her head.

Rhone gently placed his index finger beneath her chin, held her so he could look into her eyes. They were lifeless. Empty. "Nicky needs you to do everything possible to help save him. You know that, right?"

She nodded weakly.

"Norton's gone from the forest. We'll need you at the house in case he tries to make contact again. Obviously he'd rather talk to you than me." Letting go of her chin, Rhone took her shoulders in his grip. "Shannen, we need your help."

"I..."

He waited.

"Feel ill."

Which meant, at least physically, she was starting to function beyond the shocked numbness. Instantly he moved behind her, holding her hair out of the way. Rhone noted that Doug blended with the trees, giving them total privacy.

A minute or so later, Rhone grabbed a handkerchief from his back pocket and handed it to her.

She gave a groan of disgust. "I can still feel him touching me, breathing on me."

Wondering, hoping that the dam of emotions had also been freed, Rhone prayed for the strength and wisdom to help her cope. "I know," he reassured her.

"He taunted and threatened. Then laughed. He wouldn't tell me anything about Nicholas except that he's safe. For now, he said." She spoke in a monotone, barely above a whisper.

Her gaze darted around. "You're certain he's gone?"

"You're safe now, Shannen."

Rhone felt the shudder that quaked through her body. "Did he say anything to you that might help us find him faster?" He hated asking, hated making her dwell on the incident, but had to. "Give you any clue as to where he's holding Nicky?"

"No. Nothing." He heard her dejection.

His eyes closed on the impotent anger that welled within him, seeking an outlet. He knew Norton enjoyed flaunting the power he wielded in Rhone's face, enjoyed making him sweat. And at the moment there wasn't a damn thing he could do about it.

"Let's go home." Rhone pressed Shannen's head against his chest, dropping a kiss onto the honeyed mass of curls.

Quietly, unobtrusively, Doug returned, signaling he and the others would be right behind them.

Rhone stood, handed Doug the recorder, then helped Shannen to her feet, seeing how badly her knees shook. He placed an arm around her back, supporting nearly her entire weight as they moved toward her house.

On their return, Brian's face showed his concern and Rhone gave a brief shake of his head. Doug motioned Brian into the kitchen and, at the bottom of the stairs, Rhone swept his wife's limp body into his arms and carried her to the bedroom, closing the door with the sole of his boot.

"I want to be clean. I've got to get rid of—"

Rhone nodded, understanding, and continued into the master bath. Bending down, he flipped the light switch with his shoulder before sliding her down his body.

She wavered. Rhone kept a steady hand around her shoulder even as he turned on the knobs, spilling steaming water from the faucets.

She gave a convulsive shiver. "I'm so cold."

He knew closing the bathroom door would have contained the steam, adding warmth. He hesitated, but only for a second, then reached out to swing it shut.

Immediately, the fleeting image that came to mind of the enclosed narrow space was enough to double his heart rate and breathing. Damn. He couldn't do it and be the calming force Shannen needed right now. He sent her an apologetic glance that failed to register.

He cursed under his breath. More than anything, he wished he could take away the internal suffering that had extinguished the light in her expression.

"Stay with me," she said.

"I wouldn't leave if you told me to."

Shannen's gaze focused on her reflection in the mirror. Her eyes widened in shock as though she saw someone she no longer recognized. A stranger. Unblinking, she began trying to finger-comb through the knots in her hair, her actions slow and jerky.

Rhone felt her slipping away again and tried to step in front of her, but suddenly she pushed him aside, grabbing for her toothbrush and mouthwash.

Feeling helpless, he adjusted the water temperature, then crossed back to her when she started scrubbing at her face with a soapy washcloth.

As he might have done in the past, he took a brush from the counter and began to ease the tangles from her hair.

"How can you stand to look at me?"

Rhone kept moving the brush in repetitive motions, but met her gaze in the mirror.

"Because I care about you. And because there's nothing Norton could do that would change the way you look in my eyes."

She turned then, burying her face in his shoulder. She began to cry in pained measures, her heated tears feeling as though they burned his skin.

"He's so disgusting," she managed in broken words.

"And he'll never touch you again." He realized he'd said the words before, but each time they meant more. While they were a promise to his wife, they were a deadly threat to the man who'd dared to touch her. Norton had stolen from Rhone for the last time.

She pushed back, meeting his gaze. "Make his touch go away." She took a deep breath. "Help me heal. Make me whole."

"Shannen, are you. . ."

She tipped back her head; he saw her swallow deeply. "If you can bear to touch me, I need you."

Rhone cussed savagely, angry that Norton made her insecure that way. He dragged her against him, lowering his mouth to hers.

She met his touch with an urgency of her own, surprising him.

Her tongue sought his, met and danced, demanding more, giving more. He felt the nip of her teeth, and the sensation served to make his own need more profound.

As much as she wanted Norton's touch erased, so did Rhone. The thought of another man hurting what was his infuriated him.

Shannen started to fumble with her buttons. Wasted years fell away, leaving them with the flame of passion that had first ignited their love affair. She wasn't moving fast enough for either of them. Rhone moved her hands aside and took over the task of disrobing her, kissing her all the while.

Shannen rose on her tiptoes, offering more of herself. Rhone stifled a groan, frantically working to remove her clothes. He had no choice but to unwillingly stop the kiss for now.

She wiggled as he tugged. Finally, when she stood before him in pastel pink panties and bra, Rhone greedily took in the sight of creamy breasts that filled cups of satin and lace. All too well, he remembered her texture, the way her nipples tightly pebbled under his ministrations. The way she so perfectly fit with him.

Rhone felt himself harden.

He helped her from the panties, then reached behind her for the clasp to her bra, unfastening it. The scrap of lace fell apart and he began to ease the straps from her shoulders. The satiny fabric hung from his finger. Then Shannen looked at him. Misery and torment lay utterly exposed. He was stopped cold.

"It hurts, way down deep inside. I'm scared for Nicholas, scared for you and frightened I may never feel clean again."

The fabric fluttered to the floor.

Rhone looked heavenward, then back at her, aware of the intimacy, the trust that accompanied her confession. Her eyes were swollen, her nose raw. Yet he'd never met anyone more brave. "I know it hurts. I know what it feels like to—no, wait. I'm not going to say that I know how you feel and trivialize it—but I know what it's like to have your basic rights taken away."

She lowered her head, as if humbled by his words.

"Look at me, Shannen." When she did, he continued. "You are one of the bravest people I've ever met. You've taken much more than one person should be expected to. You're a survivor and I'm proud of you."

"You are?"

"More than words can say. And right now I'll do everything in my power to help you heal and feel clean. In the meantime, I can't tell you not to worry about Nicholas, and I'm honored that you're concerned about me, but I am asking that you try very hard not to let it consume you. Concentrate instead on taking things one step at a time. Can you do that?"

She nodded.

Rhone scooped her into his arms and carried her to the bathtub. Kneeling beside her, he reached for the detachable shower head. After making sure the water felt warm, he wet her hair, then worked shampoo in, massaging her scalp.

"I'm not being too rough?"

"No."

After rinsing the bubbles, he grabbed a huge sponge and squeezed lavender-scented bath gel onto it. Shannen shyly smiled, and he worked up a lather. Tenderly, yet thoroughly, he started with her nape, then worked down to her shoulders, then soaped her back.

Under his thorough attention, he felt some of the tension begin to ease from her shoulders, wishing the motion did the same for him. As much as he wanted to be here, with her, another part of him recognized the burden of inactivity, knew Norton was out there with Nicky.

Thankfully, Rhone trusted Doug implicitly. While Rhone was busy, so was Doug.

Rhone moved to her front. "Tip back your head." She did and he took the time to explore the graceful column of her neck, the hollow of her shoulders.

Slowly, with deliberation, he soaped her breasts, going in lazy circles around her nipples.

Shannen let out a little cry, allowed her eyes to shut, hopefully allowed the horror of what she'd been through to vanish, if just for a few seconds. Rhone knew how fleeting internal peace was, and he wished her as much as possible.

Unmindful that he soaked his own shirt, he took the sponge below the water's surface, stroking her legs, thighs, then higher.

"Rhone, I—that is..."

"Hmm?" His groin tightened. He shifted uncomfortably, his erection chafing against the tight denim and an unyielding zipper.

"I...want you."

Rhone shuddered. He stood, adjusted the front of his jeans, then grabbed a towel from the rack. He held it up and wrapped it around her when she stood.

He carried her to the bed, then stripped from his clothes quickly, joining her beneath the covers.

"Rhone? Make love to me. *Now.*"

The mattress sank under his weight and she opened her arms, reaching up for him. He'd been prepared to offer slow and easy, an agonizing build of sensual pleasure. But Shannen needed more. Needed the bad memories to be chased away.

"I don't want to hurt you."

"The only way you'll hurt me is if you tell me no."

Rhone stroked the inside of her thigh, moving higher and higher as she started to squirm. With a gentle caress, he made certain she was ready. She arched beneath his hand, silently pleading for him.

Rhone bathed her breasts with gentle kisses, then moved over her, feeling sweat bead on his forehead with the effort of restraint. He lowered himself gently, barely brushed her with his tip. Rhone nearly yelped when her fingernails bit into the sensitive skin on his back. "Shan..."

She reached for his buttocks, urgently driving him closer.

Further restraint impossible, he buried himself deeply inside her in a single, powerful stroke.

"Stay like that for a minute?"

"Yeah," he agreed, hoping he was capable of fulfilling the promise.

Seconds seemed to swirl into minutes, the need for release building inside him. He supported the majority of his own weight as he gently fingered damp strands of hair away from her cheeks. "You're sensational."

"So are you."

She began to move then, slowly, seemingly drawing him deeper inside her, threatening his hard-won control.

"Take me, Rhone," she said, her husky pitch all but sending him over the edge. "Take me to that special place where only you can."

Shannen lifted her hips in all the invitation he needed. Anxiously, he began to move in tandem with her. Her soft moans made heat coil deep inside him, and he felt the urgent build of his own climax.

He captured her lips, her kiss, her unspoken words. He thrusted and she met the motion with a soft cry. Sweat trickled down his spine. The tips of her fingernails bit into his flesh, the warmth of her body welcomed his.

They moved together for several more seconds until Shannen twisted to the side, burying the sounds of her climax into the pillow. Immediately afterward, he followed suit, allowing his pent-up frustration and unbelievable relief to find release.

It wasn't until later, much later, that he moved to the side. Their breaths were short and irregular, but Shannen held on to him.

"Thank you," she whispered, fingering the hair at his nape.

He feathered a kiss onto her forehead, unable to forget, that if it wasn't for him, she wouldn't have had to go through any of this today.

Guilt tasted bitter.

He knew the only way to get rid of it was to nail Norton and return Nicholas to the loving arms of his mother.

"I'm sorry I fell to pieces."

"Shannen, almost anyone would have fallen to pieces. *You* didn't. You kept calm and rational."

"But…"

"You did exceptionally well. You can be my partner anytime."

She reached for him, kissed him with a power that left him feeling dizzy.

All too soon, though, she ended it. "Thanks for everything."

"My pleasure." He gave a quick grin.

Rhone's mind drifted, reality forging its way in.

"How much longer, Rhone? When can we go after Nicky? Norton can't be that far away."

He nodded, not surprised her thoughts followed the same track as his own. Before he could answer, the ding of the doorbell shattered the near silence.

Rolling away from her, Rhone grabbed for his pants, tossing a robe toward Shannen.

"I'll see you downstairs."

She agreed.

They shared a lingering look that said a million things and left as many unsaid.

Hastily, he shoved his feet into his boots, grabbed a clean flannel shirt from his duffel bag, then jogged down the stairs. Hearing a murmur of voices, he went to find Doug in the kitchen.

"Is Shannen okay?" Doug asked.

Rhone leaned against the counter. "I think she'll be all right." But he wondered if she would. Now that he'd rediscovered her, he wasn't certain he could let her go again.

"Jack Norton's file just arrived by courier. Must have pulled some fancy footwork to get hold of that. Heard it was sealed when he turned traitor."

"I don't think there's anything in it, but..."

"Brian says he's staying here with Shannen when we move out. I can't wait to see you pull that one off, buddy." Doug hid a grin behind the soda can he drank from.

Like Doug, Rhone knew Shannen wouldn't take staying behind lying down. He couldn't say he blamed her; he wouldn't, either. But for her safety she had to.

"Any idea when you're heading out?" Brian asked, entering the room.

Rhone shook his head. "When I get the first piece of reliable information." Taking a cup of coffee, he went into the living room and started culling through the file. Service record. Academy grades. Instructor remarks. Personal information.

Aware of the sounds of Shannen moving about above him and her restless need to have her child back, he gave a cursory glance to each piece of information. He winced when his own name showed up, along with the fact he might have been one of ten to put the fatal bullet in Norton's hideous hide.

Rhone flipped to the bottom of the information, reading Norton's family history: a twin brother, deceased parents, divorced, no children.

Then Rhone spotted it.

Norton had owned a cabin in Colorado. Undoubtedly, neglect to pay the taxes had long since forfeited ownership—not that Jimmy would care. Or Rhone. The cabin was a link, the first viable lead they'd had.

Shannen joined him on the couch, taking a sip from his coffee. "What?" she asked.

Doug and Brian echoed her question.

Rhone glanced up at their expectant expressions. "Jack owned a cabin near Winter Park." Taking the report with him, Rhone met Doug at the map they'd placed on the wall days before.

Colored dots marked the locations where anonymous tips had indicated Norton's location. They were scattered all over the state. While the televised report had been painful to face, it had opened a door in the investigation, though nothing had panned out.

"Here it is—roughly fifty to sixty miles northeast," Doug said, marking the location of Jack's cabin.

"Then let's go," Shannen said, her excitement communicating through the grip she held on Rhone's arm.

"He's not there," Rhone said quietly, continuing to stare at the map.

"But..."

"It's too easy. Norton would expect us to look there."

"We have to check it out," Doug inserted.

Rhone nodded, turning. "Tell Cox and the others to be ready to move in thirty minutes. I think it's a waste of time and manpower, but you're right. We've got to check it out."

Doug headed for the back door.

"I'll finish loading the Jeep Cherokee," Brian said, trailing after Doug.

The fax machine spit out a sheet of paper. Shannen collected it, adding it to the stack that had already come through. She carried the papers back to Rhone, reading as she walked.

"Anything?" Rhone asked, more than willing to delay telling her she wouldn't be going with them.

She reread the paper. "State Patrol had to break off the high-speed pursuit of a white truck when lives were endangered. Norton?" she asked.

"Possibly." Rhone saw her flinch. "Norton knows the chase is on," he continued, "and he'd be in a hurry to get back to wherever he's holed up."

Rhone saw the expression of anticipation on Shannen's face. "Shan, listen, don't get your hopes up."

"This is it, Rhone. I know it."

So did he. Couldn't have explained how he knew it, but there it was. Heartbeats increased, indicating an adrenaline rush. The same feeling—instinct—that warned of imminent danger, the internal warning he'd cultivated, respected and trusted.

Norton had made himself known because he wanted to up the stakes. Obviously, he tired of the game, just like Rhone. It was time for a victor to emerge.

Rhone would be it.

And he would have his son safe, too.

Shannen thrust the papers at him. "I'll get Nicky's stuff," she tossed over her shoulder as she dashed up the stairs.

With reluctance, and feeling like the coward he was, Rhone followed his wife. He closed the door behind him and leaned against it. "There's something you should know."

She didn't stop long enough to look at him.

"Shannen, you're not going."

She stopped then, pinning him with a stare that made him wonder if their intimacy had been real at all. "Rhone, you've shut me out of everything for long enough." She jerked open a zippered duffel bag. "Just try and stop me."

He closed the distance in a few strides and took her shoulders between his palms.

"Get your hands off me."

"Shannen, listen to me."

"Don't patronize me. I won't stand for it."

"I'm not trying to—"

"Security."

He frowned. "What?"

"I can't go because it'll threaten security."

"Well, that's—"

"I fell for that line too many times to count. Now take your hands off me."

"Security has nothing to do with this."

She arched a brow. "No?"

Rhone fought for courage to admit the truth. "I'm the one who has everything to do with this decision, and I'm not willing to risk your getting hurt." He knew the admission made his voice scratchy. Gruff. "I care about you too much."

"That's nice."

He'd done it—exposed his innermost fears, only to have her throw them back in his face.

"I'm going to find my son, and you're not going to stop me."

"The hell I won't."

"Rhone, get your hands off me."

With a ragged exhalation, he did. "It's for your own good," he said, helplessly dropping his hands to his sides.

"I'll make that decision."

"I won't fight over this."

She shoved Nicky's belongings and her own into a canvas bag and met his gaze. "Good. Then it's settled."

Knowing the battle wasn't over, he went back downstairs and started to fill a thermos with coffee.

"Didn't go too well?" Doug surmised, obviously interpreting Rhone's dark expression and the reason for it.

Rhone shook his head.

"Can you really blame her?" Doug asked. "In her position, would *you* stay behind?"

"That's different. You know as well as I do anything can happen. This is Jimmy Norton we're dealing with. Whatever he dreams up next is limited only by his demented imagination. I don't want Shannen any closer to him than she's already been. I want her here. Where she'll be safe."

Doug shrugged, inclining his head toward the door. "Convince Shannen, not me."

Rhone looked up. Shannen's unyielding expression dared him to try. His glance swept over her. She'd traded canvas shoes for leather boots that gave the illusion of lengthening her legs. In jeans and V-neck sweater, he decided she was the most incredibly sexy woman he'd ever known. It wasn't that the clothes she wore enhanced her femininity, but more the other way around.

"I appreciate your concern," she said softly. "But I'm a grown-up, capable of making my own decisions." With an expression that begged for his understanding but promised a fight, she added, "Please respect the fact I know what I'm doing."

Damn, he wished all this was behind them. Wished all the ugliness was forgotten so they could begin a new life. Together. With their son. Then the thought occurred to him that if he was lucky, very, very lucky, maybe they had made a baby brother or sister for Nicky. If they had, surely Shannen wouldn't be too quick to toss Rhone out of her life.

The realization that asking him to leave remained a possibility ate at him. Shortened a temper already stretched to the breaking point. He cast another glance to the bags at her feet. A breath hissed between his teeth. "Leave one," he commanded. "Traveling light is essential."

Shannen nodded at Brian, who hovered nearby. "Take them both."

"I said—" Rhone began.

Shannen shook her head and moved forward, purpose in every step. In front of Rhone, she stopped, speaking for his ears only. "I have no idea what to expect when we find Nicholas. Undoubtedly, he needs clean clothes, blankets, diapers. Maybe food, medicine, I don't know, but by God, I *do* know I will be prepared to meet his needs."

You selfish fool. Have you forgotten this isn't only about protecting your wife but also about rescuing your son?

"You're right," Rhone admitted. He gave a concise nod to Brian, who lifted Shannen's bags and headed for the door.

Following, Rhone waited while Shannen locked up. "All set?" he asked when she turned, pocketing the key.

"Not quite."

"Did you forget something?"

"No, but I think you have. I want to make something perfectly clear, Rhone Mitchell. There will be no more secrets like your little plan to leave me here. As a part of this operation to get *our* son back, I deserve to know what's going on. I'm not an idiot, and I'm not a child. I will not be treated like one. I've been patient up to this point, staying in the background, letting you guys plot and plan, but no more. Either you include me completely or, I swear, I'll take matters into my own hands."

"The hell you will," Rhone exploded.

"Try me."

Standing toe-to-toe, he couldn't help but admire her spunk, but this time she was way out of her league. Damn woman. Rhone rolled his eyes skyward. *Give me strength,* he prayed silently. He didn't doubt for a minute that out of blind desperation she would follow through with her threat. Terrifying thought.

Out of understanding, his anger subsided. He reached out, lightly running the back of his hand over her cheek and jaw. He felt her tension ease, too, having made her point, as she tilted her head into his palm, accepting the casual caress. Too bad he couldn't successfully lock her in her house where she couldn't bring harm to herself—or anyone else trying to protect her.

He sighed. Along with independence, his wife had obviously mastered the art of coercion. He put his hand on the small of her back as they headed toward the Jeep.

"Shan, this is no friendly camp-out where the wildlife is the only danger."

He felt her tremor and knew the cause was more than the night's chill in the air.

"I know that," she said.

"You asked me to respect that you're fully aware of what you're doing. I do. Know that I want you to stay behind for your safety and my peace of mind."

"I do respect your concerns, Rhone."

"But you're not going to be dissuaded."

"No."

With that, she climbed into the front seat. Getting in beside her, he immediately felt the closeness in the crowded vehicle and lowered the window halfway. Damned unfortunate, he thought, that there wasn't a pill he could take to make the claustrophobic nightmare disappear, or diminish the terror that confining spaces induced.

While he drove, Rhone sensed Shannen's worry, her fear. He reached over to take her hand, enfolding frigid fingers within his grasp. "We'll find Nicky. Soon. Norton's getting antsy. He's ready to lay his cards on the table."

"Instinct?"

He nodded.

"Good enough for me. I trust you."

Simple words. Yet they spoke volumes. How many people, Rhone wondered, truly understood or felt the meaning of those three words when they exchanged their vows? But then, how many could possibly know to what extremes the promises they gave to one another would be tested? And could they be held responsible, or even blamed, if those extremes were more than they could handle?

He gave Shannen's hand a squeeze. No, he decided. They couldn't.

An hour and a half later, as the map indicated, Rhone turned off the highway onto a county road. Washboard slowed his pace and that of the cargo van that followed.

"You know the sheriff and his deputies will be ticked we didn't invite them along."

Rhone heard the smile in Brian's voice.

"Handled," Doug answered from the back seat. "Jenkins has his men chasing down leads while he's monitoring all radio transmissions. It goes without saying Norton has his own shortwave setup. Rhone, just up ahead, on your left," Doug added, lowering infrared binoculars.

Rhone checked his odometer. "That's it," he said.

He switched off the headlights as he turned. Overgrowth narrowed the one-lane road. Inside the passenger compartment, tension thickened. Rhone stopped, pushed a button that lowered all the windows and listened for anything out of the ordinary. He heard the tick of Shannen's watch, the sounds of breathing.

In his rearview mirror, he saw six shadows emerge from the van. They disappeared immediately among the trees, so quietly, Shannen remained unaware they were being surrounded by some of the best-trained men in the country.

Accustomed to the darkness, Rhone put the vehicle in gear, driving slowly.

Not more than five minutes later, Doug spoke quietly. "Twelve o'clock."

"I see it." Rhone made out the solitary cabin straight ahead.

He pulled off the road into a small clearing several feet away and cut the ignition. "Stay here," he told Shannen. "We'll go have a look around."

Shannen gripped his arm. "I'd feel safer if I could go with you."

He frowned, wanting to argue, knew it would be no use. "Stay close to me." He turned to the two men in the back seat. "Ready?"

Stepping away from the Jeep, the three men drew guns. With Shannen at Rhone's side, the foursome moved cautiously toward the cabin. Gauging from the exterior, Rhone guessed it to be no bigger than four or five rooms on the inside. The windows were boarded up and ground cover choked the foundation.

The occasional sound of chirping crickets broke the silence. Silence that seemed accustomed to the vacancy of human life.

"No one's here, Rhone. What do we do now? Where do we go next?"

He heard the disappointment in Shannen's voice. He kept his eyes moving, inventorying their surroundings, automatically committing them to memory. "Oh, Norton's been here, all right."

Her voice dropped to a hoarse whisper. "How do you know?"

"Tracks," Doug supplied.

"That he's tried to conceal, but in his rush, didn't quite succeed. Or—didn't on purpose," Rhone added. He knelt down and flipped on his flashlight. "They're a couple days old."

A few feet away, Rhone turned to Shannen. "Wait with Brian while Doug and I check out the interior."

She seemed about to argue, then apparently changed her mind.

Rhone heard distinct sounds that separated themselves from normal night noises, alerting him that his team of sharpshooters were in place.

Positioning themselves at opposite corners of the small wooden structure, Rhone and Doug crouched, inching toward the door. Flanking it, Doug poised, weapon raised and nodded to Rhone.

Rhone reached around to the handle, finding that it turned with ease. He winced as thirsty hinges protested with a loud squawk. Making eye contact with Doug, Rhone raised his own weapon, swung around toward the opening and lowered the barrel. Without making a sound, he crossed the threshold, moving the gun from side to side. Within seconds, Doug joined him.

In a methodical pattern, they checked all four rooms, finding more dust and rodent droppings than furniture or anything else.

Returning to the living room, Rhone lowered his weapon and turned on the flashlight, circling the beam for a final check. Nothing out of the ordinary. Rhone gave a snort of disgust. He knew Norton had been there. The foul odor of day's-old sweat lingered in the stale air and was as good as his calling card.

Then Rhone saw the footprints, recognized the distinctive figuration. When Jimmy walked, he dragged the right tip of his shoe an inch or two, trailing a short line above the imprint.

For a second, the light wavered. Rhone's hand tremored briefly in reaction to his own expectancy. The prints led to the far end of the room, to a crudely built wooden table.

The funnel of light skimmed over the contents on top.

The butcher knife plunged into the surface was a vulgar contrast to the half-filled baby bottle that sat nearby.

Rhone began a savage curse until his throat tightened, the realization truly hitting him for the first time that his son could very well be injured. Or dead.

Doug squeezed Rhone's shoulder, the pressure conveying his friend's own anger and frustration before he turned and walked away. As though from a distance, Rhone heard Doug call out an all-clear.

Harsh reality, based on an almost intimate knowledge of their enemy, reminded Rhone of the facts. In trying to abate Shannen's anxiety with words of comfort, laced with confidence that he would get Nicholas back, Rhone had made a critical error. He'd started believing his own words, forgetting the most important fact of all.

Jimmy Norton was utterly capable of *anything*.

Chapter 12

"Damn it, Rhone, move."

Resolutely, he shook his head.

Her anger built. Logically, Shannen knew he only wanted to protect her, shield her from more hurt. But she was tired of him treating her this way. "He's my son, too."

"Shannen," Doug said, "Rhone's right."

She folded her arms across her chest. Ever since Rhone had rescued her, he'd become tenfold more protective. Shutting her out had always been one of their biggest problems. No more, if she could help it.

Despite the way he acted, as if he wanted their marriage to work, Shannen realized, with a painful stab, that love wasn't enough.

But as she stood there, facing down two very determined males, her own determination grew. "Rhone, you've got to stop doing this."

"Doing what?"

She sighed in exasperation. "Treating me the way you've been treating me."

"Shannen, after—"

"Stop! I'm a grown woman. I have as much at stake here as you do." She dropped her voice, begging him to understand.

Rhone's brow furrowed as a war of indecision waged over his features. She saw his concern, and her logic, battle for supremacy.

"You're not going to like what you see."

She reached a hand toward him, then pulled it back, feeling helpless. "I need to see," she implored.

Without a word, Doug left Shannen and Rhone alone. The tension between them pulled even tauter.

"Shannen, please, trust me on this."

Rhone's voice held a grainy undercurrent of something she found difficult to identify. Panic?

"Rhone, this is about my baby."

"This isn't about your baby," he insisted. "It's about *our* child and Jimmy Norton. And how Norton can exact his revenge."

"Obviously, he's doing a good job," she said hoarsely. "Rhone, you asked me to trust you, but it works both ways—you've got to trust me," she whispered. "You've got to believe I'm strong enough to face this."

She saw his shudder, felt tension radiate from his body. This was about more than the cabin, more than the kidnapping. It was about their relationship and the reasons it failed the first time.

Tightly, he nodded.

Her pulse thudded in response.

Without another word Rhone moved aside.

She squeezed her eyes shut, suddenly afraid. Shannen heard the constant, if unsteady, draw of Rhone's breath. She'd asked him to let her be strong. Now she hoped she was equal to the challenge.

Feeling as though a hand had wrapped around her heart and squeezed, she forced her eyelids apart.

And what she saw made her stagger back a step.

In an instant he was there, holding her, wrapping his arms tightly around her, as if the motion could help deaden the ache.

It couldn't.

"He's sick," Rhone insisted, the words ringing harshly in her ear.

He didn't say, "I told you so," didn't offer any recriminations. Instead, he stroked her hair reassuringly while visions of Nicky's nearly empty bottle flashed through her mind.

The knife was the worst.

The silver blade was darkened by rust stains that her tortured brain imagined were really blood.

She allowed herself to be cradled for a few seconds. Shannen waited for the first wave of agony to pass.

It didn't. In fact, it just seemed to hurt worse, not in a debilitating way, but in a mind-numbing, grief-filled way.

"What does—" she sucked in a shallow breath, looked at him "—this mean?"

Soundlessly, Rhone reached for the bottle and offered it to her.

"He's playing with us, Shannen, wanting us to sweat. It's an elaborate game to him."

"A game?"

"A combination of hide-and-seek and a scavenger hunt." Rhone draped his arm across her shoulder; she gratefully accepted the support.

She ran her finger down the plastic bottle, tracing the raised lettering, as if it could bring her closer to the son she desperately needed to hold in her arms.

"It's working, Rhone." She looked at him, saw the same haunted expression in his eyes she knew hovered in hers.

For a second, he looked as though he might shut her out, then, opening up, he found the guts to admit, "Yeah, I know."

Her breath rushed out. The sight of her husband, normally so strong and brave, now trembling, scared her more than anything she'd endured. "We'll win, won't we?"

"He'll screw up."

Drawing courage from Rhone, tapping into the emotion she swore was strong enough to handle what had happened, what had yet to come, she nodded and asked, "What do we do now?"

Rhone released her. "Nail the son of a bitch."

The radio clipped to Rhone's belt crackled. Taking Shannen by the wrist, he headed outside. Palming the radio, he responded, "Mitchell here."

"We've got the abandoned truck," Sheriff Jenkins stated.

Shannen's heart did double time. Nicky was close; she knew it, felt it.

Brian scribbled down the coordinates the man gave, then Rhone signed off.

"Let's move," Doug said.

She expected to see a smile of triumph on Rhone's face. She didn't. Grim resolve painted him as a stranger once again.

Suddenly the sound of hideous laughter emitted from the radio Rhone still held. Doug and Rhone exchanged incredulous looks. Shannen fought the urge to scream. The same sound that she'd been forced to listen to in the forest, chilled her again, seeping in and haunting her every thought. *The man had her son.*

"Catch me, catch me, catch me if you can."

A pulse throbbed in Rhone's temple.

"Chicken, Mitchell? Not like the old days, huh? This time you had to bring the entire calvary with you." He cackled. "Guess you ain't man enough to face me alone no more."

Norton cackled again. "Don't feel as powerful now that I have your son, huh, Mitchell? How's it feel to know you're about to lose someone you love?"

Shannen's knees sagged, and she began to weave back and forth as her head swam.

"You killed my brother."

"You can't know that. No one knows."

"I know," Norton said in a clipped tone. "But I'm willin' to make a little deal."

"No deals."

The sound of Nicky's terrified scream split the air. Shannen couldn't breathe, and she fell to her knees. Rhone moved behind her, placing a hand on her shoulder. She struggled to fill her lungs, to accept the comfort Rhone tried to give. Couldn't. All that consumed her senses was the soul-wrenching sob of her baby.

"Maa-Maa!"

Hot tears cascaded down her cheeks.

"Deal?" Norton taunted.

Rhone's succinct curse blended with Doug's. "Name your terms."

Nicky's sobs stifled, as if Norton had shoved his hand over the tiny mouth.

"I want you and the woman."

"You get me alone."

Nicholas screamed again.

Rhone's hand tightened on her shoulder; through her own anguish, his was telepathed. She forced herself to nod weakly. Rhone shook his head. Nicky's cries continued to fill the tense air.

Finally Rhone relented. When he spoke, his voice was terse, dripping with hatred. "Where and when?"

Norton silenced their son. "Call off the boys."

"Done."

"You still a good tracker?"

Black fog enshrouded her, obliterating everything except the searing heat of desperation.

"Can hold my own."

"Catch me, catch me, catch me if you can."

Then, entombing silence shattered her. Norton was gone. Along with her fragile connection to Nicky.

For long minutes, no one said a word. Shannen's soft cries were the only haunting sound in the clearing.

Apparently mindless of the half dozen men surrounding them, waiting for his direction, Rhone knelt in front of her. He took her hands, searched her eyes. "You don't have to do this, Shan."

She fought for control, told herself how much depended on her. Norton meant business. If she didn't pull herself together, she might never have the opportunity to be with her son again. "I have to."

"Listen to me...."

She squeezed her eyes shut, trying to block the terror. "I *need* to go." Fear clogged her throat, made it difficult to speak. "Please don't shut me out."

"I can't anticipate what Norton plans."

"It won't be any easier if I'm here worrying."

His sigh sounded as if it worked itself up from the very bottom of his heart. "I guess I'd be wasting time if I ask you to stay."

Her breaths burned in her lungs. "Please don't."

They were surrounded by people, yet it felt as though she and Rhone were all alone in the world.

"I don't recall that Norton gave us a choice," she added.

He glared. Undoubtedly he wanted to argue the point. She appreciated where he was coming from, but there was no other way. "I want my Nicky back. Don't make me be the reason Norton kills him." She tried to sound determined, but knew her words were much weaker than she wanted.

His hands trembled. "He's an animal."

"Then we can outwit him."

Rhone released one of her hands, then raked his fingers through his hair. "Ready?"

While Shannen tried to pull herself together, Rhone began issuing orders, adding that a new command post would be set up at the site of the abandoned truck. To Cox he added, "Make sure Jenkins and his men stay off the radio. The less Norton knows, the better."

Doug and Brian insisted on accompanying them as far as possible.

"Sorry," Rhone objected. "To do so compromises Nicky's safety."

"Not doing so compromises your safety," Doug countered. "And Shannen's."

"We're going alone."

Doug shook his head. "We'll go as far as possible with you. When we get close enough to the rat to smell him, we'll back off."

"Rhone, Doug's right," Shannen said.

"It's too dangerous."

"So you let yourself walk into another Norton trap?" Doug challenged.

Her husband's face paled.

"You can't do it all alone, partner."

She shared Rhone's pain, anguish and the realization Doug was right. Tightly, Rhone gave a brief nod.

A few minutes later, they arrived at the coordinates Jenkins had given. They met the sheriff there, noting the truck had been left where the road dead-ended. Dense forest and rugged mountains surrounded them.

"This is going to be a chore," Brian remarked with a low whistle.

Doug nodded. Shannen glanced around. Doubts began to eat at her, shaking the small amount of confidence she possessed.

After sliding her a "chin up" glance, Rhone grabbed his backpack and the weapons he could carry.

"It isn't safe to let you all do this," Sheriff Jenkins stated flatly. With a sweep of his hand, he indicated the various mountains. "You don't know what he's got up there."

"He's got my son," Rhone countered.

"Know what you mean." The sheriff released his breath and nodded reluctantly. "Got me two little girls."

Brian reached for maps while Doug concentrated on checking out the terrain. After his equipment was ready, Rhone turned to the sheriff. "You know the area," Rhone said. "Where would you hide?"

The man scratched his beard. Looked in the distance. "Reckon I'd head to the abandoned mines."

"Show me," Brian instructed, holding a flashlight over the maps he spread across the hood of the Jeep.

Her hopes plummeted. How Rhone managed to keep going forward stunned her. Made her realize how different she and her husband truly were.

Rhone moved closer to the Jeep; she followed suit, surprised when Rhone moved behind her so that he looked at the maps over her shoulder.

"There's at least four different mines," she said dejectedly.

The sheriff nodded. "And there ain't a one of them that's safe."

"Rhone!" Doug called from where he crouched several feet away.

"Much obliged for your help," Rhone told the sheriff.

"We'll hold down the fort from here." The man patted Shannen's hand. "Best of luck getting your boy back."

She managed a tight nod.

Rhone jogged to Doug's side. Rhone nodded. She joined them, looking at the area of ground Doug showed Rhone and saw nothing.

"Tracks. Unmistakable depressions."

Try as she might, she couldn't see them, but both men seemed satisfied. Wordlessly, they gathered their equipment from the duffel bag, Rhone helped Shannen distribute baby supplies into each of their backpacks. He slung one over his shoulders, and helped Shannen do the same.

"Got it?" he asked.

"Yeah."

He gave a half smile of approval.

She wasn't sure exactly how long they hiked, or even if they were traveling in circles. Doug and Rhone stopped periodically, listened, looked at the trees, examined the carpet of pinecones and decaying timber. Twice they reversed their course when no more clues were found.

Her shoulders ached from the unfamiliar weight of the pack. Night thickened in the forest, making it more difficult to see the canopy of trees obliterating the sky. The men took out their infrared binoculars and pushed on. Shannen's fear boiled into tangible anger and frustration.

How dare Jimmy play with them? Act as though this was nothing but an elaborate game for his personal enjoyment? Damn it, this was her life, her son's life...Rhone's life.

"You okay?"

She glanced back at Rhone, his expression dark, unreadable in the night. His words had reached her from close...closer than she'd thought he was.

"Is that backpack too heavy?"

"It's fine." She'd automatically lowered her voice to match the pitch of his.

Obviously—with astuteness she wished he'd shown when they lived together, trying to make an infant marriage work—he'd picked up on her mood. "Talk to me Shannen," he encouraged.

"I'm mad, Rhone, madder than hell."

"Yeah. I know how you feel." He fell in step next to her, then grabbed her elbow and pulled her down a few inches when a branch threatened to slap her face. "Don't let it eat you, babe. It'll consume you until there's nothing left."

"The voice of experience again." She knew bitterness tinged her voice, but couldn't help it. She was mad, hurt, angry. And desperate for this whole thing to be over.

He didn't respond.

After several silent seconds, he released her, dropping back a couple of feet behind her.

The thrum of tension surrounded her, making her jump every time a night noise tore at the air.

A few minutes later, he promised, "We'll stop for the night soon."

She nodded, then realized Rhone probably couldn't see the motion. A few minutes turned into an hour or more. Her thigh muscles constricted agonizingly and her feet hurt where the unforgiving leather of her boots rubbed her skin raw.

Then, as if by unspoken accord, Doug and Rhone stopped, Brian joining them from his position in the rear. The dim glow from a lantern barely helped her make out shapes of trees, but the three men acted as though it was high noon. Efficiently, Doug unzipped one of the packs and handed sandwiches to everyone.

She said a soft thanks, realizing her stomach protested the fact they'd been on the run without stopping to eat. Hastily she pulled the sandwich from its wrapper and bit into it. Shannen grimaced as soggy bread met expectant taste buds. None of the men seemed to notice. Or care.

She forced herself to chew and swallow several bites before rewrapping the remains and tossing them into a small grocery bag. The food was bad, she admitted that, but worse were the knots in her stomach that had made it difficult to eat much of anything the past few days. She knew she'd already lost a few pounds—the looseness at the waist of her jeans was indication of that.

Doug rooted fruit from the pack and offered her an apple. Shaking her head, she wandered a few feet away, wrapping her arms around her middle, as much to ward off overwhelming worry about Nicky as to keep warm.

In an instant, Rhone stood beside her. She hadn't heard his approach.

He shrugged from his jacket and draped it around her shoulders, the subtly intoxicating scent of him clinging to the material.

"This is nothing new to you, is it?" she asked, oddly hollow now that she was in his world.

"Old hat."

It was no wonder she and Rhone had difficulty making their relationship work, if he felt as alien in her world as she did in his.

"It gets old, Shannen," he commented, as if reading her mind. Rhone moved behind her, folding his arms around her and pulling her back against him.

She unlocked her arms, then placed her palms on his forearm, his flannel shirt warm against her hands.

"You get tired of looking behind every bush, wondering if someone's hiding high in the treetops, waiting to drop on you."

Doug glanced in their direction, then set about making up a makeshift camp.

"I need to help," she said, any distraction better than listening to the night sounds and imagining all the things that could be happening to Nicky.

"You need to relax," Rhone countered, tightening his hold on her.

"But..."

"Doug and Brian have it covered. Remember, it's old hat to Doug, too."

"Are you saying I'd be in the way?"

"There's that possibility."

He slackened the hold a little, but she didn't take the opportunity to bolt. Instead, she leaned her head back against his shoulder, able to hear the steady beat of his heart.

"I don't know how much more of this I can take," she admitted.

"You're strong, Shannen. You keep proving it."

"I always thought so. I thought being married to you showed my strength."

"Ouch."

Shannen almost felt his wince. "That's not what I meant," she said. "It was hell, Rhone. At least I thought it was, wondering if you were coming back to me, never knowing if you were dead or alive. But this..."

"Go on."

His arms had tightened around her again. She felt the strength of his chest, of his grip. She felt safe and protected. And never more frightened in her life. "I realized I couldn't live like that, that it would be less painful to try and cut you out of my heart."

Shannen wondered if he realized how hard he now held her. "I couldn't," she admitted, the words wrung from her very depths. "I tried to go on with life, but I wasn't living. Not really. I was functioning, making a new home, but there was always a hollow, empty feeling where you'd lived inside me."

She felt him bury his face in her hair, felt the warmth of his kiss on her crown.

She turned to face him, stroking her fingertips down the side of his cheek in unspoken apology. "I'm scared, Rhone, more frightened than I've ever been about anything in my life."

Rhone captured her wrist, stilling her movements.

"But I thank God I have you here, beside me."

"Do you realize what you're saying?" His voice was hoarse with suppressed emotion.

She swallowed the tightness constricting her throat. "Yes."

"Shannen..."

"I'm saying I don't blame you, Rhone." She blinked, looking up at him, wishing she could completely read his expression. But then, if she didn't have the anonymity of darkness for cover, she might not be able to find the courage to confess what had been burning inside. "I did at first, but I don't anymore."

"I've placed our child's life in danger, maybe our lives, too."

She didn't need light to see his self-inflicted blame. It was jaggedly etched into each word.

"I knew who you were when I married you, Rhone. I knew the risks."

His other arm went around her, dragging her flush against his chest. "You're saying you forgive me? No matter what else we have to face?"

She nodded, the feel of soft flannel and hard male consuming her. "I don't know what the future holds, but I know you would have given anything to keep me and Nicky safe. You arrived as soon as you could—"

"Not soon enough," he countered bitterly.

"You were there for me, Rhone." She felt her insides being ripped to shreds. She didn't need to heap guilt on him; he'd done more than enough for a dozen people. "When I needed you most, you were there."

"It's not over," he warned.

"As much as you want to be, as much as you'd like to pretend to be, you're not a superman, Rhone. You're doing everything humanly possible." She reached her hands around his neck, feeling the longish length of his hair tangling through her fingers.

"You're the most incredible woman I've ever met."

With that, and obviously not caring whether Doug or Brian looked on, Rhone kissed her fully, leaving her hungry for more. Now that she'd rediscovered her husband, she didn't know if she could let him go a second time. Worse was the fear she wouldn't have a choice.

She'd always been the play-it-safe type. The fact she'd married Rhone in the first place surprised no one more than her. But she was discovering the error of her ways. Wasn't all-consuming love worth the risks? Life was short, and memories might be the only thing that helped one survive. She'd definitely learned that the hard way.

An obviously reluctant Doug cleared his throat, then approached. "Sorry, partner, but duty calls."

Rhone released Shannen. "I'll take first watch," he said.

"Twist my arm," Doug replied, then bent and tossed a couple of sleeping bags in their direction. The flashlight followed.

"I think Doug's tired," Shannen commented.

"He knows I'm not going to sleep anytime soon, anyway." Rhone spread the sleeping bags out.

"Why don't you zip them together?"

"I was afraid you'd never ask." With a few, deft motions, he secured the bags together. Pushing up from his crouch, he finished, "I'll climb in when my watch is over. Try and get some rest."

"I'll wait up with you."

"There's nothing more boring than trying to stay awake and alert while everyone else is sleeping."

"All the more reason for you to have company."

They moved away from the area where Doug and Brian had spread their sleeping bags. Rhone poured them both coffee, black, and nearly espresso strength, with only a hint of sugar to take away the caffeine's bite.

After handing her a metal cup, he asked, "Have you always been this stubborn? Or maybe I just don't remember."

"I've changed in the last couple of years. You, on the other hand, have always been bossy."

"Me?"

"You," she responded, in the same, mock-horror tone he'd used.

"I think I liked things better when you were more malleable."

"Did you?"

"Honestly?" he asked, turning to place the cup on a huge rock. Gently, Rhone feathered back hair that had escaped from her ponytail.

The roughness of his fingertip abraded her skin, sending a dance of desire through her.

With a breath, he continued, "No. You've got a well of strength now, not that you weren't strong before. It's just different somehow."

"Being a mother changes you."

"Maybe that's it. Maybe getting away from me was good for you."

"Don't say that," she demanded. "If I have strength now, it's because of you. From you. You're my inspiration, Rhone."

He placed his palms on either side of her cheeks, cradling her chin where his hands joined together. "Thank you for that. You can't imagine what it means to me."

With infinite tenderness, unbelievable coming from a man this size, this hardened, he dropped a kiss on her lips. She shuddered, wanting more, wishing things were different, hoping things would work out.

Shannen could never recall being bombarded by so many overwhelming feelings at the same time. Fear, panic, love, joy, despair and anger. It left her drained, but simultaneously ready to fight if she needed to.

She heard a groan, as if it came from all the way deep inside him. With obvious reluctance, he dropped his hands. "As much as I want to hold you, taste you, I've got to check our perimeter. Ready?"

The fact he hadn't arrogantly assumed she would stay near the camp thrilled her.

Not a fool, though, she stayed close, stopping when he did, cocking her head to the side to listen. Fifteen or twenty minutes passed before they returned to camp, Rhone obviously satisfied Norton didn't lurk behind the trees, watching their every move.

She gratefully accepted a refill of the coffee as she sank onto the sleeping bag. Twigs had reached up and slapped her shins while low-lying branches had grabbed for her hair. After this was over, she knew she never wanted to camp again. And if Nicky wanted to, well, he'd just have to go with his father....

The thought brought her head up.

How easy it was to picture a happily-ever-after for them. And, as yet, how impossible it seemed.

Rhone dropped down next to her. He winced, trying to adjust and hold his coffee steady at the same time. "Damn. I forgot how much I hate doing this. Nothing feels worse than a sharp rock digging into your—"

"Behind," she supplied.

"Right." He shook hot liquid off his hand.

They drank their sugar-laced coffee in companionable quiet, her mind once again supplying teasing images of them sitting in front of a fire, sharing the events of the day while their child slept soundly upstairs.

Thoughts of Nicky led naturally to her worries. "I wonder if he's asleep."

Rhone didn't respond.

"Nicky, that is. Or if he's awake like we are."

Rhone swore.

"How can he do this to us, Rhone? How can any man steal a baby from his mother?" She knew he'd followed her leap of conversation.

"I wish I could answer that."

"I'm angry." She didn't resist when Rhone put his arm around her shoulder. "Who the hell does Norton think he is?" She took a long swallow. "I wish I could get my hands on him."

"The idea is to keep you away from him."

She said bitterly, "I'd kill him, Rhone, I swear I would."

"Shannen, you've got to listen to me. A certain amount of anger is just fine, understandable, even necessary. But don't let it blind you. Passion, of any kind, can be deadly in the field. You've got to bottle it up and shove it away."

"Is that what you do?"

"That's what I *try* to do. Giving in can get you hurt."

"Is that what happened in Colombia?"

"Yeah," he admitted. "I'd have done anything to get Menendez. In the end, that same determination got me."

She wasn't sure she could shove away the loathing if she saw Norton again. The urge to kill him would be stronger than anything. But Shannen couldn't admit that to Rhone. It would just make his protective instincts surge to the surface again.

An owl hooted and Doug sat up in a single, fluid, all-alert motion. Shannen recognized the movement. She'd seen it from Rhone plenty when he used to sleep at home. She wisely stayed where she was until Doug blinked reality into focus.

Rhone flipped on the flashlight.

More than a little sheepishly, Doug slipped his gun back in its holster.

"Sleeping out here never gets easy, does it, partner?" Rhone asked.

"In my next life I'm gonna be a banker," Doug insisted, walking to the thermos and pouring a cup of coffee for himself.

"And I'm gonna be an accountant," Rhone seconded.

It still amazed her that the two were so comfortable in the dark, moving unhesitatingly. Her vision had accustomed to night, but not nearly enough to maneuver effortlessly.

"Last time you said you wanted to be a dishwasher repairman," Doug reminded him.

"At least I have dreams, bud. You've always wanted to be a banker."

They continued in a lighthearted tone, both always keeping a wary eye on the area around them. "It's time for another perimeter check," Rhone said. "Want me to do it?"

"No. I need some exercise anyway. You and Shannen catch forty winks while you can."

Within minutes, Shannen had snuggled against Rhone, using his chest as the pillow she didn't have. Rhone propped one arm behind his head, letting the other skim down her spine.

She didn't expect to sleep. But the rhythmic beat of Rhone's breaths and the warmth from his body lulled her into a brief nap.

When she woke, coming instantly awake as she'd seen Doug do earlier, she realized a cold chill had wound its way around her. Rhone was gone.

She pushed to sitting, heart pounding unnaturally. All three men were loading supplies into backpacks. All the other sleeping bags had been rolled and readied for the day.

"You should have woke me," she said, shoving unruly hair from her face.

"We still have work to do," Brian said. "No worries."

Rhone joined her, offering coffee. No steam rose from the top of the cup. "It's warm," he said, dropping to a squat in front of her, "but not much more than that."

She accepted, fighting to find the good mood she usually woke up in. But the burning in her eyes, the chilly temperature, predawn skies and the fact she'd overslept, combined with all the things she'd been through, made a smile impossible.

Wisely, Rhone disappeared, joining the other men and helping Brian to situate a larger pack on his back. She finger-combed her hair, redid the ponytail, tucked her V-neck sweater back into her jeans, then pulled on her boots.

"We've got beef jerky if you're hungry."

She wrinkled her nose, stomach instantly protesting the thought of jerky and tepid coffee. "Pass." After buttoning her jacket, she unzipped the two sleeping bags, refastening and rolling one while Rhone worked on the other.

"Do you have any idea which way we should head?" Shannen asked.

"There's a mine to the west of here. It's worth checking out. If nothing else, maybe we can pick up his trail."

Doug nodded agreement.

Within five minutes, not a single trace of their stay remained.

She thought their trek through the woods in daylight would be easier. It wasn't. Her muscles burned, her feet sported blisters, which stung with every step, and bugs buzzed around her head. The sun made the exercise uncomfortably hot.

No one spoke during the morning, and hardly a dozen words were exchanged when they stopped for lunch. When they'd walked for hours with no sign of Norton, tempers began to wane. Shannen wondered if they were heading in the right direction or if they were giving Norton his jollies by running all over in a wild-goose chase.

And wondered if Nicky was still alive.

Gritting her teeth, she picked her way over yet another moss-eaten rock. Only positive thoughts of Nicky's firsts kept her going. She slipped, green fuzz staining her jeans and palms.

Rhone's hands came around her waist, helping hold her steady while she recovered her footing.

At the front of the line, Brian abruptly stopped, raising a hand. Nervously she glanced around, suddenly feeling as though a hundred pairs of eyes were staring at her. A shiver traced between her shoulder blades. Setting her firmly on the ground, Rhone hurried to where Brian stood, his footsteps making no sound on the pine-needle-carpeted ground.

Following, she stopped short, the morning's coffee curdling in her stomach.

Hanging from a tree branch was the shirt Nicky had been wearing when he was abducted, a note pinned where Nicky's heart would beat against the fabric. "Can't catch me," it read.

Rage stabbed her. "No!" she screamed, suddenly not caring if anyone heard. Let the sick bastard come after them. She was desperate to fight, desperate to hold her son again, desperate for the insanity to be over.

In a swift motion, she pushed to the front of the men, grabbing hold of the shirt and yanking it free with a loud rip. She saw the three men exchange a glance. "Don't worry," she said, her voice strained, "I'm okay. I'm not going to freak out on you just because my son was wearing this shirt when the bastard stole him from my house."

"Shannen . . ."

She pretended not to hear, holding the material against her cheek.

Rhone disentangled the shirt, easing the material from her numb-feeling fingers.

With efficiency that seemed callous to her, Brian dug in his backpack for a plastic bag. He opened the top and Rhone dropped the shirt in.

Evidence.

The word ricocheted in her mind.

Evidence.

As far as she was concerned, they didn't need evidence. Norton wouldn't live long enough to make it to court.

"He's trying to wear us down," Rhone told her, bitingly digging his fingers into her shoulders.

The sharp pain distracted her. She looked up at him, his eyes containing a mixture of tyrannical determination and compassion.

"It's psychological warfare. He wants anger to blind us so we screw up."

Her hands shook. She watched Brian seal the bag and scribble a notation on the side. Then he zipped the backpack closed with a single, tearing sound.

"Shan, I knew he'd do this. That's why I wanted you to stay at the command post."

He'd said the words harshly, intentionally goading her. Rhone Mitchell knew how to push her buttons and had no compunction about doing it.

"We can't let him weaken us, Shannen. The four of us are only as strong as our weakest link."

"And that's me."

"Is it?" he asked softly.

Angry and hurt, she forced her spine into a rigid line. "No. I won't let you down."

"I knew you wouldn't." Looking at Doug, he raised three fingers, then ticked them down one by one.

Doug nodded, taking the lead.

She felt as though a summer tornado gathered force around them. All three men had their guns drawn, their movements tight and controlled. Every time they found another clue, another sign of Norton's presence, Rhone, Doug and Brian performed the same ritual.

Looking around, trying to see things as they did, Shannen noticed branches were broken from trees. A wild animal? Or Norton? Adrenaline crashed through her bloodstream and her pulse roared in her head so that she heard little else.

Walking farther, the sun directly overhead, she knew they were getting close. Felt it.

She glanced back at Rhone. He frowned, his eyes narrow slits, mouth set in a determined line. His tension was almost palpable. It wasn't her imagination. Something was going to happen.

Within the next sixty seconds, it did.

Still walking, Doug made a hand signal. Rhone instantly grabbed her, tossing her to the unyielding ground, a million pine needles digging into her body. The weight of Rhone on top of her only intensified the feeling.

She struggled to gulp air into her lungs.

From above her, she heard Rhone's vivid four-letter curse. Then he got off her, offering a hand up. Suddenly, the idea of keeping her head buried seemed like a good one.

But she forced herself to look.

Then wished she hadn't.

"Lord, Rhone, he's been in my house, in my bedroom! And he's still got Nicky."

She squeezed her eyes against the searing pain of seeing her son's beloved Bear's head grotesquely pinned between the jagged metal teeth of a wild animal trap.

With furious but efficient motions, the corners of his mouth turned in a frigid sneer, Rhone set to work on the trap, dismantling the damn thing, piece by piece.

She stood there, terror rooting her immobilized.

Before Brian could repeat the procedure of bagging the evidence, she picked up Bear, one of its eyes dangling by a thread from a fuzzy face. Stuffing oozed from the hole in his neck.

Shannen wondered where the tears were.

There were none.

She didn't have a clue where to start fighting this kind of mental torture. Doug and Rhone seemed more angry.

Goose bumps stood rigidly at attention on her skin, but other than that she felt completely numb, worn-out. Worn down.

"Aw, hell!"

Hearing the rare mix of anger and frustration in Doug's voice, Shannen glanced up. Now what? she wondered.

A crack of gunfire exploded around them.

"Watch out!"

Chapter 13

Doug's shout of warning echoed in Rhone's ears. A fraction of a second later, he heard the repeat of a semi-automatic. In a flurry of motion, Brian lunged forward, blocking Rhone's path.

There was no time to think or evaluate. Only act. Grabbing Shannen, Rhone shielded her body with his own. In a fluid motion, both dropped into a crouched position. He could have sworn he heard the whiz of a passing bullet splitting the air near his head. Cursing aloud, Rhone backed up, drawing Shannen into a more dense cover of trees.

As quickly as the ambush began, it ended. In the ensuing quiet, Rhone heard Shannen's adrenaline-induced gasps for air. His own chest rose and fell in rapid succession for the same reasons. The difference was, he'd long ago learned how to contain his terror, and now he tamped it down with practiced resolve.

He glanced across the space that separated them from Doug and Brian. At Doug's signal that he was all right, Rhone exhaled his sense of relief.

Then familiar dread took its place.

In a prone position on his side, Brian didn't move.

Doug realized it at the same time. "I'm going after Norton," he said, rising.

"No!" Rhone surveyed their surroundings, moving with guarded care toward Brian. "He's long gone," Rhone assured Doug. "What's more important now is getting the kid to a hospital." If it isn't too late, Rhone added silently.

The radio at his side screamed to life.

"I told you to come alone!"

Then silence.

Rhone fisted his hands. He cursed. Recrimination washed over him. He should never have allowed anyone to accompany them.

"We'd have been right here, with or without your blessing," Doug stated. "If the situation was reversed, so would you have."

It didn't make the self-disgust diminish.

Brian's moan urged Rhone into action.

Gently, with Doug's help, Rhone rolled Brian onto his back and dusted dirt from a face turned ashen, brushing away pine needles from lips tinged with blue. He felt sickened when his gaze took in the gaping chest wound.

Rhone reached for Brian's wrist, fingers finding a weak pulse. Rhone's gaze met with Doug's. "This kid, crazy idiot, purposely stepped in front of me. Why would he do such a fool thing?"

Doug squeezed Rhone's shoulder and let go. "I'd have done the same. So would you."

Rhone heard and acknowledged the simple truth.

"Oh, God." Shannen's incredulous whisper reminded Rhone of her presence. His first instinct was to shield her from the ugliness, protect her from reality that brutally defined the depth of violence that stalked them.

She didn't give him a chance.

Falling to her knees, she unbuttoned Brian's shirt, her fingers moving swift and sure. Doug ripped open packages of sterile gauze pads, handing them to Rhone. He held them against the wound, applying pressure to stop the flow of blood.

Brian's lids fluttered open, his eyes glazed with agony.

Rhone spoke, forcing the words through the tightness in his throat. "And just what the hell did you think you were doing, Yarrow?" He heard the gruffness, the concern and strived for a lighter tone. "When I need a bodyguard, I'll let you know first."

Brian winced, then gave a weak smile. "Norton practices what you preached at the academy. 'Don't aim to maim,' you always said. He'd have killed you, Rhone. I couldn't let that happen. You're one of the best."

Rhone swallowed. Hard. "So are you, kid. So are you."

"Hey, boss? No regrets, huh? I wanted to come." Yarrow coughed. "Now I can tell everyone I saved your butt."

Out of the corner of his eye, Rhone saw Shannen's eyes widen as she cut a glance in his direction. As the impact of Brian's words sank in, Rhone sensed her withdrawal, felt the protective barrier he'd struggled so hard to penetrate fall into place once again. He closed his mind to defensive explanations he doubted she would accept anyway. Frustrated, he wanted to shake her. Most of all, he saved his irritation for himself. He knew about traps, shouldn't have allowed others to walk in with him.

In tense silence, he and Shannen bandaged Brian's chest. Doug stood apart, having no option but to use his radio to call for help. Norton would know the outcome of his ambush, but it couldn't be helped.

"You're going with Doug and Brian," Rhone told Shannen.

"Wrong. I'm going with you."

"The subject isn't open for discussion."

"I couldn't agree more." Shannen dampened a square of gauze with water from the canteen, holding it to Brian's lips. Slipping in and out of consciousness, he sent her an appreciative glance.

"Don't be stupid. You could have just as easily been hurt."

"Don't be stupid!" Shannen raged, somehow managing to keep her voice barely above a whisper. "Norton wants us and he wants us alone. That's what he'll get."

Rhone shook his head, wanting to argue, needing to convince her.

Brian's bandage intact, Rhone sat back on his haunches, resting his elbow on his knee. With thumb and forefinger, he rubbed his closed eyes. "Why do I waste my breath?" he asked on a weary sigh.

Doug saved Shannen from having to reply. "Mountain Rescue is on the way. I hate to leave you two, but someone should go with Brian. I'm the logical choice. Both of you have too much at stake here."

Rhone nodded.

"I'll be right behind you. In the meantime, monitor our frequency."

Rhone agreed, then gave his friend a firm pat on the back. "You'll be okay until help arrives? We need to get moving before we lose any more daylight."

"Now, what do you think?" Doug didn't expect an answer.

Slipping his backpack over his shoulders, Rhone helped Shannen do the same. "You're sure I can't convince you to go with Doug and Brian?"

Shannen glanced over her shoulder. "Like Doug said, what do you think?"

When Rhone didn't immediately respond, she turned around to face him.

"I think," he answered with deliberate calm, "you're going to be needing this." He watched her tense as she saw what he held.

Shannen realized the cold metal represented a lot more than a perfunctory necessity.

Her heart skipped a couple of beats and her breathing became shallow as she reached for the handle of the gun. With efficient motions, he offered an ammo clip. "Twelve bullets," he said.

Trying to still the slight trembling of her fingers, she accepted the clip and snapped it into place.

He nodded. "Ready?"

"Yes," she said, stiffening her shoulders in order to hide the fear that shook her all the way to the center of her being.

"Stick close to me. Be ready to drop and take cover on command."

She heard a trace of trepidation in his tone.

"I think I'd die if anything happened to you."

"I won't let you down, Rhone." She met his gaze squarely. "I swear, no heroics. I'll follow every command implicitly."

He reached for her, giving a quick, nearly brutal kiss that telegraphed a million things he seemed to want to say but didn't, or couldn't.

Following his lead, she fingered the unfamiliar bulge in her waistband. For the first time since he'd arrived in Colorado—heck, for the first time since she'd met him— he was treating her as though she had the capabilities to handle danger. At his side.

That thrilled her—and made her nervous. What if she failed him?

Vowing to do what it took, she ignored the lance of chills that claimed her.

The horrific events of the morning replayed over and over in her mind, in vivid detail and with a slowness that made her think she could have acted quicker, done something, anything, to stop the carnage. But that hadn't been possible, she told herself.

The mind had an odd way of working, playing deceptive tricks until you questioned your own sanity. With resolve and determination, she shoved aside the horrible images, the pasty look on Brian's face, the utter devastation on her husband's features.

She had to function the best she could. Rhone counted on it. Both their lives—and that of their son, too—might depend on it.

Rhone set a slower pace than before, seemingly having the alertness of ten men. In that moment, she wanted to offer comfort, encouragement, to give instead of receive.

The day dragged interminably. Each noise made her jump, every branch looked broken. Her muscles ached, mosquito bites itched and blisters had long since popped, no longer cushioning sore heels from uncompromising leather.

Yet she refused to stop or complain, knowing how much was riding on her, and how much depended on Rhone being able to concentrate.

Her foot caught on a rock and she winced, giving Rhone a watery smile when he glanced back.

Nightfall fought to conquer daylight when he finally halved the length of his strides. She gratefully followed suit. Periodically he stopped, peering through the darkness with his binoculars.

He stopped a few minutes later, unscrewing the cap on the canteen, offering her the water first. Nothing had ever tasted so good. When her throat no longer burned, she handed the canteen back to him.

"We'll stop for the night as soon as I find a good spot."
He tipped his head back and swallowed deeply. "You
hanging in there?"

"Fine." She forced the lie past a tongue that wanted to
shape the words and yell the truth.

"You're doing great," he said, closing the canteen with
a decisive twist of the cap. "I'm proud of you, Shan."

She never imagined those words could mean so much.
He'd said them more than once of late, but she never
thought they'd have so much impact. Suddenly she felt as
if she could climb the tallest mountain, walk all night—
whatever he wanted from her.

Nearly an hour passed before they came across a small
abandoned shack nestled among a stand of trees.

Breath clogged her throat. *Norton.*

He had to have been there.

Her blood froze.

Rhone studied the building and its surroundings.
Without looking back, he managed to close his hand
around her wrist, then draw her forward until she stood
even with him.

"It looks deserted—the area is secure. Still, we need to
check it out," he said carefully. "I don't want to be surprised a second time."

"Want me to wait here?"

"No. Separating us might be the opportunity Norton's
waiting for." He reassuringly squeezed her hand before
releasing her.

Approaching the door, he hesitated.

"Something wrong?"

Rhone shrugged.

Her heart hammered so loudly, she was certain she
wouldn't have heard a 747 thunder by.

With the toe of his boot, he nudged the bottom of the
door. It didn't budge.

"Damn." Ducking low, he moved to the other side of the door, leaning a shoulder against the jamb. With his free hand, he tried the knob.

She'd been wrong about the 747.

The sound of the knob seemed to shred the night air.

In the faint light from the millions of dots of light in the cloudless sky, she saw Rhone hold up three fingers. Knowing what to expect, she nodded, then was rewarded by his flash of approval in the shape of a thumb's-up sign.

Hours seemed to drag as he ticked down from three to one.

The door flew open, snapping against the inside wall.

She heard the deafening sound of a gun crack.

Then realized it was nothing more than the door bouncing back.

Petrified, she ducked inside, following Rhone.

The cabin consisted of a single room, which Rhone quickly surveyed, even pulling back the curtains and shining a flashlight beneath the bed.

"What is it?" she asked.

"Strange."

"What?"

"He hasn't been here. Not even a trace. This is obviously a ski hut, and the dust here hasn't been disturbed in months, most likely since last winter. He couldn't have gotten in and out without so much as disturbing a cobweb or leaving a single footprint."

Her breath whooshed in audible relief. "He hasn't been here?"

"No. Which isn't logical." He raked a hand through wind-washed hair. "Hell." He sighed, the sound audible in the stillness.

"What's wrong with that?"

"Maybe we're on the wrong track. Maybe we took a wrong turn. Maybe I don't know where the hell he is after all."

"We're not on the wrong track," she insisted. "Don't ask me how I know. I just have a gut feeling that he doesn't want to be found yet." She sank onto the edge of the bed. "Didn't you say Norton spent time in the jungle, too?"

"Yeah. He's a regular Rambo."

"Like you said, he's waging psychological warfare, Rhone. Surely keeping you—us—guessing is part of it."

"But he hasn't spent as much time in the jungle as I have, and I'm getting damn sick of his games. Damn sick."

"Do you think we're safe here for the night?" The inviting comfort of the mattress tempted her.

"As safe as outside, and at least there's some protection here."

"Then we'll stay here?" She hoped she didn't sound as anxious as she felt.

"We'll stay," he agreed.

She shucked the backpack, then rotated her shoulders, not realizing until then how badly the pack had pulled her muscles.

With an apologetic glance, Rhone opened the window that faced the front and pulled the burlap curtain aside far enough to feel a stirring of air in the room.

"Unfortunately, the accommodations don't include indoor plumbing." He shot her a rueful grin.

He turned the lantern to low and placed it on the single table. "I don't want to risk starting a fire," he explained.

"Let me guess.... Foil packages for dinner?"

"Sorry. Next time we go camping, I promise to get a fully loaded trailer and stuff it full with real food."

He looked at her, the air hanging heavily with the unspoken idea they may have a future together.

Breaking eye contact, she washed up with the wipes, then read the unappetizing label on the food pack.

"Not a good idea."

She raised a brow.

"Much better to close your eyes and swallow."

"And here I was, thinking your job contained all the promised fun and adventure."

"Now you know, kid," he said, doing a bad Bogey imitation spiced with an even worse John Wayne.

The fact he could still crack unfunny jokes endeared him even more. She appreciated what he tried to do: take her mind off Nicky. When she finished the food that didn't taste a thing like the package said, she shoved the remains into a plastic bag. "You know what I think?"

"Hmm?"

"I think all those meals are exactly the same and they just change the ink on the printer."

He examined the outside of his package. "Is that what they do? I've been trying to figure it out for years."

He finished, then cleaned up his own mess.

"I'm not sure how great I'd be at standing watch, but I'm willing to do it while you try and sleep."

"Thanks, babe, but there's no way I'm going to sleep anyway." With an economy of motion, he zipped their bags together and spread them on top of the mattress.

Shannen tugged off her boots. Instantly she wished she hadn't. Circulation returned with a painful rush. "Man," she said.

"What's wrong?"

"Nothing that a long soak in Epsom salts and a pair of fluffy slippers wouldn't solve."

"Why didn't you say something earlier?" he demanded. He dropped to his knees in front of her and gently peeled off her socks.

"Because you didn't have time to play doctor."

Her feeble attempt at humor didn't seem to amuse him.

"Really, Rhone, it's okay. If we just put a bandage on each foot, I'll be fine."

He shoved to his feet, grabbed a small first-aid kit from his backpack, then returned. As he bandaged her feet, she had an urge to tangle her fingers through his hair, the way she might have when they first married.

She tried to resist the impulse, then gave in.

His movements arrested as he looked up at her. Her hands stilled. "Do you have any idea how much I missed you?"

"Maybe... maybe half as much as I missed you?"

He surged to his feet in a fluid motion, pulling her up with him. "Lord, Shannen, I want to hold you, make love with you, make the wrongs go away."

"I want that, too," she admitted, the confession not as difficult as she thought it would be.

"That was always good between us," he said hoarsely.

She stroked her fingers against the stubble on his face. His eyes held sorrow, regret, exhaustion.

"Still is," he said.

"Yes," she whispered, the memory of rediscovery still fresh and thrilling.

"We can't take the chance tonight," Rhone said. Expansively, he raised a hand, communicating their danger.

"I know." She wondered if the joy would remain as strong, or whether it would become bittersweet in the years to come.

"It wouldn't be wrong to hold me, would it?"

"No one, no one, could stop me from doing that." He scooped her into his arms, carrying her the few feet to the bed.

"Put your gun on the nightstand," he said.

She did.

"Reach for it."

Unhesitatingly she did.

"When you put it down, put it down the same way you picked it up, so there's no fumbling if you need it in an emergency."

"Right, boss."

He left her for a few seconds, extinguishing the lantern, then walking back, his boots echoing off the bare wooden floor.

Rhone joined her on the bed, propping his shoulders against the headboard, while she curled up next to him, familiarly resting her head on his shoulder.

"How do you do it?"

"Do what?" he asked.

"Survive this kind of life-style? How can you bear to watch people you know getting shot?"

Beneath her ear, she heard the rapid acceleration of his heart. "I'm sorry, Rhone. I didn't mean to touch a nerve."

"It's okay," he said, but the words emerged on a jagged burst of air. "Truth is, I can't tolerate this kind of life-style."

For a second, her mind supplied an enticing "what if" scenario.

"Any more than I can give it up. I can't stand watching people get shot, but I can't sit home watching the news, knowing others are out there fighting, making a difference, while I'm pretending the nastiness and ugliness don't exist."

"You know, Rhone, for the first time, I truly understand."

"Shannen—"

"No, wait," she hurriedly interrupted. "I understand how you can't not be involved, but I can't live with it any more than I ever could. I used to think it would get easier, that I'd get used to it, but I didn't."

The arm he had around her tightened.

He bit out a curse that served to tell her how deeply the pain ran, but how shallow it was buried. "I know." The two words were shrouded with despair, with resignation.

Instead of saying anything further, he took a tried-and-true track, like he always had. He changed the subject. "I can't believe that idiot took the bullet."

The thought of what would have happened if Brian hadn't tried to act the hero struck her with horror. But what was the point of expressing her feelings? Rhone would only discount them.

"He respects you."

He stroked her hair. Tension and stress began to drain from her body. He continued to talk in a low tone that soothed her, lulled her. She couldn't tell where reality ended and fantasy began.

"But one thing's never changed, Shannen."

She didn't respond, couldn't, as exhaustion claimed her. She struggled to stay awake but the dream that overtook her consciousness was too compelling.

"I love you, Shannen." Darkness absorbed the whispered words. "With my heart and soul. With what's left of them, anyway."

Morning came too soon. She opened her eyes, looking at the man who'd seemed so accessible last night, so remote this morning. She remembered the dream and wished it'd been real.

"Morning," he said, barely looking up from the pack he was zipping.

She sat up, realizing he was nearly ready to go. "A ghost doesn't move as quietly as you," she said, rubbing her hand over gritty eyes.

"Practice," he responded. "Lucky you, I found an apple in the bottom of the pack. It's a little bruised, but..."

"Manna from the gods." Despite being groggy, she snagged the piece of fruit he tossed in midair.

"I've seen graduating members of the academy who didn't have reflexes like yours."

"It was a good toss," she said, giving him his due. After devouring the fruit, she started rolling her socks back on. "You sure you're not holding out on the Epsom salts?"

"Sorry."

It felt as though her boots were two sizes too small. Still, she persevered. Going barefoot six months of the year and wearing moccasins the other six, hadn't left her prepared for the torture.

She grabbed her gun. "I'll be right back," she said.

"Where are you going?"

She scowled at him.

"I'll walk out with you."

"Thanks, but I can do this alone."

"Humor me."

Outside, he performed a quick check of the area.

Shannen pulled on the outhouse door handle, surprised when the door quickly opened. A dull thunk sounded.

She glanced down.

Screamed.

A woman's body fell at Shannen's feet, a dried pool of blood matted in her hair.

Instantly, Rhone was at Shannen's side, gun tightly cupped in his palm.

She looked away, fists clutching the fabric of Rhone's shirt. "It's the woman who was with Norton."

Chapter 14

The sun slipped into the sky, bloodred, and dripping with the promise of retribution.

Jimmy stood beneath that sky, rage threatening to destroy all he'd worked for. He tipped back his head and roared into the uncaring heavens.

He screamed, the pain slicing his heart into tiny scraps that his mind then fed to him.

Because of Rhone Mitchell, Jimmy had lost everything important. He grabbed a knife strapped to his thigh and stabbed it into the trunk of a tree.

Over and over. Over and over.

"Your family for my brother." With a final yank, he ripped the blade free, wiping the sticky sap from the gleaming metal, not caring that he left his own blood behind. Jimmy the Brain had to think. Had to have a plan.

That's right. Had to have a plan.

In a stupor, Shannen failed to respond.

Rhone saw the vacant expression in her eyes and fought

a desperate urge to shake her until it disappeared. He hated the feeling of helplessness that swamped him, hated worse the fear that any hope they'd had of reconciling had been smothered, cruelly snuffed out by the actions of a madman.

It had been Rhone's experience that revenge fought countless battles and won few.

How had Norton won this one?

Every muscle in Rhone's body grew taut as rage and a fierce need for a chance to balance the scales coursed through him. The realization that he had nothing to lose and everything to gain made retaliation boil beneath the surface. It wasn't revenge that drove him. It was survival of a dream he couldn't bear to let go.

Rhone holstered his gun and moved forward, stepping between the dead woman and his wife, blocking her view. He wanted her attention, needed to replace the emptiness. "Get a grip, Shannen. I don't have time to coddle you while you go to pieces."

"Well, *excuse me.*" She glared up at him, reacting to his harsh tone as he'd wanted her to, though in part, he'd meant his last remark. Norton had been too close for comfort—would continue to be as long as he lived.

"I'm not as accustomed to seeing . . ." Faltering, Shannen pointed, unable or unwilling to say the words.

Anger sparked his own. "And you really think I am?" He could see she thought him callous, unfeeling.

"You'd have to be—to do what you do." She shuddered, wrapping her arms around herself. "I hate it, Rhone. I hate it."

He nodded tightly. "Yeah, I know," he said wearily. "You never get used to it, Shannen." Rhone looked at her intently. "Through the years, you were constantly on me for my chosen profession. Obviously, had I chosen a different path, we wouldn't be standing here on the side of this mountain having this conversation, much less these problems. My profession has been the crux of our problems from the very beginning. Finding a way to explain the importance of why I do what I do eludes me. I can only say that if you don't understand by now, it's probably safe to assume you never will. I can't change who I am, Shannen. Just as I can't change who you are.''

With weariness, he added, "Go back to the cabin. Get your gear and bring me the radio.''

Not looking back, Shannen strode away. As soon as she was out of sight, he knelt by the woman. Though common sense told him it wasn't necessary, he felt for a pulse. Finding none, he shook his head in disgust. Another senseless waste of human life.

Gently he eased the woman's upper body back into the wooden structure and closed the door, protecting her from scavenging wildlife.

The image of a child—an innocent grin captured on film—formed in Rhone's mind. Fervently he prayed for his son's safety, prayed for infinite guidance to reach Nicholas before it was too late.

Shannen met him halfway, handing him the radio. She remained at his side while Rhone made contact with Doug, informing him of the latest developments.

"Roger," Doug acknowledged. "You and Shannen okay?''

"Affirmative. How's Yarrow?''

"After two hours in surgery, he's critical but stable. Prognosis looks great. What's your heading?" Doug asked.

Like Doug, Rhone knew secrecy was moot on the air— Norton knew exactly where they were, where they were going. A blind man could've followed the tracks.

"West-southwest," Rhone answered.

Signing off, Rhone clipped the radio to his belt and reached for the backpack Shannen held out to him.

Her glance darted around him. He heard what he supposed was a sigh of relief when she discovered the body was no longer in sight.

Rhone absently reached out to tuck a strand of windblown hair behind her ear. She looked dejected, alone. Feelings he could relate to. In spite of himself, he wanted to hold her. And never let go.

She nodded, seeming to understand.

"Where to from here?" Shannen asked, adjusting her pack.

Rhone pointed up the steep, rocky incline behind her.

"No," she corrected hesitantly. "I meant with us. Where do we go from here?"

Rhone shrugged. "If you'd asked me that this morning, I'd have told you it was up to you. Now, honestly, I don't have a clue."

The glare of the sun overhead made him squint as he studied Shannen's face. Digging sunglasses out of the breast pocket of his shirt, he put them on.

He watched a play of emotions cross her face, recognizing the ones that lingered, having experienced them himself. How many times had he also wished things were different or wished he'd had the control to change them? Too many to count.

It was the feelings she tried so hard to hide that interested him most. They were the ones too painful to face, the ones to avoid whenever possible. They were the ones that truly told the story of what resided in the heart. And the harder you tried to suppress them, the more vigorous their battle to surface became. How well he knew. And understood.

"Ready?" he asked with feigned nonchalance. At Shannen's nod, he turned, picking their way over loose rock and around brush and boulders.

He knew Shannen loved him. He'd seen it in her eyes. Yet for reasons known only to her, she failed to say the words. Not that it mattered. It was too late. He and Shannen were like the proverbial two ships...so close and yet miles apart.

Twice, they stopped to rest. Shannen was strong, he knew, but she wasn't used to day-long treks over mountains and through forests. She was holding up well, and when he told her so, she beamed, though she avoided looking directly at him.

Rhone uncapped his canteen, offering it to her.

She took a long drink, and sighed, leaning against a sun-warmed boulder. "Thanks," she said, handing back the water. "How much farther, do you think?"

"I'm not certain. I'm surprised Jimmy hasn't left any recent signs or clues—Shannen!"

She'd moved against the rock, trying to lever herself onto it. Unbalanced, the rock shifted.

Scrambling toward him, her foot slipped. "Rhone! Help me, I'm stuck. The rock—Rhone, it's moving!"

In three long strides, he was at her side as the boulder tipped precariously. Concentrating his strength on moving the smaller rocks that held Shannen's foot captive, he watched the boulder out of the corner of his eye. In what seemed like slow motion, it began to roll to its side. Or maybe he was the one moving in slow motion. Like in a nightmare.

Rhone saw Shannen wince, but she didn't yell. He did, for both of them—at the same time, yanking and pulling the last rock out of the way. Finally freeing her, he half carried, half dragged her from the path of the giant chunk of granite that had begun its descent toward them. Picking up speed, the ground vibrated as it thundered past. Chips of rock and dust spewed in its wake.

A safe distance away, Rhone found a grassy area and set Shannen down. Before he could tell her not to, she put her weight on the injured foot. Crying out, she doubled over.

At the same time, favoring her ankle, she lost her balance. Rhone caught her, lowering her to the ground.

"It's best if you don't try to stand on a foot supported by a sprained, or possibly, broken ankle," he told her dryly.

She closed her eyes on the pain as he probed gently. "I wasn't thinking. It's not broken, is it?"

"I can't tell with your boot on. Shannen, we need to take it off."

She pushed his hands away. "Uh-uh. Hurts too much."

"Not wimping out on me, are you?"

"Goading me will get you nowhere this time."

"I promise you when it swells, it's going to hurt worse if we don't get it off now. Not to mention it'll be a lot harder to remove."

In response to his advice, she grimaced. Then apparently concluding there was no other way, she took a steadying breath. To help brace herself, she wrapped her hands around her shin, supporting her leg, trying to hold her foot still.

"What was that you were saying about no signs or clues from Norton?" she asked.

Rhone took in her pallor, noted pain-filled eyes.

"As much as I'd like to blame Norton, I don't think he was responsible. He couldn't have moved that boulder into so shaky a position without help."

"You're probably right. Erosion is most likely the culprit."

He saw Shannen's eyes widen when he withdrew the steel blade from inside his boot. "Don't worry. I'm reasonably certain we can save your foot. However, your boot's about to become history."

Shannen glared. "I'm glad you find this so amusing."

After effortlessly slicing a seam down the front of the brown leather, he sheathed the knife. "Would you rather I complain about how your timing stinks?"

Frustration mingled with her discomfort. "It does, I know," she said.

Rhone got up to grab his backpack. Returning to her, he eased the boot away from her foot. Cradling it in one hand, he carefully examined the swollen ankle. When he touched the area just above her instep, she flinched.

"Well, the good news is, you seem to have one bad sprain. Unfortunately, sprains tend to be worse than breaks. I don't think I need to tell you how important it is to stay off it."

"No, you don't. Listen to me, Rhone. I want you to go on without me. We've wasted so much time as it is."

He reached for an elastic bandage, wrapping it snugly in a figure-eight pattern around her ankle. "When we're close, I'll leave you nearby, but I'm not about to leave you here." He shook aspirin into his palm and handed them to her along with the canteen. "These'll help the pain. Wish we had something stronger."

"I wouldn't have taken it. We don't know what's ahead of us."

When the first-aid box and canteen were packed away, Rhone handed Shannen the canvas bag. Still in a crouched position, he turned, presenting his back to her. "Let's go find out," he told her.

"This is crazy, you know." Hobbling on one foot, Shannen leaned over, wrapping an arm around his neck. "You really should leave me here."

"Forget it." Rhone didn't want to offer false hope, but he felt sure they were close to Norton.

So sure, that a couple hours later, Rhone chose a more wooded route as they neared the top of the mountain. Not ten yards back, he'd noticed a tree. Part of its trunk had been mutilated. Rhone didn't doubt for a minute the damage had been caused by a wild animal—but not the four-legged variety. The marks on the tree weren't from sharp claws but from the blade of a knife. Not wanting to frighten Shannen any more than she already was, he kept the information to himself.

Near the summit, Rhone found an area thick with brush and buffalo grass, surrounded by huge boulders.

Shannen glanced at the rock formation with skepticism. Seeing it, Rhone reassured her. "These are near-permanent fixtures. It would take dynamite to budge them."

Her features were drawn, her coloring still pale. He easily read the mix of anguish, exhaustion and tension that registered in her gaze as she looked up at him from the protective cover. "If you say so."

"I'm going to have a look around." Rhone set his backpack within her reach. "Here's the radio," he said, unclipping it and handing it to her.

"What if Norton's listening?"

"If you have cause to use it, it won't matter." He gave cursory instructions on using the piece of equipment. "Got your gun?"

Brows drawn together, she said, "Rhone, you're scaring me. You're only going to look around, right? We're not on Norton's doorstep, are we?"

He hesitated, debating. Bravery was a fine tool to motivate one into action, but when finally faced with the confrontation, it was often a different matter entirely. Nevertheless, concealing the truth didn't prepare her for possible consequences. Besides, he needed as much backup as she could provide, even if it was only by using the radio.

"He's in the vicinity—which means, so is Nicholas. We're close, Shannen. We're so close to getting back our son."

At his words, Shannen's shoulders straightened and the fear he'd seen moments before faded to steely determination. In answer to his question, she withdrew her gun, laying it on her lap.

Rhone nodded. Though he'd taught her how, he knelt, taking her gun to check the clip. Satisfied, he clicked the magazine back into place and returned it to her. "If you hear or see *anything* out of the ordinary, use the radio to call Doug. Likewise, he may contact us shortly. I think you've got everything else you need."

In his mind, he checked off water, first-aid kit with aspirin, spare ammo, flare gun. Yep. She was set.

He rose, taking a few steps backward.

In the silence that fell between them, gazes roved freely, hungrily, as though needing to commit the image, the uniqueness of the other, to memory.

Rhone wanted to tell her she was beautiful. That he loved her. That everything would be okay.

He said nothing.

Shannen opened her mouth to speak.

"Come back to me, Rhone. For good this time."

Her comment surprised him, catching him off guard. She'd spoken so quietly, he could almost believe he'd misunderstood. That her invitation had cost her a great deal was evident. Her hands twisted together while she nipped at her bottom lip. Even so, her glance met his.

More than anything, he wished he could go back. Wished she could accept him for who and what he was…that she'd said the words he'd ached to hear for two long years.

Wished it wasn't too late.

A shot punched a hole in the sky.

Birds stopped their chatter and the forest air hung still with tense expectancy.

Oh God, not again. Not again.

The sight of the woman's body flashed in Shannen's thoughts, only to be superimposed by the memory of Brian crumpling in a heap.

She shoved to her feet, tears matting on her eyelashes at the piercing pain. But she had to get to Rhone. She took a step, and another. Then crashed to the ground.

She tried to push herself up, but failed. Excruciating agony ripped up her leg, settling in her stomach until nausea threatened her. Cold perspiration racing down her back, she forced herself to draw deep breaths into her lungs.

Rhone's all right, she told herself. He had to be. He wouldn't fall at Norton's hand. "Please," she prayed, nearly sobbing on her frustration and agony. Tenaciously, she clung to the belief Rhone was okay, that he'd return for her at any minute.... Blindly she fumbled for the radio, remembering Rhone's instructions to call for help if anything went wrong.

A rustle behind her grabbed her attention. She dropped the radio into the open canvas bag. Relief flooded her— it sounded as if Rhone were returning, unerringly remembering where he'd left her.

She turned quickly, already ordering her heart to return to a more normal beat.

Several more branches broke and twigs snapped. The familiar rush of fear snaked up her spine. *Rhone was never that noisy.*

Her pulse began to pound at the thought Rhone might have been the victim of the gunshot. If so, Rhone wasn't heading for her.

Panic held her momentarily paralyzed.

Galvanized into action by a burst of adrenaline, she palmed her gun in a single rush. She was frustrated by the way her hands shook.

Seconds later, Norton's twistedly ugly face came into view. Frantic, she looked for signs of her son, her heart sinking when she realized Norton was alone.

"Stop," she said, dredging the note of authority she didn't know she possessed.

The look of startled surprise in his eyes gave her momentary satisfaction, but the look disappeared quickly, replaced by a sneer meant to intimidate.

Suddenly she remembered the feel of his hands on her, the revulsion as his breath swam over her, the anguish of a life without Nicky.

With a flick, she released the safety. *Twelve bullets.*

He threw up his hands. The sneer vanished. "You wouldn't shoot ole Jimmy in cold blood, would you?"

His scratchy tone held a whine that made her skin crawl. A thousand thoughts crowded her mind, each battling to be uppermost.

"Now would ya?"

"Where's my son? Where's Rhone?" Keep him talking, she told herself. She had to gather her wits, sort through the confusion and figure out how to help her husband.

"I'll take you to him, show you where he is."

She wouldn't fall for it. This was crazy. The man had abducted her son, maybe killed her husband.

He advanced.

She blinked.

"Come on, sugar," he wheedled. "Your husband needs you."

"Stop."

"You wouldn't shoot Jimmy, not really." A triumphant smile began to play at the corners of his mouth. Obviously seeing her indecision, he took another step closer.

"Don't," she commanded, trying to still the wavering. Damn, damn. She shouldn't let him push her buttons.

"Mitchell's lying in a pool of his own blood," Jimmy said with a touch of pure glee. "He was askin' for you. I'll take you. I'll show you. Maybe you can save his life."

She supported her wrist with the opposite hand, fighting nausea and blinding pain as she tried to shore herself against the rock.

"If ya loved him, ya'd go to him."

Her hand shook. The gun wobbled. She couldn't do it. Dear God, she couldn't do it.

As if he stood next to her, she heard the echo of her husband's words as he'd patiently taught her everything she knew about the semiautomatic pistol in her hand.

"Commitment," he'd said. "You have to commit to use it, to follow through. Two things turn private citizens who try to defend themselves with guns into victims. One is lack of knowledge and training." She'd had both. "The second," he'd added, "is commitment to use it."

Finding hidden strength, her hands steadied.

Jimmy didn't seem to notice. He laughed cruelly. "Mebbe I'd let you live, even though ya lied to me." He arched an eyebrow as if in deep, contemplative thought. Jimmy's tongue darted out and he licked his lower lip. "So as you can bury your husband next to his brat."

She flinched—dying a little as the meaning of each word sank in as he intended. With stunning clarity, she now understood what Rhone went through when doing his job.

She'd never seen it before, never even caught a glimpse of the myriad of things that had gone into his decision to return to Colombia.

Cold metal curved into her palm, becoming one with her. She knew if Norton ever escaped after having harmed her son or husband, she wouldn't rest until he'd been stopped.

Rhone was no different.

Norton had abducted Rhone's son and tortured his wife.

No, she couldn't ask Rhone to give it up. Couldn't be selfish enough to demand it of him. A hurting soul, a burning desire to right the wrongs inflicted with casual disdain, none of them could be ignored.

They'd all made Rhone the man she loved.

But now she might never have a chance to tell him how she felt.

The cost of her foolishness, she realized with twisting bitterness, threatened to blur her vision.

Her selfish stubbornness could well have cost her the man she loved. Certainly her demands had cost them any chance of a happily-ever-after.

In less than a blink of an eye, Norton pulled a gun.

He laughed. Blood-lust crazed his eyes.

He aimed.

She gulped for air. Fought panic. Prayed she was faster.

Then pulled the trigger.

In a haze, Rhone heard the gunshot. Knocked down but not out, he struggled to his feet. His head pounded. It was impossible to fill his lungs. His vision doubled, then cleared as he ran, stumbling between the trees.

Dear God, not Shannen, too. But in Rhone's heart he knew she didn't stand a chance against Norton's barbaric skill.

Rhone remembered thinking earlier that he had nothing to lose and everything to gain. He'd been wrong. So wrong. He had everything to lose.

Everything.

Unable to bear the suspense, unwilling to picture her dead, he yelled her name. Panic gripped his heart and squeezed when he heard no response.

Red-hot jabs of pain slowed his progress as he ran up the slope, panting, toward the cover where he'd left her.

Uncertain of Norton's whereabouts, Rhone thought to slow his pace and move cautiously. His injured body demanded it, but reaching Shannen took precedence over safety for himself, took precedence over the agony of ripped skin.

"Rhone!"

At the same time he heard her call his name, he saw Norton facedown in the dirt several feet away. Rhone nudged the still form with his boot, his gun held firmly in both hands.

Somehow managing to rise, Shannen hopped forward. "I shot him. I know he's dead."

Fighting off blackness, he didn't bother to confirm the obvious. Instead, he bent to drag Norton's body out of view, all the while knowing the act taxed his remaining strength.

When he turned back to his wife, he fully understood the internal battle she'd endured.

Rhone caught her against him. She pressed closer to him, seeking comfort; he gave it, even though he had to fight off the waves of nausea the hug caused. "It's okay, babe. You did what you had to do."

"I could do it again," she said without hesitation.

Her response took him by surprise.

Shannen drew her hand back from his side. Blood covered her palm. "Oh my God, you're hurt!"

"In a struggle for Norton's gun, it went off. The bullet grazed me. It's nothing," he stated. Compared to what he'd been through in Colombia, it was nothing.

"But—"

"A stitch or two will take take care of it later." The fact her focus was on him rather than on having shot Norton convinced Rhone she was truly all right. Relief flooded through him. But the sensation was only temporary.

Ignoring what felt like heated barbed wire sinking into his flesh, he squeezed her tightly. "I'll be fine."

"I have to bandage it at least."

Rhone's gut twisted with enough intensity to match the injury.

Tears welled in her eyes. "You'll pass out," she stated.

Though he tried to deny her truth, he couldn't. Wooziness swept through him. With great reluctance he nodded. He'd be no good to her—or Nicholas—if blood loss overtook him.

He eased to the ground with her, unbuttoned his shirt. He ground his back teeth together when she gingerly pulled the flannel away from jagged skin.

"Sorry."

He nodded.

His head spun when she doused the area with tepid water from the canteen. It's only a flesh wound, he reminded himself.

Closing his eyes, escaping to a world without suffering, he allowed her to tape gauze onto the jagged tear.

"You okay?"

The softly haunting tone of her voice dragged him back. He read horror and anguish in her gaze, knew he'd give anything to erase both. "I'll survive."

When she was finished, he told her, "Nicky wasn't with Norton." Even he heard the quiet grief that edged his words.

Shannen moved back to look up at him. Stark fear, unvoiced, reflected his own feelings.

She gulped. "Norton was headed that way," she said, pointing the opposite direction. "He seemed fixed on his destination before he spotted me." Her voice shook with a combination of fear, dread and hope.

The same feelings overwhelmed Rhone, rendering him speechless. "If I support you, can you hop on one foot?"

Shannen nodded.

They didn't have far to go. Camouflaged with tree limbs and dried brush, Rhone spotted the entrance to a mine shaft the same time Shannen did.

Rhone helped her to a tree. She sat, using the trunk for support, waiting while he cleared the entrance.

Rotted timber framed darkness that stretched into the bowels of the mountain. He glanced over his shoulder, unable to hide the same concern he saw in Shannen's eyes. "This is it."

She turned her attention toward the opening that men had long ago carved into the mountainside, staring into the pitch blackness. Hours and days of pent-up emotion split the air, the single word piercing the quietude with disturbing precision.

"Nicholas!"

Chapter 15

"Maa-Maa?"

The echo of Nicky's faint response emerged from the jet-black cavity, but only barely. It was enough.

Rhone met Shannen's wide-eyed gaze. His throat tightened. Shannen's broken voice as she'd shouted their son's name had ripped his heart. Now, hearing the answer to their prayers from Nicholas himself and seeing the joy, the triumph in Shannen's eyes brought tears to his own.

Was it possible, Rhone wondered briefly, that Norton had had even a shred of decency? How very easy it would have been for him to take Nicky's life—the cruelest revenge of all.

Rhone's relief that Nicky was alive rapidly became despair. And panic.

Damn.

For the first time, Rhone saw—really saw—the yawning darkness that separated him from Nicholas. It might as well have been a million miles. He could think of at least as many dangers he would rather confront than the strangling fear of closed-in places.

As though reading his mind, Shannen said, "Rhone, what are we going to do?" Her expression revealed her concern for Nicholas, her angst over the predicament Rhone faced.

In her understanding, he found strength—and out of their mutual concern for the well-being of their son, he found courage. "*I* am going after our son. Unfortunately, once again, you'll have to wait."

She cast a rueful glance at her ankle before giving an accepting nod. "Rhone, I would go if I could."

He forced a smile. "You know, Shan, I believe everything in this life happens for a reason. Sometimes we're lucky enough to get to know what it is. Need I say more?"

Shannen shook her head. He saw the glisten of moisture in her eyes. He wanted to go to her, hold her, pour out all the feeling in his heart, to ask if there was a chance for a future together.

But he held back and kept his distance. Instead, he needed to cling to the belief that there was a chance—real or imaginary. Believing there was a future for them to share would light his way through the darkness. Just as thoughts and memories of Shannen had gotten him through hell before, belief that a future together was finally going to be reality would get him through again.

He radioed Doug with an update, asked for reinforcements.

Doug promised he would be there with a chopper within thirty minutes.

"I don't want to wait," Rhone told Shannen.

She nodded slowly, as if torn between his safety and needing her son. He understood all too well.

With a final glance back, Rhone smiled, knowing it was as much a grimace. To compensate, he gave a thumbs-up.

At last, facing his demon of darkness, he took a step, immediately struggling to ignore the corresponding churning in his stomach and pain in his side. He took several slow deep breaths.

"Rhone."

He turned his head to glance back at Shannen, keeping his face in shadow, needing the obscurity, knowing whatever color had resided beneath his tan had since faded.

"I'm with you," she told him. "Every step of the way."

Greedily, he gathered her words of encouragement close, drawing strength from them before he answered, "Babe, you always have been."

Rhone disappeared from view.

As long as she lived, she knew she would never forget the pure panic in his eyes, mixed with steely determination to see this through.

More than anything, she wanted to do this for him, wanted to spare him the agony of confronting his claustrophobia head-on in the coal darkness of an underground cavern.

His expression had been tight, his complexion devoid of any color.

She shivered.

Her pulse thundered as the events of the previous days took their heavy toll.

Shannen felt as though someone had climbed inside and grabbed her heart, ripping it in two. She wanted her son, wanted him with an intensity that shook her to the core, but the price to her husband seemed more than any human should have to pay.

It was as though Norton had uncovered Rhone's weakness with the razor-sharp edge of a butcher knife and sliced him bare. Even from the grave, Norton had the last laugh.

Seconds that seemed like minutes dragged into eternity. She cursed her ankle, angered by the fact she had to patiently sit and wait, depending on Rhone to save their son . . . and her sanity.

Shannen knotted her fingers into fists as emotions bombarded her shattered mind and body.

She would never forget the way Rhone had looked when he'd been forced to leave her alone when going to confront Norton. The anguish in her heart had been tattooed on his features, too.

In the past, she'd said things to Rhone that she didn't mean, things she wished she could take back. She realized now, compared with love and being together, no matter how short that time together was, it was better to take a chance.

If he wanted to head out into the field, she knew she'd find a way to build her strength and allow him to do that. Their tender reunions and shared memories would make it worthwhile.

Burying herself and pretending he didn't exist had been a shallow way to live. Rhone had taught her the meaning of life, of joy, of hope and despair, all of which made their love deeper, more lasting.

Never again would she be so afraid, so hesitant. It had been wrong to deprive Rhone and Nicholas of each other's presence. Because of her fear, she'd cost both of them a bonding experience.

"I swear," she whispered aloud to the waning sun and teasing breeze, "if you give us one more chance, I'll make it work."

The whistle of wind through towering pines was her only answer.

"Come on, Doug," she said, again wishing Rhone had waited for Doug before taking a breath and plunging into the stony unyielding fortress of solid mountain.

Shannen hadn't protested too much, though, she thought with a twinge of guilt. She'd wanted Nicholas back in her arms, wanted him with desperation that made the misery truly an unbearable Catch-22.

A sudden crash, the unearthly echo of mountain giving way, captured her attention.

"Rhone!"

A cloud of dirt burst from the mouth of the mine.

They couldn't have made it this far only to fail. Surely no force was that unutterably cruel.

"Damn you, Doug, where are you?"

Tears stinging her eyes, Shannen struggled to her elbow and grabbed for the radio, needing to urge Doug faster. Her fingers shook worse than when she'd stared down the sight of the pistol.

Huge sobs choked her.

She had to have help, had to reach Doug. Rhone and Nicholas were depending on her. Taking the walkie-talkie-shaped radio into her hand, she turned it on. When it emitted a loud hissing noise, she turned another dial, trying to squelch the sound. In the frenzy of her efforts, combined with her lack of experience, she accidentally punched a button that switched the channel from the one Rhone had used when talking to Doug earlier. Distraught, she pushed buttons, pausing long enough between each to speak into the mike, trying to find the channel Rhone had been using. Loud static was her reward.

What was taking so long?

Frustrated beyond words, Shannen tossed the radio back into the pack. Rooting around, her searching fingers felt for the flares and gun to shoot them with. Biting the inside of her lip, she focused, firing one straight up into the sky, all the while praying someone in the promised helicopter would see it.

Her ankle throbbed and her heart ached almost more than she could bear. Shannen pulled herself into a tight ball, praying with fevered passion for the sound of the chopper.

The ceiling was low and Rhone had to stoop as he walked. Inching forward was more like it, he decided. He'd once heard of the superstitions miners had regarding the lamp on their hard hats. As the beam of Rhone's flashlight sliced through the inky darkness, he understood firsthand a miner's terminal fear of his lamp going out.

At the same time, Rhone didn't know which was worse—feeling his way through pitch blackness or having just enough light to show how close the walls were. Either way reminded him of his imprisonment.

His face and neck already drenched, he felt rivulets of sweat trail in a steady stream over his back and chest, even though the air in the mine was cool and damp.

Wave after wave of nausea swept through him, each worse than the one before. He gulped huge amounts of air, no longer noticing the strong musty scent, and exhaled slowly. To his disgust and frustration, twice he had to stop, squatting down to put his head between his knees. Willing the illness to pass, the dizziness to subside, he forced himself to concentrate on Shannen and Nicholas.

Rhone lost all perception of time. It felt like hours had passed but a quick glance at his watch revealed it'd only been twenty—

Something—a noise—interrupted his thoughts.

Rhone cocked his head to listen. There it was again. A whimpering sound. Though distant and weak, it was unmistakable.

"Nicholas?" Rhone called out. Words of comfort formed on Rhone's tongue, but he didn't say them.

The whimpering stopped. There was no sound at all. In a flash, Rhone realized Nicky could well be frightened of a male voice, or even of Rhone, especially if Norton's treatment had been rough.

Damn. A complication Rhone hadn't thought of...

Because he didn't know what else to do and because he hoped it would help calm Nicky's fears, Rhone started talking, discovering that doing so also helped take his mind off his own discomforts.

Rounding a bend, the walls narrowed more. The beam of light startled a small colony of bats. Rhone flipped one away from his head instinctively. When another touched him, he turned off the light. He tried to stand still until the bats quieted, but dizziness momentarily had him swaying. His injured side brushed against the wall. He groaned aloud hearing, before he felt, the rotted timber start to crumble, giving way.

No longer caring about the bats and their plight, Rhone flipped the light on and, quickly as he dared, moved forward to avoid getting hit.

A safe distance away, Rhone had to wait for the dust to settle before he could assess the damage. He uttered a curse. Not only was the path he'd just taken obstructed—so was three-quarters of the one that lay ahead of him. Somehow he managed to ignore the realization he was trapped. Getting to his son and getting him to safety was priority. He had no idea how much of the tunnel ahead of him had caved in. Knowing it could fall like neatly stacked dominoes was no reassurance.

Talk, Rhone coached himself. Holding the claustrophobia at bay, he refused to accept the possibility the cave-in was more than localized. Keeping his voice calm, rhythmic, he moved the debris aside with care, not wanting to encourage more collapse.

With the flashlight positioned beside him, he frantically dug at the pile of rock.

Finally he breathed a sigh of relief.

Able to climb over the rubble, he grabbed the cylinder of light and moved forward. How much farther? Rhone wondered. "Nicholas, everything will be okay. Mommy is waiting for us."

No response.

He wanted to run ahead but safety forced him to walk.

When he spoke again, he had to force the words around the knot in his throat. "You don't know me yet, Nicholas, but you will."

More silence.

"Don't hate me for not being here. I didn't know, or I would have been."

Rhone rounded a corner. And froze in his tracks.

Nicky.

Of late, he'd dreamed of this moment on countless occasions, and still he was unprepared for the sight that greeted him.

A playpen sat in a small area off to the side of the tunnel. A sliver of light filtered through cracks in the rock wall, weakly illuminating the room.

Rhone's heart performed somersaults.

Nicky stood, childish hands gripped on the upper edge of the playpen. A track of tears laced through the dirt on his face. His lower lip quivered. And he began to whimper.

Understanding his son's hesitancy, Rhone stepped forward slowly, not wanting to startle the boy anymore. He paused when Nicholas drew back, Rhone's expression mirroring his son's confusion. What now?

Glancing around them, Rhone scowled and quickly hid his reaction to the arsenal Norton had stashed against one wall. Undoubtedly, he'd planned to kill them all. He'd only been waiting to do it when Rhone, Shannen and Nicholas were together. Rhone swallowed a vile curse. So much for thinking Norton had had a strand of decency. The man hadn't begun to know the meaning of the word.

Rhone turned his back to the weaponry that represented the control and violence that he'd fought so hard against. The sight of his child suddenly, sharply, brought Rhone's life into focus. He was no longer interested in continuing the fight. He'd done his share and he'd done his best. It was time to pass the torch to someone else, time to move on.

Time to bring his family together.

He looked down at the miniature reflection of himself and shrugged helplessly. Knowing he couldn't delay any longer, that Shannen was outside, consumed with worry, Rhone reached for Nicky, pretending the wound didn't hurt, and trying not to take it personally when his son pushed away. "Be patient with me," Rhone encouraged with soft tones. "I'm new to this daddy business."

Nicholas squirmed, twisting about to closer inspect the stranger that held him. After a while, surprising Rhone, tiny fingers began exploring his face with hesitant curiosity.

Rhone closed his eyes on emotions so intense—a sweet pain like none other he'd ever experienced.

With the pad of his thumb, Rhone lightly wiped the moisture from Nicky's tear-swollen eyes.

Holding Nicholas close, Rhone reentered the dark corridor. He noticed the beam of light was steadier. Come to think of it, he was more aware of the warmth of the small body cradled against his chest than he was of the cold and damp tunnel. Rhone was more focused on the coming reunion outside than he was of the close quarters. Gone was the nausea. Gone was the tension. And he knew he wore a goofy smile. Meeting his son, holding him, *feeling* him, meant more than words could possibly describe, and that was all he could think about.

Until they reached the solid wall of crumbled rock that blocked their path to freedom. And Shannen.

Surveying their dilemma, Rhone acknowledged they were trapped and automatically braced himself for the all-too-familiar reaction.

It never came.

Granted, he wasn't thrilled with the situation. Admitting the truth to himself, he was aware his breathing and pulse rates had increased—probably always would in close areas, but the milestone was in the fact he could somewhat control his response. Rhone felt like laughing out loud. He was no longer debilitated, no longer a slave to the master of dark confinement.

Setting Nicky down, Rhone dug at the loose rock with bare hands. Working from the top, rock and dirt cascaded to the ground, the dust choking them both.

Rhone resorted to using an unloaded rifle from Norton's stash to dig with, progress noted by the growing pile of debris at Rhone's feet. He paused to take a breath. When he did, he heard someone digging from the other side. He also heard voices—one he recognized.

"We'll be out of here soon, Nicky, if your future godfather has anything to do with it. You'll like Doug," Rhone went on to explain, aware Nicholas didn't have a clue as to what Rhone was saying.

Less than an hour later, both men broke through the dense clutter of rock and timber, meeting in the middle, a narrow path cleared over the top.

Rhone grinned at his friend. "About time you got here. What took you so long?"

"Ever tried to find a needle in a haystack?" At Rhone's grimace, Doug continued, "Shannen shot a flare that got our attention. She's a fine soldier, Rhone. She can cover my back anytime."

Rhone narrowed his eyes, sending his friend a mock glare of warning. "The only back she's covering will be mine."

"About time." Doug grinned. "What took *you* so long?"

Knowing Doug didn't expect an answer, Rhone pushed and shoved aside a boulder and chunks of wood, finally gaining enough room for him and Nicky to crawl out.

"I'm sending Nicky through first."

This time, when Rhone reached for him, Nicky raised his arms rather than pulling back. A tremor of joy jolted through Rhone.

When Nicky was safely in Doug's embrace, Rhone followed, crawling on his belly.

The first thing he noticed when he reached the other side was the scent of fresh air that drifted from the entrance around the bend. He thought it had never smelled so good.

"So," Doug said, handing Nicholas to Rhone, "this is what you looked like as a youngster."

Rhone glanced down and was immediately rewarded with a smile that sent his heart leaping with pure pride. "Almost."

"Where's the difference?" Doug's tone was disbelieving as he led the way out of the cavern.

"Nicholas is going to grow up with parents who love him, who'll encourage him to be himself, who'll pick him up and dust him off when he falls." Rhone's voice grew husky as they exited.

Blinking in the light of early evening, his eyes settled on the love of his life, the mother of his son as she stood where he'd left her to wait. "Nicky will have parents who'll always be there to support him," Rhone went on, "no matter what."

Shannen clasped her hands together, bringing her fingertips up to cover her lips, tears streaming unheeded.

"Maa-Maa!" Nicholas shouted with excitement and squirmed with determination to be set free.

When only a couple feet of fairly even ground separated them, Rhone stood Nicky on his feet. The reunion between mother and son followed the script of Rhone's dreams. Gathering each other close, hugs, tears and kisses said it all. Rhone felt the warmth of his own tears as he stood apart and watched.

Leaning against the tree for support, Shannen shifted Nicholas onto her hip with practiced ease. Meeting her husband's gaze, she undoubtedly saw the raw need he made no attempt to hide. She extended her other arm to him, her eyes communicating volumes.

In the span of a heartbeat, Rhone was at her side, injury forgotten in the pleasure of gathering his wife and son close.

"I thought I lost you, Rhone. I thought I'd lost you both."

"Shh, it's all right now, sweetheart. Everything is going to be fine."

Shannen drew back, her hand wiping the moisture from his cheek.

If an eagle could describe what it felt like to soar through a cloudless sky, skim the tops of majestic peaks, Rhone was certain it could feel no different than the way he felt at this moment. For the first time in his life, he knew peace of mind. And freedom.

"Is it? Are we?" Shannen glanced at Nicholas, including him in her appeal to Rhone.

Two sets of eyes turned expectantly to his. As though he'd been doing it forever, as though Nicky were accustomed to it, Rhone took his son, settling him against his chest, relieving Shannen of her beloved burden.

When her arms were free, she wrapped them around Rhone's waist. In the hug she gave him, he felt strength and determination as fierce as his own. He dropped a kiss, first on Nicky's forehead, then Shannen's. She turned her face up to his. Rhone needed no encouragement as he lowered his head, his lips hungrily seeking hers.

Urgency canceled gentleness. Need for need, ache for ache, they gave to one another.

Promise for promise, they took with greedy abandon. The answer to their future was no longer in question, each knowing eternal fulfillment lay on the horizon of a love born to endure.

Breathless, they peppered kisses over one another's faces, laughing when Nicholas mimicked them.

"Shannen, there's something we need to clear up."

Instantly her expression sobered.

"I told you once I'd never forgive you."

She squeezed her eyes shut momentarily.

"I was wrong, Shannen. Wrong to blame you. Wrong to want to punish you."

"Oh, Rhone."

"Say you'll forgive me."

Tears threatened to spill from her eyes. "There's nothing to forgive."

"Then you'll be my wife again? Share my life?"

He held his breath, nothing he had ever encountered prepared him for the tension of waiting for her answer.

"There's one more thing we need to discuss."

Rhone frowned, his insides becoming a churning mass of panic. What if, after all this, she refused him?

"I know I've said it before, but there can be no more secrets between us, Rhone. Ever. Everything I am, everything that I can be, I want to share with you. Doing so, for me, completes the circle of our love. I'm not asking you to share anything you're uncomfortable with. And I'm not asking for what's in the depths of your heart and soul. I already know I have your love. What I *am* asking for is your explicit trust in me—in us. Furthermore, I won't hold you back from pursuing your career. I fully understand now what drives you. I love you and I want to be together, to be a family. That's all I need."

With exquisite gentleness, Rhone kissed her. He swallowed her moan, and she his, as they released lingering fears and doubts.

He drew back, needing to watch her expression as he spoke. "Trusting you was never an issue with me. Apparently, I went overboard in my attempts to protect you, giving you the impression I didn't trust you. Still, in spite of my efforts, life-threatening danger landed on your doorstep. A chance I will never allow to happen again.

"I love you, Shannen. You *are* my heart and soul. You are the other half of me that makes me complete. There is nothing, *nothing* I don't want to share with you. We already have the foundation of a good marriage. Thank God it was stronger than either of us believed. Building on it with shared hopes and goals that will take a lifetime to fulfill is, for me, a dream come true."

Doug cleared his throat as he approached. "Speaking of dreams, I wouldn't mind having a few in the comforts of my own bed tonight, and you two need to see Dr. Peterson." He looked at Rhone. "We got Norton's informant. Couple guys from the Rocky Mountain field office hunted him down."

Rhone's breath whooshed out. It was over. Finally over.

Doug's smile was rimmed with understanding.

"If you two have had enough fun and frivolity, what say we move off this mountain before nightfall?" He bent, lifting Shannen.

"Doug," she said, her glance holding Rhone's, "how do you feel about being Nicky's godfather?"

Beside them, carrying their son toward the waiting chopper, Rhone laughed out loud. "Learning to read minds?"

Shannen shrugged, a grin tugging at the corners of her mouth.

He sent her a mock glare. "I'll have to remember that."

She mirrored his expression. "See that you do."

Epilogue

"You look..."

Rhone trailed off. Their eyes, meeting in the mirror, locked. She arched a brow, waiting. Unconsciously, she drew in her breath and held it. Even after all this time, his opinion still meant so much.

He took a step closer to her, the snowy white of his shirt bright next to the contrast of his tan. Even in reflection, she noticed that the grooves around his eyes no longer seemed pronounced and the haunted look had disappeared from his face. The time they'd spent together in Florida in a small beach house donated by a now-defunct drug dealer, had made all the difference in the world.

The three of them had spent more than a month together, without any daily intrusions, rediscovering and deepening their love.

Then, months later, Rhone had been there to hold her hand during the long, torturous hours of labor. He'd been there to give Jessica the very first hug of her life.

When Rhone placed the blanket-wrapped infant in her arms, Shannen had seen the sheen of tears covering his eyes. And in that moment, beyond any doubt, she'd known everything would be fine between them.

Rhone had faced his demons.

And walked away the victor.

Now Shannen placed the brush on the dresser top, reaching her hand over her shoulder. Rhone took it, then exerted just enough pressure to turn her.

Her breaths doubled.

The mirror hadn't properly shown the range of emotions now laid bare in his eyes.

"Stunning," he finished, tilting her head back for his kiss.

"But I just had a baby," she protested when she could finally speak again.

"Doesn't show," he said, smoothing a hand down her stomach. "How much longer did the doctor say we have to wait?"

"Six weeks is up today." She smiled.

"God, I was hoping my math hadn't been off."

An ear-piercing scream split the sensual tension.

He groaned. "Timing is everything."

"And Jessica's is better than most."

"I'll go," he said. "Then I'll meet you downstairs."

"Don't forget the diaper bag this time."

"Never again," he vowed. Rhone dropped another quick kiss on her forehead.

"Baby cry," Nicholas said, barging into the room.

"Thanks, honey," Shannen said. "Daddy's going to get her."

With a look of promise commingling with hunger, Rhone responded to the imperial summons.

Shannen scooped the wiggling Nicholas and Bear into her arms.

Nine months ago, she'd been forced to stitch together the ragtag stuffed animal. It had hardly been out of

Nicky's hands since. Shannen sat him on the dresser, then ran a comb through his hair for the third time that morning. "Where are your shoes and socks?"

He shrugged. "Dunno."

"Suits don't look good without shoes and socks." She adjusted the navy tie knotted at his neck.

"Jessy not."

"She's barely six weeks old. Besides, she has satin shoes that match her christening gown."

Rhone popped his head in, Jessica balanced like a precious bundle in his arms. "Found these by the front door." He held up shoes and socks.

Nicholas scowled.

The clock chimed, a reminder of how late they were. Carrying Nicky in one arm and scooping up the shoes in the other, Shannen headed for the front door of the house they'd had built on Long Island.

After belting both kids into their car seats, Rhone gave Jessy a pacifier, which she noisily fastened on to. Rhone slid a hand up Shannen's nylon-clad leg, making her gasp in surprise before he closed the door. Then he slid behind the wheel and headed into town and toward the small, whitewashed church that had become sanctuary to both of them.

The morning sun shone brightly and the scent of blooming flowers filtered through the windows.

"Happy?" he asked.

"Never more so," she agreed.

The absence of traffic made the drive easy, and they arrived at the church with a couple of minutes to spare. Doug and Brian stood near the door, both conspicuously handsome in suits and ties.

"I'm glad you could get away," Rhone said, juggling his daughter with ease as he offered a hand to Doug and Brian.

"Wouldn't miss being a godfather for the second time for anything," Doug said.

Shannen smiled. Doug looked almost as proud as Rhone.

"Thanks for sending that new kid to me," Doug said. "He's gonna be great. Has a knack for defense."

Rhone nodded. "Glad he's working out."

"No one's like you, though."

"When you fall in love and have a baby, I'll hire you at my firm," Rhone said.

"I'd have to have one foot in the grave to accept the kind of mundane job you're offering."

"It's not so bad," Brian supplied. "There's still plenty of excitement. In fact—"

"Yarrow," Rhone warned.

"Gentlemen, please," Shannen interrupted. "There's a christening going on here."

The three exchanged sheepish looks.

Rhone handed Jessica to Shannen, then went back to the car to lock and close the door. Some things would never change, she realized, as she saw Rhone and Doug give cursory glances around the church's exterior.

Danger hadn't been completely eliminated. As long as Rhone had contacts in the business, the risk would never be totally gone. But she felt safe and secure. Their new home was reminiscent of the one they'd left behind in Colorado. But Rhone had taken precautions by installing a sophisticated alarm system.

Though she hadn't expected to like New York life a second time, she did. Rhone was close to his new job, training agents in special tactics, but they were far enough away from the city that home truly felt like home.

The minister met them, smiling at his new parishioners.

"*¡Hola! ¡Hola!*" Maria called, hurrying over. She left her sister behind as she rushed to Shannen and Jessica. "Oh, that baby, she's a beautiful one!" Maria cooed.

Shannen managed to give the woman a big hug. Then Maria dropped to her knees and Nicholas ran over, nearly tripping over untied laces. "Gramma!" he called, having bestowed the honorary title Maria was more than proud to wear.

Though Maria hadn't moved from Colorado, she'd retired and now traveled with Shannen and Rhone when necessary. Reluctant to fly alone, she and her sister had visited several times, just to see Nicky.

The minister discreetly cleared his throat.

They took their places as rehearsed, Jessy tucked in the crook of Doug's arm. Nicky rode on Brian's shoulders. Rhone's arm slid around her waist. A feeling of peace and contentment stole over her, enhanced by the pristine surroundings.

She allowed the minister's words to warm her heart. He was right—they'd been blessed in ways far too numerous to count.

When the ceremony was over, Jessica started to fuss. "I'll take her in the back and feed her," she told Rhone, cherishing the stolen moments with her daughter.

"We'll have cake downstairs when you're ready."

She found a private room and fed her daughter, knowing that downstairs, Nicky would indulge in nuts and candies some of the church ladies had thoughtfully provided.

When Jessica was fed and once again asleep in her mother's arms, Shannen joined the others. Rhone had gotten the carrier and Jessy fussed only minimally when Shannen put her in it.

While she and Rhone cut the cake, Brian snapped pictures. Maria insisted on doing the serving and then Nicky demanded Rhone's attention for a matter daddies handled much better than mommies did.

A few minutes later, Shannen saw Doug standing off to the side, an expression in his eyes that might have been regret. She knew he cared too much for both her and Rhone for it to be envy, but certainly a longing, and a flash of pain, resided there.

Shannen crossed to Doug, a cup of coffee in hand. The second he became aware of her concern, he painted a false smile on his face. Knowing him as she did, she had no doubt the smile was an imposter. Otherwise, regrets wouldn't linger around his eyes.

Happy as she was for herself and Rhone, she couldn't help but regret their friend had no one to hold during the cold long nights when demons of the dark returned to play their torturous games.

"Beautiful baby you've got there," he commented.

"Thanks. Coffee?"

He took it with the same detachment she used to see in Rhone's eyes. "Rhone meant it when he offered you a job."

Doug's smile was more requisite than sincere. "I'm not ready to give it up, Shannen."

She nodded, understanding now in a way that wouldn't have been possible a year ago. She curled her fingers around his wrist and gave an affectionate squeeze. "We think of you a lot."

"Likewise."

"Anytime you need a friend . . ."

"I appreciate the offer. More than you'll know."

Sensing he didn't want to talk any further, she left him—a solitary warrior to his solitary battle.

An hour or so later, the festivities wrapped up. Brian drove Maria and her sister to their hotel while Doug headed for the airport. The exhausted children slept soundly in the back seat.

After dinner that night, Rhone was on bath duty down the hall while she slipped into their bedroom. Comforting sounds of childish laughter and squeals of delight met her ears, filling her with warmth.

Knowing Rhone would be joining her soon, she knelt to pull out the bottom drawer of the dresser.

As she touched the tissue-wrapped lingerie, she experienced a flash of painful remembrance. She recalled a conversation that had cut a channel in her soul. "I dreamed of you," Rhone had said, "walking to me, a sexy smile on your lips, a feminine sway to your hip, and invitation in your expression. Yeah, I made it because of you."

Tonight she intended to banish their last ghost.

Hearing his footfalls in the hallway, she disappeared into their bathroom, locking the door. Hands and fingers trembling, she fumbled with the unfamiliar garter fasteners.

"Shannen?"

"I'll be right there."

Several minutes later, insides twisting into a tight knot, she opened the door.

Rhone instantly glanced over from the bed.

Then whistled.

Long.

And soft.

She smiled hesitantly, hoping she looked sexy. Hoping she resembled the heroine of his dreams after all.

When he grinned back, like a man who'd died and gone to heaven, she knew her smile became genuine. Emboldened by the appreciation in his eyes, she walked to him, stopping within reaching distance.

Rhone sat up and she saw his Adam's apple move as he gulped. "Oh, yeah," he said huskily, so sexily—like velvet dragged across sandpaper—all doubts were vanquished.

He stood, capturing her shoulders in the unyielding bite of his fingers. Her eyes drooped closed with the promise she saw in his eyes, the love in his expression.

When he started to speak, she opened her eyes again, not wanting to miss a single second of this reunion.

"Oh, yeah, babe." He stroked her hair possessively. His voice was grating and raw. "I made it because of you."

* * * * *

INTIMATE MOMENTS®
TM Silhouette®

COMING NEXT MONTH

#679 HIDE IN PLAIN SIGHT—Sara Orwig
Heartbreakers
Safeguarding single mom Rebecca Bolen and her two cuddly kids from a crazed killer was tying Detective Jake Delancy into some serious knots. He'd had worse assignments, more crafty adversaries, but he'd *never* before taken his work to heart—or fallen in love....

#680 FIVE KIDS, ONE CHRISTMAS—Terese Ramin
They'd married for the sake of the children, but Helen wanted more. She *needed* Nat Crockett as surely as any love-struck bride. Only problem was, Nat didn't seem to share her newlywed notions. But with mistletoe and five darling matchmakers, Helen vowed to change his mind.

#681 A MAN TO DIE FOR—Suzanne Brockmann
One minute her life was normal, the next Carrie Brooks was on the run with a man she hardly knew. Felipe Salazar *was* dangerous, but he'd somehow captured her trust. And while she knew in her heart to stand by him, only the face of death revealed the extent of her devotion.

#682 TOGETHER AGAIN—Laura Parker
Rogues' Gallery
How dare he? Meryl Wallis knew James Brant for the power-hungry tycoon he was. She'd loved him once, only to be betrayed. Now he *needed* her to save his reputation. Well, she had control this time around—of everything but herself....

#683 THE MOM WHO CAME TO STAY—Nancy Morse
Native American Trace McCall had done his best, but there were some things he simply couldn't teach his preteen daughter. So when Jenna Ward took an interest in his parenting dilemma, he figured there was no harm in letting her "play" a maternal role. Then he found he wanted her—for real.

#684 THE LAST REAL COWBOY—Becky Barker
Jillian Brandt knew there was no place safer than Trey Langden's remote ranchland—and rugged embrace. Her enemies were getting closer, and her life depended on staying out of sight. But hiding away with her former love posed problems of a very different sort....

We've got more of the men you love to love in the Heartbreakers lineup this winter. Among them are Linda Howard's Zane Mackenzie, a member of her immensely popular Mackenzie family, and Jack Ramsey, an *Extra*-special hero.

In December—HIDE IN PLAIN SIGHT, by Sara Orwig: Detective Jake Delancy was used to dissecting the criminal mind, not analyzing his own troubled heart. But Rebecca Bolen and her two cuddly kids had become so much more than a routine assignment....

In January—TIME AND AGAIN, by Kathryn Jensen, *Intimate Moments Extra:* Jack Ramsey had broken the boundaries of time to seek Kate Fenwick's help. Only this woman could change the course of their destinies—and enable them both to love.

In February—MACKENZIE'S PLEASURE, by Linda Howard: Barrie Lovejoy needed a savior, and out of the darkness Zane Mackenzie emerged. He'd brought her to safety, loved her desperately, yet danger was never more than a heartbeat away— even as Barrie felt the stirrings of new life growing within her....

Nora Roberts

THE PRIDE OF JARED MACKADE
(December 1995)

The MacKade Brothers are back! This month,
Jared MacKade's pride is on the line when he
sets his heart on a woman with a past.

If you liked THE RETURN OF RAFE MACKADE (Silhouette
Intimate Moments #631), you'll love Jared's story. Be on
the lookout for the next book in the series, THE HEART OF
DEVIN MACKADE (Silhouette Intimate Moments #697)
in March 1996—with the last MacKade brother's story,
THE FALL OF SHANE MACKADE, coming in April 1996
from Silhouette Special Edition.

 These sexy, trouble-loving men
will be heading out to you in
alternating books from Silhouette
Intimate Moments and Silhouette Special Edition.

NR-MACK2

**This December,
discover a match made
in heaven with**

Help Wanted: Angels!

All they needed was a little divine intervention....

Three complete novels by three of your favorite
authors—all in one special collection!

**A LOVING SPIRIT by Annette Broadrick
EARTH ANGEL by Christine Rimmer
ANGEL FOR HIRE by Justine Davis**

Available wherever

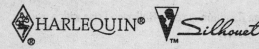
HARLEQUIN® Silhouette®

books are sold.

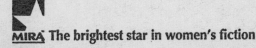